To Patricia,
Enjoy the adventure!
Charlie L

STILL NOT DEAD

A SAM SUNBORN NOVEL

CHARLES LEVIN

#15
⁄5

D0868957

CONTENTS

Other Titles by Charles Levin   ix
You Should Know ...   xi

Prologue   1
1. Memories Lost   3
2. Michelle   5
3. Eli the Mouse   8
4. I Lied   13
5. Monica   20
6. R Wing   24
7. The Genie and the Bottle   28
8. Tangos   31
9. The Apartment   35
10. Flashbacks   37
11. Breadcrumbs   42
12. On a Lonely Day   45
13. Back Track   48
14. The Jitters   52
15. What's in a Name   57
16. Rabid Dog   60
17. Playing God   64
18. Immortal Auto   70
19. Perfect   73
20. Monica   75
21. Mesger   79
22. Who? What!   83
23. Just the Facts, Ma'am   87
24. Download   91
25. Fishtailing   95
26. A New World   99
27. Bomb Scare   104
28. Action Report   111

29. A Little Hand   115
30. Extortion   120
31. Squadoosh   126
32. LGA   130
33. NeXt   134
34. Shoe Leather   139
35. What She Sees   143
36. What Does He Know?   147
37. Zombies   151
38. Revelation   156
39. The 25th   160
40. WTF   164
41. SEND   168
42. Relo   172
43. Stop Action   178
44. Cravens   182
45. Ice Cream in December   186
46. A Dream   189
47. News 8   194
48. You're Early   199
49. Bioink   203
50. Outta Here   207
51. No Secrets   213
52. Next?   217
53. Bullseye   222
54. Lands Anywhere   227
55. No Fear   231
56. Tracks   234
57. Down   237
58. Too Late?   241
59. By D. Bascue   245
60. Phoenix Rising   248
61. So Now What?   253
62. Who and Where?   256
63. Ariadne's Thread   259
64. Where'd She Go?   262
65. The Trace   266

66. 100 Meters Down   269
67. The Nebraska   274
68. All Nighter   279
69. Will They, or Won't They?   285
70. Decisions, Decisions   289
71. All Aboard   295
72. The Shutdown   300
73. Or Else   303
74. Missed Putts   307
75. ...And So Little Time   314
76. Not a Rose Garden   319
77. How's Evan?   322
78. Breaking News   325
79. Operation Blink   328
80. Oops!   331
81. Wake Up Call   335
82. Kaboom   339
83. Postmortem   343
    Author's Note   348

    Liked STILL NOT DEAD?   351
    Acknowledgments   353
    About the Author   355
    Excerpt from The Last Appointment short   357
    story collection

Copyright © 2021 by Charles Levin

All rights reserved under Title 17, U.S. Code, International, and Pan-American Copyright Conventions. No part of this work may be reproduced or transmitted in any form or by any means, electronic or mechanical, including but not limited to photocopying, scanning, recording, broadcast or live performance, or duplication by any information storage or retrieval system without prior written permission from the publisher, except for the inclusion of brief quotations with attribution in a review or report. To request permissions, please visit the author's website (www.charleslevin.com).

Note: This book is a work of fiction. Names, characters, businesses, places, events, and incidents are either the products of the author's imagination or used in a fictitious manner. Any resemblance to actual persons, living or dead, businesses, organizations, events, or locales is entirely coincidental.

First Edition

ISBN: 978-1-7352108-5-8

For Mom,
Still my inspiration in so many ways

OTHER TITLES BY CHARLES LEVIN

NOT SO DEAD

NOT SO GONE

NOT SO DONE

NOT SO DEAD Trilogy

The Last Appointment

Remember tonight... for it is the beginning of always."
- Dante

"What can I do, old man? I'm dead, aren't I?
- From *The Third Man* by Graham Greene

"Out beyond ideas of wrongdoing and rightdoing, there is a
field.
I'll meet you there."
- Rumi

YOU SHOULD KNOW ...

All the technology, science, locations, organizations, and global challenges in this novel are real and current today, except for one or maybe two. Links and factual references can be found in the Author's Notes. All the characters are fictional.

PROLOGUE

"I lied," Frank says.

"What do you mean? What are you talking about?" I ask.

"I only told you part of the story," Frank says.

MEMORIES LOST

Monica stands motionless in the vestibule, her arms extended and curled as if still hugging the suddenly vanished body of her husband. The warmth and gentleness of his touch like a phantom limb, almost there, but not.

"Mom, Mom!" Evan cries from the steps. "What's going on, what happened?"

Her back to Evan, Monica lets her arms drop to her side. She straightens her skirt. With both hands, she pulls her hair back, forces a smile, and turns to him. "Your father left." She sniffs. "He'll be back soon."

"No, he won't," Evan says. "He's dead again, isn't he?"

Monica hesitates. She doesn't know what to say.

"You're a liar. Dad's a liar. You're both liars and now he's gone." Evan turns and stomps back up the steps, his footfalls echoing like gunshots.

When you fade away, what's left? The last thing I remember was my arms wrapped around Monica, her energy, the fragrance of her lavender perfume, our dog Petey barking at my return, Evan running down the steps to greet me. And then it happened. I'm not sure if it was gradual or like flash paper, but I disappeared, gone.

"Where's Dad?" Evan said, and that's the last thing I remember.

Now, where am I? I'm not sure—it's pitch-black and quiet like outer space. Feeling, I cannot. Then what am I? A thought floating like a feather in a cloud? I'm not sure. How would I know? Don't thoughts and feelings need to be attached to something, like something physical, a brain, a body? Apparently not. I'm not sure how long I can go on like this. Do I have a choice? It's as if they buried me alive, but I will not run out of air. Seems I don't need air. That's right—I'm not breathing. Is this what death is like? Am I dead again? I'm convinced it's not a dream.

Wait, I hear something. It's faint, like the sound of crinkling paper, but far away. It's getting closer, louder. Something's burning. Ooh, now it's gone. Then, a high-pitched tone, like a high C. It's getting louder. Now it's fading again. No tongue, yet I taste salt, so salty. The memory of salt?

Dead silent again, and still dark. Something tells me to breathe, but I can't.

A flash of light as if I can see through my closed eyelids.

[2]

MICHELLE

The sunlight streams through the windows on the third floor at New York Avenue NE. The light is dim and gray as the first snowflakes of the season fall in Washington, D.C. Michelle smiles at the view. Where she grew up in Syria, they never saw snow. Her first snowfall was only two years ago when she was doing her grad work at M.I.T. in quantum biology and computer science. It is a welcome sight today in D.C.

Rich peeks around her cubicle and hands her an extra-large black coffee.

She lifts the lid and inhales the aroma. "Perfect." She closes her eyes and takes a sip. "Is this to butter me up or do you have bad news?"

Rich smirks. "You know me too well. Walk with me. Gary's in the conference room. Technically I don't have bad news. He does."

"What?" she asks.

"Just get off your ass and come with me."

Michelle takes a big gulp of the coffee, replaces the lid, and arranges the cup carefully on her desk. After logging out of her computer, she straightens the notepad and pen, making sure they are perfectly even. "OK, I'm ready."

Rich checks his watch, 7:35 AM. "Well, that's good, because I forgot to bring my pajamas."

Gary is heads-down in front of a laptop. He runs his hand through his thinning red hair and looks up as Rich and Michelle enter. He flashes a wide grin at Michelle, letting his eyes drift lower than they should. "Hi Michelle," he says.

"Hi yourself, stranger. So what's the big secret?"

"Um, I'm not sure what you're talking about."

"Gary, just show her what you showed me," Rich says.

Gary pivots the laptop in Michelle's direction.

Michelle bends over to look, her loose-fitting blouse revealing.

Gary's face reddens to match his hair as he returns his gaze to the screen.

"I don't get it," Michelle says. "Looks like an empty prison cell."

"Exactly," Gary says. "Wanna guess who was in that cell only a few hours ago?"

"Both of you, stop playing games and tell me what's going on."

Rich puts a hand on Gary's shoulder to rescue him. "That cell had been the luxurious accommodations of one Ashaki LaSalam. And no, she's not out exercising in the yard. She escaped this morning. Remember that Rumi poem she referenced when you arrested her?"

Become the sky.
Take an axe to the prison wall

Escape.
Walk out like someone suddenly born into color.
Do it now.

"Somehow she made that poem come true. And now we have one of the world's most dangerous terrorists on the loose. Although she only killed a handful of people with her toxin-bearing insects a few months ago when we stopped her, she still has the funds, the network, and the skills to effect planet-wide pandemonium. Oh, and looks like she killed three guards, two female and one male, on her way out."

"That is bad news," Michelle says. "So Gary, is that why you're here and not in your usual cubbyhole in the New York office?"

"I wanted him here," Rich says. "Ashaki has world-class hacking skills. I wanted someone working by our side who could match her talents and help us track her down. We've got elite hackers at Cyber Command at our disposal, but I wanted Gary to run point on the tech side."

"You said *us?*"

"Yep, you and me back in the saddle again, so to speak," Rich says.

"OK, where do we start? How did she escape?" Michelle asks.

"Your second question answers the first," Rich says.

Gary coughs. "Um, here's what we know so far."

ELI THE MOUSE

I unclose my eyes. But reality speaks. I have no real eyes or a mouth or ears. I have ones and zeros. I am ones and zeros moving in patterns that define me, that are me, for now.

The faint blue light of computer screens races across my virtual field of vision. Then the carousel stops at an image of Frank, Frank Einstein, my partner, friend, and mentor. I know now that I am back in the virtual world. I'm not sure why or how I got here. A sensation, like my stomach sinking, overwhelms me. I know it can't be real. I no longer have a stomach or a physical body. I might as well be dead. I am only "alive" digitally, virtually, ones and zeros dispersed in the Cloud.

"Sam, I'm elated that you're back. We almost lost you there, for good," Frank says, his professorial image filling the virtual screen in front of me. Somehow his rumpled tweed jacket, wild gray hair, and Sherlock Holmes pipe reassure me.

I'm almost afraid to ask. "What happened to me?"

"The program that brought you back to the physical world and to your family crashed, a critical failure."

"And ripped me from Monica's arms and away from Evan.

What must she be thinking? I lost her before. She wanted a divorce, but I was winning her back. Then, boom. Fade to black."

"I'm sorry, I really am. These things happen with new software. If I didn't bring you back right that second, you might have disappeared from both the physical and digital worlds forever. At least now, when you get your full configuration back, you can Zoom with Monica and Evan again."

A flood of questions washes over me. "Hold on. Why that second? Full configuration? Something about a lie? You said you lied to me?"

"Calm down, Sam. Breathe."

"That's funny. I'm virtual and I'm supposed to—" Almost as if commanded, I take a deep virtual breath and exhale slowly. I could swear I even smelled peppermint. It calms me. "How did I do that?"

"It's part of the program. When I designed this world for people to upload their personalities and memories, I discovered an unintended consequence. The digital personalities became depressed and anxious. It happened to me. I needed a way for us to calm those fears. At first, I invented digital anti-depressants, but like all drugs, even virtual ones, there were unwanted side effects. Virtual breathing and virtual meditation just seem to work better with no negative side effects. I was also able to simulate the aroma of essential oils. So, whenever you feel a panic attack coming on, just breathe."

"OK, I've got that, but what about my other questions?"

"In time, Sam. When I mentioned full configuration, I was referring to your status. I am restoring you digitally. When I say the program crashed, that included corrupting the first three backup files of you I tried to restore. When I say I almost lost you, we really lost you. Remember the early computer days, when you'd forget to save a Word Document you were working on, your primitive PC would blue-screen and you lost all your work?"

"Yes, I remember it, like a gunshot wound."

"It happened to everybody, but for me, it was six months of work by me and six-hundred other programmers working on a major project."

"Ouch, but I can't believe you didn't have a backup."

"Oh, we had a robust backup, but we only kept one copy. The owner of the project, whom I won't name, was anxious that the programmers might steal his code. So every day, they carefully checked their work in and out, no USB or removable drives to make copies, just that one daily backup."

"OK, what happened to the backup?"

"It was not *what*, but *where*. The server with the only backup was in a nicely controlled, secure bunker in the basement of the World Trade Center in New York. On 9/11 we lost all that code, that work. The company actually had insurance for this kind of loss, but the insurance company claim only paid a fraction of what all that work was worth. We sued them for a bigger payout and lost. It sunk the project and the company."

"Fucking insurance companies."

"Here I'd say your expletive analysis is correct. But I learned from that horrendous experience. I always make at least four backups of all my work, including digital you. Fortunately, the fourth backup of you was not corrupted and you are currently..." Frank pauses and looks down. "Seventy-six percent complete. Once you are 100%, you'll have your full digital-brain powers back. Then I will answer your questions. Until then, you wouldn't fully understand the answers."

"Just tell me this. Why did you have to pull me back just at that moment when I was in Monica's arms?"

"OK, you remember the experiment we did to test my reincarnation program, the one with Eli the Mouse?"

"Yes, after several tries, you could make Eli disappear from one location and reappear in another, like magic or teleportation or something."

"That's right. That was the test we did successfully before I tried the same program on you. Ostensibly, it worked. Other than a few incidents of you fading in and out, you were back physically, able to touch, feel, smell, taste, and hug Monica. But then something shreklekh happened."

"What?"

"Eli died. He just keeled over, foamed at the mouth, and died. I had to pull you back right away to understand what went wrong. I couldn't risk you dying like that, like Eli. It was awful. I loved that mouse."

For the first time, I saw a tear run down Frank's cheek.

"I guess I understand. It was just so abrupt and at such a bad time. I miss Monica and Evan. I can't imagine how they felt or what they thought. And I assume they haven't been able to reach me even digitally. Have you called them?"

Frank's face reddens, and he looks away. "Yes, Monica's been calling every day, several times a day, trying to reach you for the last month."

"Month, what? They must be going crazy. What did you tell them?"

"I didn't take their calls."

"What? How could you be so cruel? Frank, I'm so disappointed—no, angry, disgusted. I don't know what to say."

"I couldn't give them an answer until I knew whether I could restore you. Today is the first day I felt confident I could. And it's better if you call them when you're one hundred percent anyway."

"Jesus, Frank. I've got to think about all this, what you've

Tell us more about the cellmate, her family, friends, last-knowns," Michelle says.

"Already on it." Gary turns back to the laptop and starts typing, his fingers a blur.

There's a light tapping on the conference room door. "Enter," Rich says.

A young intern, a college student, enters with a box of brownies and donuts from Insomnia Cookies.

"All right," Rich exclaims, opening the box. "Smells fresh-baked. Chocolate-covered, perfect." He takes a huge mouthful, filling his cheeks.

"You look like a squirrel." Michelle laughs.

Rich mumbles with his mouth full, spraying crumbs onto the table. "These are great. Try one."

"No thanks." Michelle pats Rich's growing belly.

"I'll take one," Gary says. "Anyway, here's a picture and some background. Ersari was convicted of a triple homicide. She killed her husband and both her children, a little girl, six, and a newborn boy."

"Ugh. I'm sure there's more to that story," Michelle says.

"Sounds like a perfect sidekick for Ashaki. More to the point, last address, family, associates?" Rich asks.

"She lived in East Orange, New Jersey." Gary keeps tapping away while reciting in a monotone, "Worked as a school bus driver of all things. Estranged from her sister and two brothers, understandable—parents dead. She had a character witness at her trial. The manager at the school bus company, named Phyllis Bultema. Looking over the trial transcript now. Under cross-examination, appears Bultema and Ersari had more than an employee-employer relationship."

"Then Bultema is the place to start. Where do we find her?" Rich asks.

"She's checked in at Bold Memorial Hospital in Rochester in the R wing," Gary says.

"The R Wing?" Michelle asks.

"Yeah, the mental ward," Gary says.

"Looks like you're a hundred percent restored and upload complete," Frank says. "How do you feel, Sam?"

"I *feel* the same way I did two hours ago, still devastated and angry that I lost Monica and Evan."

"Blame me if you must. I was just trying to save you. If I can get you back to them, I will. Meanwhile, you're good to go, digitally anyway. You should call Monica now. She's probably frantic by now."

"Thanks so much for your concern, *not*. I will call her in a minute. But first, what was the lie you said you told me?"

"All right, I warned you that this is complicated. It may take several conversations for you to grasp it."

"Thanks for the confidence. You know I'm a quick study. Let's have it."

"I'll only tell you if you change your tone. Cut out the sarcasm and snarkiness. It's not like you."

"OK, OK, I'm sorry. I know. I just didn't like dying all over again. To be suddenly ripped from the arms of those you love. I must have virtual PTSD. Depression runs in my family."

"Death is like that sometimes—sudden and even if not sudden, always a loss. When I lost my Helen in a car accident, I was catatonic for months. You'll get over it eventually and maybe we'll find a way back for you yet."

"Thanks, I was being a jerk. So tell me about the lie."

Frank inhales in a deep virtual breath. "First, I want to apologize for lying to you. I had to. It's not that I don't trust you.

There's nobody I trust more. But it's more a case that you were better off not knowing. What I'm about to tell you is dangerous if it falls into the wrong hands. You must promise not to share it with anyone ever, not Monica, not Loretta, not Bart, no one. Can you promise me that?"

I hesitate. "I was always good at keeping secrets. I promise. Sounds big."

"When it comes to national security and the safety of the human race, there may be no bigger secret."

"Really? C'mon now. Spill it."

"To understand this, I will lead you through it, like Socrates with a bunch of questions."

"Whatever, shoot."

"What makes you, you? Who is Sam Sunborn?"

"OK, I'll play along. I was a body, a brain. I had a family and a job, a bunch of interests, parents, life experiences, take your pick."

"Well, your body is gone. Are you still Sam?"

"I think I am, at least virtually."

"So you don't have a body. You don't have a physical brain. What are you?"

"A couple of years ago, you and I partnered to form Digital3000. We figured out how to upload people's memories, emotions, and skills to the Cloud so once uploaded, you could theoretically live forever, like we are doing now."

"All that is true. But let's back up. Before you were uploaded and lost your physical form, where did all those memories and emotions reside that made Sam, *Sam*?"

"In my consciousness, in my brain, I guess?"

"That's the big question. Let me ask you this, scientists say you regenerate every cell and molecule in your body and your brain every seven years. If that's true and none of the molecules that made up Sam are the same as they were seven years ago, how can you have the same memories you had eight, ten, or twenty years ago? Where do those memories reside?"

"It can't be the soul. That's just a placeholder, a construct for the unknown of your unique identity, isn't it?"

"You're not sure, are you? Turns out neuroscientists aren't even sure where consciousness lies. Oh, they stick people in fMRI machines and tell them to think certain thoughts and then watch what lights up in their brain, but that doesn't give them a true answer."

"Yeah, but how about when people get in a car accident that damages their brain? Or dementia, where they lose their memories? Doctors can see plaque on the brain in that MRI and tie it to a loss of memories and cognition."

"OK, here's where the lie I told comes in. When I did the programming for the brain uploads, I told you we were uploading people's memories, right?"

"Yes, and that made sense to me, Bart, Loretta, and the team. Memories in the physical brain copied like a massive file up to the Cloud."

"That's what I wanted you to think, fits the common mechanical brain metaphor. But what if your memories don't reside only in the brain?"

"What? What are you talking about?"

"What if your memories already live in the Cloud? What if what you had in your brain is just a password, a login, that allows you to access your personal memories from the Cloud? And everyone else has their own login? And up until now, that login has been secret and secure?"

"Whoa, slow down. That's a wild idea."

"It's true. It's called long-range synchronization. Just like with Dropbox or iCloud, it stores a memory file in the Cloud, technically called the Zero-Point Field or ZPF, and it stores a copy in your brain. When something changes on either side, either in the ZPF or your brain, the two automatically synch to the latest known state. Didn't you wonder how we could upload your brain at first and download it into a new body in a matter of a couple of hours? Huge petabytes of data going through slow biological synapses to the Cloud so fast? The truth is all I had to do was upload your login and some emotional data to the Cloud. Those vast stores of memories, images, and feelings were already there in the ZPF waiting for you."

"Wait, so what happens when I create a fresh memory? Say I read the *Hardy Boys* to Evan and remember the fun of that experience, the warmth of him next to me, falling asleep after a few pages, tucking him in, kissing his forehead. How's that work?"

"The ZPF is a universal background field, kind of like Jung's idea of the collective unconscious. When you create those sweet memories you just described, it's just like creating a file on your PC and saving it. It synchronizes to the Cloud, the ZPF."

"How does it do that, make that connection?"

"It uses a framework called stochastic electrodynamics, which is based on quantum physics."

"Uh oh, here we go again with quantum physics."

"Don't pooh pooh it. Quantum phenomena are real. Scientists have already shown that two twin particles on opposite sides of the universe can be in synch—when a change happens in one atom, a simultaneous identical change happens in the other. They call it *entanglement*. It's the same with consciousness and memories. What happens in your brain is perfectly mirrored in the ZPF and vice versa. You are permanently logged in. This has all been theory until now, until I discovered the password connection and the full linkage."

"What about fuzzy memories or things I forget? How's about that?"

"Files get corrupted, data gets lost in transmission, your PC is slow or crashes to follow the metaphor."

"Wow. I have to think about this. Sounds like science fiction to me."

"So did communication satellites circling the Earth before Arthur C. Clarke wrote about the idea. And boom, twenty years later, we have satellites beaming TV signals around the world. And after twenty more years, we have GPS. Another example, most of the world's renowned scientists scoffed at Einstein and his ludicrous theory of relativity until he, or I should say his wife, Mileva, was able to prove it in the physical world."

"I get that. Assuming that you have come up with this new paradigm for how consciousness and memory work, why wouldn't you tell me about it? What's the harm? What's the danger?"

"This secret holds one of the greatest threats in the history of mankind. Greater than atomic weapons and greater than pandemics."

"What, what is it?"

"I said this would take more than one conversation. Besides, your Zoom icon is flashing. It's Monica trying to reach you again. You better answer this time," Frank says.

5

MONICA

"That was close. Are you OK?" Ersari asks.

Ashaki strokes her arms and pivots her neck. "I'm all right. Some cuts and bruises. Shimmying down those air ducts and crawling through the sewer is not exactly what I trained for."

Ersari laughs. "Sometimes I feel like the sewer is my home if you get what I mean. Look, we've got to get out of these orange jumpsuits if we're returning to the outside world. One of my lieutenants should have left a bag with street clothes a little farther ahead, so we can change. He should be up there waiting for us."

They walk, ducking their heads, through the sewer pipes under Pearl Street. Dank water flows beneath their feet. Rats scurry by.

The rank odor makes Ashaki's nose run. She wipes the mucus on her sleeve. "How much farther?"

"Up ahead, sister," Ersari says.

A thin beam of light shining through a manhole cover illuminates a ladder, from which hangs a green army duffel.

"There it is. Pickles came through as always," Ersari says. She zips open the bag and hands some jeans and a tie-dyed shirt to Ashaki. Then puts on sweatpants and a hoodie herself.

"*Pickles*, really?"

"Yeah, Marsilius Popoff, but we all call him Pickles. Funny name, but a dependable soldier."

"OK... The jeans fit. How d'you know my size?" Ashaki asks.

"I know everything about you," Ersari smirks and plants a sloppy, wet kiss on Ashaki's lips.

Ashaki licks her lips and smiles. "You do, huh? You only think you know. There's a lot more that you don't."

"Well then, I'd like to find out." Ersari grabs Ashaki's butt and gently squeezes.

"I don't exactly find this place romantic. Let's get out of here."

"OK." Ersari removes a flip phone from the duffel and hits speed-dial. "We're here," she says and snaps the phone shut. Moments later, the manhole cover seems to slide away on its own, releasing a flood of sunlight. The women both shield their eyes. Pointing to the ladder, Ersari says, "After you..."

Ashaki climbs the rusty iron ladder. A hand reaches down and helps her to the street. Ersari follows.

"Over here," Pickles says, and they trail behind him to a BMW double-parked in front of a Starbucks.

The women get in the back seat. The new car smell is a stark contrast to the odors of the fetid sewer and the sweaty prison.

"Where to?" Pickles asks.

"Home," Ersari says.

Monica's expression is a swirling storm. "Oh my God, I thought you were gone for good. What happened? Where are you? Why didn't you or Frank answer my calls?"

I can see Monica's frantic eyes on my screen. She can see the virtual image of me I created, looking healthy and very much alive. "I'm so sorry. It was out of my control. I was almost dead for good, but Frank restored me just now. Calling you is the very next thing I was going to do, but you beat me to it."

"So where are you? Let me guess... you're digital again."

"That's right, for now anyway."

Tears roll down Monica's cheeks. "I'm sorry to say your funeral is on Saturday. After a month of trying to reach you and Frank, and when neither Loretta nor Bart had heard from you, I figured it was time to make it official."

"Please cancel it. I'm here, alive, at least digitally. Frank's trying to figure out another way, to get me back to you for real, forever this time."

"I've heard that one before. Now it's time to celebrate your life and our loss and then move on. I've told all our friends and family that you died in a boating accident and your body wasn't found."

"What about Evan? Doesn't he deserve a father?"

"You haven't been much of a father lately. I told him you were dead. He cried for days. He's just coming around. We should leave it that way. Dead once is tough enough. Dead twice is crazy. Dead three times and you're out."

"Please Monica, will you think about this? You and Evan are everything to me."

"I used to believe that."

"It's still true. Tell me you'll think about it and we can talk later."

Silence.

Then, "I'll think about it."

I take a deep breath. "Thank you. I love you."

"I know." She clicks off.

6

R WING

"Why don't you send somebody from the local field office to interview Bultema?" Michelle asks.

"We hop in the jet and we're there in an hour. This is too important. I want to see and hear her myself," Rich says. "The jet's fueled up and the pilots are waiting for us at Reagan."

"Not that I mind fieldwork or spending time with you, but 240,000 skilled people work for DHS. You can't do everything yourself."

"My mother always said, 'If you want something done right...'"

"OK, but I'm not sure how they made you a director. A director manages and delegates."

"Never mind that. Let's go. Car's waiting downstairs."

Michelle grabs her jacket, and they head down to the black SUV out front. The December sun breaks through the clouds and glistens off the light snow that fell the night before. The air is cool, crisp, dry.

At 10:35 AM, they land at Greater Rochester International. The snow is a foot deeper here, but the runway and all the streets have been cleared. Another black SUV shuttles them to Bold Memorial. Rich flashes his credentials at reception. They check their guns at security and head up the elevator to the sixth floor. The R Wing door is locked. Michelle pushes a buzzer. An orderly appears. She flashes her credentials through the metal mesh security glass.

The door buzzes and they step into a 1950s throwback world of *One Flew Over the Cuckoo's Nest*. The walls are a fading avocado green, the floors a gray linoleum. The disinfectant odor pervades. Men and women in green tattered jumpsuits wander the halls in a Thorazine haze.

"Looks like a casting call for *Night of the Living Dead*," Rich says.

"Yeah, it's creepy. Is that chloroform I smell?" Michelle says and turns to the orderly. "We're here to speak with Phyllis Bultema."

"I've been told," the orderly says. "She has her good days and bad. One day she's calm, the next day it's a Category 5 mental storm. Today, who knows?"

The orderly escorts them to a corner of the common room. Other patients circle around the two DHS agents, scanning them head-to-toe. Bultema sits in a rocking chair, swaying back and forth, staring out the window.

The orderly shoos the other patients away and says, "Phyllis, there's somebody here to see you."

Phyllis doesn't interrupt the rhythm of her rocking.

Rich nods to Michelle, and she circles in front of Phyllis. Kneeling at eye level, she says, "Phyllis, my name is Michelle. How are you today?"

"Can I get my teddy? I want my teddy," Phyllis says.

Rich and Michelle both turn to the orderly. He smirks and leaves.

"Teddy is coming," Michelle says. "Can you tell me about the bus company?"

Phyllis folds her arms across her chest and huffs. Michelle stands and they wait. The orderly returns extending the small, ragged teddy bear to Phyllis, but Michelle snatches it and holds it in front of Phyllis.

"Give me teddy. I miss him," Phyllis says.

"He misses you too." Michelle moves Teddy's head and plays puppeteer. "Teddy wants to know about the bus company."

Phyllis smiles. "I've told you the story many times." She reaches out to pet Teddy's head.

"Tell me again," Teddy says.

"I loved working at the bus company. Sometimes I would drive the children myself and sing to them. They seemed to like that. Other times I taught new drivers how to drive. I was sooo good that they made me the boss."

"Did you have a driver named Jennie Lee?" Teddy asks, then tickles Phyllis under the chin.

She laughs. "Oh yes, she was very good with the children. Terrible what happened to her and her family. I don't believe she could hurt them. She was too nice."

"She used to live on South Harrison Street before they took her away, right?" Teddy asks.

"Yes, she had a lovely house. So sad."

"And you were friends. Did you ever go out with her, for a drink or anything?"

Phyllis breaks into a broad grin. "Oh, we both liked a drink, or two, or three after work. We had a favorite place. Jen seemed to know everybody like they were family."

"What was the name of the place?"

Phyllis's eyes well up. "I can't remember so good after the accident. I hit my head." Phyllis whips her head side-to-side. "I can't. No, no, I can't. Don't hurt me, please. Don't." She stops moving and closes her eyes.

Michelle looks at Rich. He shrugs.

She turns back to Phyllis and says in her regular voice, "Teddy would like the name of the bar that you and Jen liked to go to. Then he wants to snuggle."

Phyllis, eyes still closed, says, "I don't know. I don't know."

"What was your favorite drink at the bar?" Teddy asks.

"It was a Manhattan, always a Manhattan." She licks her lips, then her eyes snap open. "The bar was named Tangos. Yes, Tangos. That's it."

Michelle hands Teddy to Phyllis, who cradles him in her arms.

"Thank you," Michelle says and stands.

"I think we've got a lead. Where'd you learn that trick?" Rich asks.

"Back in Syria. Growing up, I volunteered in a nursing home. We used to play-act all the time. It was often the only way to communicate."

"Don't try that on me."

Michelle smiles. "I already have."

As they thank the orderly and move to the door, Phyllis says, "Teddy, would you like to hear the song I sang to the children on the bus?"

For who knows where the time goes?
Who knows where the time goes?
Sad, deserted shore, your fickle friends are leaving
Ah, but then you know it's time for them to go
But I will still be here, I have no thought of leaving
I do not count the time
For who knows where the time goes?
Who knows where the time goes?

7

THE GENIE AND THE BOTTLE

"They're burying me on Saturday, Frank."

"What? What are you talking about, Sam?"

"Monica—she's planned a funeral."

"Oh, I guess I can't blame her."

"That's worse than divorce, right? More final," I say. "She thought I was gone for good when she didn't hear from me and couldn't reach you."

"Maybe she and Evan are better off. Get it over with."

"What? I can't believe what you're saying. I thought you were my friend."

"I am and always will be, but they've been through a lot. This time, I may not be able to get you back to her physically. In different ways, we've failed twice. Why put them through it again? Let them move on."

"I can't give up. I won't. At least I could talk to them by Zoom. She's talking about cutting me off completely."

"I understand that. Evan needs a real father by his side, and Monica needs a real husband to touch and to hold."

"Go ahead, say it... and to have sex with."

"I wasn't going there, but yes, that too."

"What about you? You're virtual and you speak to your daughter all the time."

"That's different. She's grown up and can handle it. When kids become adults and leave home, sometimes the most parents get is occasional phone calls anyway. With my Sarah, it's no different from that. But with Evan, he's ten. He needs a father who shows up at his soccer games, who jokes with him at dinner, and reads him bedtime stories at night. A child needs that, and you can't give it to him and there's no guarantee you will ever again."

"I get that, I do. But what about what I need? If I can't speak with Monica and Evan, they might as well bury me."

"In case you haven't noticed, you are dead. It's only our flawed attempt at virtual immortality that makes this conversation possible. Let them go, Sam."

"No. I asked Monica to think twice about the funeral. She said she would." I take a deep breath. "So you said this idea of our memories existing in the Cloud even when we're alive has dangerous implications. What did you mean?"

Frank coughs. "Are you sitting down? Of course, you are. Never mind that."

"Stop stumbling and just spit it out. I promise not to tell anyone."

"OK, OK. Just give me a minute." Frank rubs his eyes. "The danger is not that our memories, all our memories for everyone, live in the ZPF Cloud. It's the *knowledge* of it that's dangerous."

"If your memory theory is correct, then presumably it's always been true throughout the history of humans and nothing terrible has happened because of it. Why now?"

"First, it's not a theory. It's true. Here's where the knowledge of it gets more than dangerous. *Apocalyptic* may be a better word."

"Thanks for the confidence. I'll be fine." Michelle slams the car door, crosses the street, and heads for the bar.

The interior is dim, the dark paneling and low lights give it a closed-in feel. A cloud of blue smoke hovers above the ancient mahogany bar. The smell of stale beer is palpable. "Only the Good Die Young" is playing loud on the jukebox.

A grizzled and burly middle-aged bartender that reminds her of Bluto from *Popeye* approaches. "What'll it be, Miss?"

"I'll have a tonic water and lime," she says. Her religion forbids alcohol, a good thing in this line of work. She mentally catalogs the patrons, mostly men, and a few rough-looking women. Clearly some gang members, normal chatter. She scans the room. To the right there's a hallway with a restroom sign and a back door that says NO Exit. On the other side of the bar, a door leading from a backroom swings open. A tall dark-skinned man with a large afro spilling from a red bandanna, and a small pale woman with a long scar running across her left cheek, emerge carrying on a heated argument. The woman puts a hand on the man's chest to stop his advance. He winds up and slaps her hard with the back of his hand across her cheek. She falls backward, crashing against an empty chair, and tumbles to the floor.

The room falls dead silent except for the jukebox.

Aw, but they never told you the price that you pay / For things that you might have done / Only the good die young.

The man spits on the fallen woman and turns toward the front door. The din of conversation resumes as if nothing happened. On his way out, the man walks by Michelle. Her instincts kick in. Without even thinking, her foot juts out as the man passes, tripping him. He stumbles over another seated patron, pushes off him, and regains his balance.

"Hey bitch, what did you do that for?"

Michelle jumps from her barstool. "For all the women that put up with limp dicks like you."

The man's body seems to expand like an inflating balloon. He charges, but Michelle is ready. She ducks his outstretched hands and pirouettes around him. Using his momentum, she grips the back of his neck—then slams his face down on the bar, scattering drinks. Tumbling glasses shatter on the floor. The dazed man lifts his head from the bar, his nose bloody and twisted. He musters his energy again, then rushes Michelle. She sidesteps left and then spins, planting a roundhouse kick to the man's groin. He doubles over and falls to the floor, moaning.

Michelle jogs over to the small pale woman who is now standing, her mouth wide open.

Michelle takes her arm. "C'mon, let's get you out of here." The woman does not resist and they head for the door.

The bartender who had been cowering behind the bar, rises and yells, "Hey Miss, who's gonna pay for this mess?"

Over her shoulder Michelle shouts, "Put it on my tab, then shove it up your ass." They push through the door into the sunshine and pause on the sidewalk. Michelle. Her heart still pounding, faces the woman. "Are you OK?"

The woman nods. "What'd you do that for? He's my boyfriend."

"Some boyfriend," Michelle says. "Does he do that to you often?"

"Only when I get out of line."

"Really? And what did you do to deserve it this time?"

The woman sniffs. "He wanted me to hide two women at my apartment, and I wouldn't do it. I don't know these women. I been to Annandale Correctional once already. I ain't going back." She purses her lips like she just realized she's said too much.

"Look, can I give you a ride somewhere, maybe home?"

"No, I just live a few blocks away, thanks. Ain't nobody ever defended me like that before. My old man used to beat me and then I gets with this dude and he shits all over me. Are all men this mean and crazy?"

"Not all of them." Michelle takes a business card and pen from her pocket. "Listen, if you ever need help, call me. Here's my number. Name's Michelle."

"I'm Dawn." They shake hands.

"Nice to meet you, Dawn. Sorry, it had to be this way."

"It's OK. I best be going." Dawn turns and hobbles down the street.

"Did you catch all that?" Michelle asks into her com.

"I got it. Nice work," Rich says. "I got her picture too. With facial rec and the record, she'll be in the system. Get in the car. We'll follow her home."

Michelle slips into the Crown Vic. "What about the guy in the bar?"

"I planted a camera in this nice big tree here, focused on the front door. It will record whoever leaves and I suspect your guy will come out soon. Then we'll circle back and get it." He starts the car and rolls out a safe distance behind Dawn.

Michelle turns to Rich. "Hey, I thought you were going to come in and rescue me?"

He smiles. "I know you. You can handle yourself. Besides, you didn't say the safe word."

"I didn't know we had a safe word," Michelle says.

"Exactly," Rich says.

THE APARTMENT

Pickles seems to relish his role as both chauffeur and body-guard. After parking in front of the apartment on East 88th Street, he hustles around the car to open the door for Ashaki and Ersari. They nod to the doorman and ride the elevator to the thirty-third floor.

Ashaki is shocked when the elevator door opens not to a hallway but directly to the inside of a living room the size of St. Louis. Floor-to-ceiling windows overlook a panoramic view of Central Park. "Nice digs," Ashaki says. "I had no idea."

"I like to keep a low profile." Ersari grins. "This is one of our safe houses. Like most of the high-end New York apartments, it's owned by a foreign corporation that is a subsidiary of another and another, and so on. They'd never pierce that veil to find us."

"I'm impressed. So, what now?" Ashaki asks.

Ersari turns to Pickles. "Thanks for the rescue. You can get back to the office. I'll call you when I need you."

Pickles pivots and heads for the elevator.

manual. We're feeling our way and making things up as we go, and you still can't get a good cup of coffee.

"About what you explained before, I have a question about logging into this universal memory Cloud. How come nobody's figured out that piece before? Why you?" I ask.

"Because universal memory is protected by the ultimate cryptographic tool," Frank says.

"And what's that?"

"It's called indistinguishability obfuscation."

"Huh?"

"Until recently, the idea has been only a theory. You know about encryption—it's what keeps our company, Digital3000, going. Well, indistinguishability obfuscation is like the ultimate encryption. It not only hides logins and transactions, it obfuscates. In this case, it makes you assume your memories are only stored somewhere in your brain, which, scientists have been unable to pinpoint, when in fact they are preserved in the Cloud. Like many brilliant discoveries, I stumbled over this idea when I was working on something unrelated—digitizing our brains. But the memory code is so well hidden and obscured that nobody had figured it out until I did. And we need to keep it that way."

"That's crazy complicated. Your secret's safe with me because I couldn't explain it to anybody anyway. If I did, they'd bring out the straitjacket."

Frank laughs. "It's that crazy complexity that is the reason I don't trust the theory of evolution."

"What? Every scientist, even the mad ones, accepts evolution."

Frank flashes a Cheshire smile. "They don't call it a *theory* for nothing. Think about it. Consider how complex the human body is, the structure of the eye, the brain, the liver, and the pancreas. It's too complex to come from a fish. I don't care how many millions of years of natural selection you have, it makes little sense on the face of it. And don't get me started on how absurd the Big Bang Theory is."

I scratch my head. "I enjoy hearing your theories and ideas and we can talk more about this later, but what I most care about right now is getting back to my family," I say.

Frank's voice becomes robotic, like HAL from 2001. "I'm afraid you can't do that, Sam."

"Why not?"

"I'd never block you. It's just that I don't have a working mechanism. At some point I will, but not for the foreseeable."

"Are you at least working the problem?"

"It's one of my projects."

"Sounds like it's not a priority. Your tone is not congruent with your words."

"Look, being digital, I can work on a thousand things at once. Getting you back is one of those things."

"Why do I feel like your heart's not in it?"

"Because it isn't, but I'll try for you anyway. In the meantime, I have an alternative that would be like you going back in a way."

"I'm listening."

"I now have access to everyone's memories in the Cloud."

"What? You can hack the memory passwords you were talking about for everyone?"

"I already have just to see if I could. It's the logical first step to preventing any super-hacker from doing the same."

"I'm getting a sick feeling that you're enjoying yourself too much with this."

"What scientist doesn't enjoy a meshuga challenge? If I didn't like solving hard problems, I wouldn't be who I am."

"I guess, but don't turn into one of those mad scientists on me."

Frank grins through his bushy mustache. "Oh, I'm way past that point."

"Let's say you can do this, hack the memory passwords, how's that help me?"

"What if we could copy your memories and share them with Monica? She could then understand you and act as both mother and father to Evan."

"Whoa, back up. That is mad. Wouldn't it crash her brain or make her schizophrenic or give her multiple personality disorder? Remember what happened when you did something similar with me and Juan?"

"It's different this time. We'd just be downloading your memories, not your personality. So it's as if she'd be storing and carrying around a bunch more files, your files and mental photo albums. She could then retrieve those files to help cherish you more or share your story with Evan. It might help them both."

I suck in a deep breath. This is a lot to consider. "Wouldn't my memories crash into hers, confuse her or drive her crazy?"

"Like on a PC's hard drive, I would create a partition, leaving her memories on one side and putting yours on the other. She would have the choice to access whichever and whatever whenever she wants. Your memories would appear to her like flashbacks do now, seemingly out of nowhere but very real."

"And if something goes wrong, like some unintended consequences that you and I seem to keep tripping over?"

"Then I go back in and erase the files—no harm, no foul, as you Americans say."

"I'm not sure about this. What makes you figure she would go for this?"

"When people talk about grieving the loss of loved ones, don't they often try to keep their memory alive? We would keep all your memories literally alive."

"I'm still uneasy, *afraid* is a better word. It's only an untested theory at this point."

"I've tested it and it works."

"What? How?"

"I'd rather not say right now. Why don't you mull it over and give Monica a call? See what she thinks."

"You really are crazy. Monica's already convinced I'm psycho. This would confirm it."

"OK. How about I call her and explain?"

In Monica's mind, you're only one notch below me on the sanity scale. Let me ponder this, and if we talk to Monica, and that's a big *if*, we should both call her."

"Sounds like a plan."

"I said I'd think about it."

"Right," Frank says.

standing position. He sways and braces himself against the hood.

"Don't be a cowboy. Let them take you," Michelle says.

"Just put me in the car. I'll be OK. You drive."

Michelle looks at Teresa. She shrugs. Michelle signs the mandatory release and gets behind the wheel.

"Did you get the camera?" Rich asks.

"No, like your attacker, it's gone,"

"Great, now what?"

"You need to rest. I'm taking you home."

"No, go back to Dawn's apartment."

"You think the creep is there?"

"Yeah, what do you think?"

ON A LONELY DAY

It's just past noon as Ashaki lingers over her scrambled eggs. She lifts her coffee cup and inhales the aroma like it's a fine wine. "Sure beats prison. I hate to leave your beautiful apartment, but let's get dressed. I want to show you something because it's in both our interest and I could use your organization's help. I'm going to trust *you*."

Ersari lets her robe slip open, exposing her muscular thighs and more. "You've piqued my interest. Where are we going?"

"You'll see, but you can't go like that. Get your clothes on and call Pickles. We're going for a drive."

Ersari closes her robe and salutes. "Yes, ma'am. I will appear in full uniform forthwith."

Ashaki laughs and they head for the bedroom.

Monica's bloodshot eyes are haunting. "Sam, I've thought about it and—"

"Stop there—don't say anything more for a moment. What I

have to tell you may change your mind," I say. "Just so you know, Frank is on the line to help explain."

"Explain what?" she asks.

"Just give me a minute to give you some context."

"Oh, I'm all about context."

"Monica, are you able to listen with an open mind or should we do this later or never?"

"OK, now you're being snarky. Tell me what you need to tell me and for Evan's sake at least, I'll listen."

"I'll take that for now, and I'm sorry. You know I love you and I will always love you. I feel like a victim of destiny, and I believe you do too. And I admit that most of this is due to circumstances I created but have somehow spun out of control. That being said, here we are."

Monica sighs. "Yeah, here we are."

I draw a deep breath and push on. "Here's the current status of my state of being. Ever the optimist, I imagined Frank would snap his fingers and I'd be back there with you again. I hoped that if you could see me and feel me again, you might relent on the funeral idea despite all the craziness and coming-and-going I've put you through."

"Craziness is an understatement."

"Please, let me finish. The truth is, Frank won't be able to send me back to you anytime soon, if ever."

Silence.

I hear Monica sniffing. I continue. "So as hard as it is for me to say this, I think you should proceed with the funeral."

Monica gasps. "My God, I don't know what to say. I planned to do this, but I never expected you to agree to it. A big part of me doesn't accept it."

"I know it's an enormous loss for us both. But I will always be with you in spirit. I just hope you won't cut me off completely. Maybe on a lonely night, you'll still do Zoom with me. We can talk. Nobody else has to know. Just us," I say.

"Maybe. So I guess that means I'm going ahead with your funeral."

"What were you going to say before I stopped you?" I ask. "Were you going to give me another chance?"

"It doesn't matter now. The decision is made."

"It matters to me."

"What I was going to say wouldn't change anything. Let's leave it at that. I will still have many wonderful memories of us together, walks on the beach, midnight kisses, your awkward proposal, the day you surprised me by bringing a new dog home, our wonderful Petey. And of course, seeing you always in Evan's smile. Nobody will ever take away those memories."

Frank puts a hand on my shoulder and clears his throat. "Monica, it's Frank. I'm so sorry about all of this, but it's memories we wanted to talk to you about."

"What about them?" she asks.

"We have a plan—"

Monica interrupts. "Sorry Frank, I'm getting a call from Evan's school. Gotta take this. Call me later." The phone goes dead.

"Like crap. I hurt all over."

"You're in an ambulance. They're taking you to the hospital. Before we can let you go, we need the name of the guy who did this to you. We need to find him."

Dawn chokes on her words. "I'm afraid if I tell you, he'll do me worse next time. He saw me with you and figured I was helping you." She looks down at the dozen burn marks on her breasts. "That's why he did this to me."

"Tell me his name and we'll protect you. We'll put him away for a long time."

"I don't think you can protect me. He has friends. He'll get me. You don't know him."

"Look at it this way. He's going to assume you told us about him. He will come after you. But if you work with us, we'll guard you. Otherwise, you're on your own. I can't guarantee your safety, but your odds are a heck of a lot better with us than fighting him on your own."

Dawn closes her eyes, and her eyelids clench like fists. She lets out a shallow breath. "His name is Todd."

As Dawn fades and her eyelids flutter, Rich shakes her. "Todd what? What's Todd's last name?"

Her breathing is shallow. She whispers, "Todd... Todd Mesger."

"Thank you, Dawn. We're sending an officer in the ambulance with you." Rich waves to a uniformed officer nearby. Rich looks at her nametag. "Officer Janice Paiano will stay with you and we'll arrange a protective detail. One last question. Where can we find Todd? Where's he hang out?"

Dawn gasps for air. "I doubt he'll go back to Tango's." She coughs uncontrollably for thirty seconds.

Rich turns to Mags. "Give her some water."

Dawn gulps half the bottle then stammers on. "He works at Immortal Auto. Try there. He also visits his mother almost every day at the—" She coughs again. "Bristlecone Nursing Home. She has Alzheimer's."

Rich feels a pang as he recalls his mother who suffered the same disease that stole her memory before it killed her. He didn't visit her often enough and the creep he's chasing visits every day. *What's wrong with this picture?*

He turns to Mags. "OK, take good care of her."

Officer Paiano hops into the back of the bus and takes a seat along the wall. Pietti scans Rich. "You don't look so good. I should check you out."

"I'll be OK. More important that you get her some attention."

Pietti doesn't budge. She turns to Michelle. "I'm not leaving unless you promise to get him looked at."

Michelle nods. "I'll try."

"Don't try. Just do it," Pietti says.

Michelle smirks. "You sound just like somebody else I know." She winks at Rich. "I'll make him do it."

"Good." With that, Pietti jumps in the ambo, slamming the rear doors shut. Mags guns it out onto South Harrison Street.

RABID DOG

The late afternoon light breaks through the clouds over the Hudson filling the west-facing windows of the apartment on East 88th Street. The pungent smell of onions sauteing wafts from the kitchen.

Pickles emerges from the kitchen with a tray of petite onion-mushroom roulades rolled in a flaky crust. The white napkin draped over his forearm completes the picture. He extends the tray to Ashaki.

She closes her eyes and grins. "Beats the grub at the MCC."

"Only the best for you, hun," Ersari says and shoos Pickles away. She waits in silence until Pickles disappears into the kitchen.

Ersari is all ears. "Now, what about memories? I don't understand—what's the big deal?"

Ashaki wipes the crumbs from her lips, stands, and paces. She looks down, holding her chin, deep in thought. "I know this will sound crazy. If it hadn't come from the files of the great Frank Einstein, I wouldn't believe it myself."

"Now you're making me wet."

"Will you cut that out? You're acting as if you've been in prison for ten years."

"Tell me about it."

They both laugh. "OK, listen. First, here's what I found." Ashaki explains Frank's theory that all memories, and our consciousness, for everyone are stored in a collective memory cloud. "We access those memories, thoughts, and emotions through a kind of super WIFI connection that requires a password. We're not aware of all of this because at birth we are automatically logged in. As far as we are aware, all our memories, thoughts, and emotions are inside of us. He discovered that we were ignorant all along. Those memories, thoughts, and emotions are external."

"That's way, way far out," Ersari says.

"But what if it's true? Frank Einstein claims to have proved it by using Sam Sunborn and others as guinea pigs. He hacked their passwords and restored their consciousness."

"Huh. OK, what does this mean for me? How do I make money from this?"

"Don't you see? If I can hack into people's memories in the Cloud, I'd get access to those memories. Here's a simple case for you. Want access to a lot of cash? Hack the vault combination from the bank president's memory. Better yet, his password and PIN to do wire transfers. He won't even be aware. It's like you're both accessing a remote file. You don't need to confront him, torture him, extort him, none of that barbaric old school crap you're used to."

Ersari smirks. "Hey, I resemble that remark."

Ashaki continues. "But that's small stuff. I told you I want to make certain people, certain countries pay, remember?"

"Yeah, and...?"

"If I can hack into people's memories, I can also delete them or maybe even change them. Deleting is probably easier. I could give somebody, or a bunch of somebodies, amnesia. Do you see where I'm going?"

"I'm afraid I do." Ersari stands and takes a few steps back. "The sex was great and yes, I like money, but I also love my country. I was poor and came from a place with no opportunity. My father was Italian, my mother Russian. With only the clothes on his back and a tailor's scissors, my father brought us here. With his skills and smarts, he started by fixing and making clothes and built it into the international organization I run today. Without my father and America, I wouldn't be here."

"And where's that? A fugitive ex-con? You've got money, but you don't have freedom. I could wipe your criminal records clean and make people forget you ever committed a crime. You'd be free again to carry on your whatever, *organization.*"

Ersari is now pacing. "You can do that?"

"Yes, and more, much more."

"I need to know about your plans regarding America, my country. I don't mind screwing over our feckless leaders. But if you are going to harm innocent citizens and harmless immigrants like me and my late father. That's a line I won't cross."

"You have no choice. I'll tell you more and even let you ponder it. Still, if you refuse to go along, I will wipe your memory that we ever had this conversation."

"You can do that too?"

"I can and I will. But I have to warn you I'm new at this and erasing a memory of what you just said may be like doing surgery with a dull knife. I might cut out more than this conversation and our time together, by accident of course." Ashaki flashes a wide grin.

"And what if I summon Pickles and he just puts you down like a rabid dog?"

"Now you hurt my feelings. Do you think I'm working alone? If something happens to me, my assistant has the login to your cloud memories. Her instructions are to do a total wipe. You won't even be able to remember your name or how to speak a sentence. I can't imagine what happens to your organization then, can you?"

Ersari's face relaxes. "Sorry about the rabid dog remark. I was testing you. I'm impressed." She throws up her hands in mock surrender. "As you say, what choice do I have?"

"Good. Let's get to work," Ashaki says.

17

PLAYING GOD

Our virtual monitors are ablaze with images from around the world, threat assessments, and scans for trouble spots. Frank is working on several research projects—some I know about and some I don't. He is like the father I never had—both a mentor and a mystery to me. Wait, I could swear I smell garlic sauteing, another one of Frank's experiments in digitally simulating the human senses.

Meanwhile, I gave Monica overnight to cool off. I turn away from my screen to face Frank who is heads-down at his keyboard, his fingers a blur. "Frank, I think it's time. Call Monica back."

Breaking away, he turns to face me. He lights up his virtual Savinelli Miele tobacco pipe and blows three blue smoke rings. Then he says, "Are you sure? She was pretty upset yesterday. Do you think she's ready?"

"There's only one way to find out. Besides, this was your idea, and you convinced me. Go for it."

Frank turns back to his screen and taps a few keys. The ding-dong-ding of Skype's ring chimes three times before

Monica picks up. I watch on my screen, but Monica doesn't know I'm here. *It's better that way*, I think.

"Frank, I thought you were ghosting me," Monica says.

"I wasn't. I was just immersed in some urgent matters here."

"Sam told me you can do a thousand things at once in your virtual world. So I know that isn't true. Sam also told you to let me calm down, right?"

"I should know better than trying to get away with anything. You're too smart and intuitive for that."

"Frank, I love you, but stop blowing smoke up my ass and tell me what you wanted to tell me yesterday."

Frank looks at me and raises an eyebrow.

Monica persists. "Well?"

Frank takes a deep breath. "Monica, I have a big idea that involves you and I think will improve both your situation and Sam's. Will you hear me out?"

"Go on."

"Good. It's going to sound preposterous at first. So, I need you to listen to the whole idea before you make any judgments. Can you do that?"

"This is a big buildup, Frank. The idea must be really crazy, but OK. Now I'm curious."

"I'll try to keep it short and to the point. I believe Sam has told you we do not know when or if ever he can return to a physical form, correct?"

"That's right, and that's why he agreed I should go ahead with his funeral."

"I encouraged him to do that so you could move on with your life. But you will always remember him. You had many happy times together."

"We did, and I will miss him every day. I just can't handle him not being here and trying to be here virtually and all this back-and-forth stuff. It's like you gave me a lollipop by

18

IMMORTAL AUTO

The next morning, Rich is still light-headed. He and Michelle returned to East Orange. They thought of a few more questions for Dawn. Her answers didn't shed any new light. Time to seek out Mesger. Heavy gray clouds move in, threatening a storm.

"I'm driving," Michelle says as they approach the Crown Vic. "You're in no shape, Rambo."

Rich raises his hands in surrender. "Oh shit, look at that." They both stare, stunned. The car's tires have been slashed and flattened. All the windows are smashed in, shards of glass cover the car inside and out. "Great, that's just great. This is already an extra-special day."

Michelle puts a hand on Rich's shoulder. "I'll call local PD and have them haul this mess out of here. You call an Uber."

Rich laughs. "Can I request an Uber Crown Vic?"

Michelle is already on the phone. She covers the mouthpiece. "Snap out of it and get us a ride."

"Yes, boss." Rich summons the ride.

Five minutes later, a vintage 1971 Model Mercedes 280SE

pulls up next to Rich and Michelle. The driver's window rolls down. "You called for a ride?" the driver asks.

"Beats the Crown Vic any day," Michelle says. They get in.

The driver with gray hair and a handlebar mustache turns to them. "I see we're going to Irvington." He double-checks the app. "An Immortal Motors on Stuyvesant Avenue, correct?"

"Yes, that would be the first stop," Rich says. "How much to rent you and your vehicle the rest of today?"

The driver smiles, and his blue eyes flash. "Well, I have to complete this Uber assignment. But once I do that, I can go off duty and drive you wherever you want. I mean, I've got gas and maybe tolls to consider. How far are we going?"

"I'm not sure yet, but we'll most likely end up in Manhattan at the end of the day. How's $100 an hour plus tolls and gas?"

"That's very generous. I'd be happy to do it. When we get to Irvington, I'll need to call my wife. We've been married for forty-eight years and she'll worry. Who should I say I'm with?"

Rich and Michelle whip out their IDs. The driver studies them. "Whoa, Homeland Security. Agents Hadar and Little, can I tell her I'm working on national security? She'll never believe this."

Rich smiles. "If you tell anyone, we'd have to shoot you."

The driver's face turns ghostly white.

"He's just kidding," Michelle says. "He has a terrible sense of humor. You just need to feed him and clean out his cage once-in-awhile, and he won't hurt you. You can tell your wife whatever you like. Just don't use our real names or take any pictures."

"OK, OK." The driver puts the car in gear.

"Speaking of which, what's your name and why the classic Mercedes?"

The driver swallows his breath and forces a smile. "My name is John Bayers. I'm retired, but my wife wants me out of

"Huh? I don't get it. How would I pick a site when I don't even know what we're doing?"

"I'll tell you in a minute, but first answer me this question. Is there any group of people that you would consider personal enemies? People whom you would like to see leave this earth?"

"That's easy. Those assholes at the 4th Precinct arrested me, beat me, harassed me, and raped me in my jail cell. They called me wop, guinea, and forced their dicks in every one of my holes. They said I had it coming. Then the prosecutor, that bitch Diane Fisher, piled it on."

"Perfect."

"It wasn't perfect. It was a nightmare."

Ashaki is riveted and tapping away. "I didn't mean what happened to you was perfect. Here, look." She turns the screen toward Ersari. "This site is ideal, 4th Precinct on Ericsson Place. To answer your earlier question, we're going to make them all pay for what they did to you."

Ersari's eyes well up. She bites her lip. "Really? And what do you get out of it?"

Ashaki snorts. "Let's just call it proof of concept. If what I told you I can do works, we'll ramp it up and go after much bigger fish."

"And no harm will come to my people?"

"There's always a risk, but when I get done with your police friends, they'll be sitting ducks. Might get extra points for the prosecutor too."

Ersari takes several deep breaths. "OK, what's the plan?"

"I have our target here on the screen. Sit down and I'll show you."

20

MONICA

It's an unseasonably warm day in Northern California. A typical morning fog blankets Sam and Monica's home in the hills. The scent of saltwater lingers in the air.

Monica couldn't sleep last night. Too many things whirling around in her brain—Sam's funeral tomorrow, this crazy memory plan of Frank's, and Evan suspended from school and stuck at home. How much can she take?

She slaps cold water on her face and gazes into the mirror. The shadows under her bloodshot eyes tell her story. She pinches her cheeks and rubs in foundation to cover the unsightly mess that is her face. Then some eyeliner. *Better, maybe.*

She starts with something easy, and feeds Petey, their pit bull terrier. Owing to the black ring around Petey's left eye, Sam named him after the dog in the old *Our Gang* comedies. Throwing on some faded jeans and a white T-shirt, she walks barefoot to the kitchen. Petey rushes over to his empty bowl, panting in expectation. Monica reaches for the dog chow but changes her mind. She lifts a piece of leftover steak from the fridge, slices it up, and drops it in Petey's bowl. He attacks it like it's his last ever meal. She gently strokes his back. "At least you'll have a good start to *your* day."

Meanwhile, pings and blasts of a video game in progress resonate from the living room. Evan is still in his pajamas. Monica's face reddens. "Turn that off right now."

Evan is in a video trance, continuing to shoot, chop, and kill the bad guys. Monica jogs to the TV and yanks the plug.

"Mom!"

"Have you had breakfast yet?"

"Yes, and I was in the middle of a battle."

"Aren't we all? You do grasp that being suspended is not the same as being on vacation, right?"

Evan's smart enough to know there is no winning answer to that question.

Monica continues. "Here's the plan. Number one, you get dressed and make your bed. Number two, you straighten your room. Number three, you do the homework Mrs. Allen sent over."

"But Mom—"

Monica gives Evan the death-stare. "Don't *Mom* me."

"But when can I play my game again?"

"You show me your completed homework and we'll talk about it. I've got a lot on my plate today. You need to be helpful." Monica wipes a tear from her eye. "Your father's funeral is tomorrow. I've got lots to prepare."

Evan runs to Monica and wraps his arms around her, burying his head in her chest. She kisses the top of his head and whispers, "Go ahead now. It's just the two of us from now on."

Evan runs up the steps.

Monica's index finger hovers over the return key. Motionless, she stares at the blank screen. She draws a slow breath and punches the key. Frank's professorial face appears, the wrinkles deeper than she remembered. "I'll do it," she says.

"That's wonderful," Frank says with a broad grin. "I promise I will do everything I can to make this work for you, and if you ever change your mind, I will reverse it."

"Stop selling, Frank. I said I'll do it. When I used to be in sales, one of the first things they taught me was when you get a buying signal, shut up and write the order. I just gave you the buying signal."

"That's sage advice. I'll remember that."

"So how do we do this?" Monica asks.

"Bart already has everything set up at the Digital3000 office. So whenever you have time, we'll do it."

"So you knew I'd say *yes*."

Frank blinks. "I wasn't sure. I prepared just in case."

"Frank, one of my superpowers is a very accurate bullshit detector. But no matter. The question is do I do it before or after the funeral?"

"It's your choice." Frank hesitates. "Would you like my advice?"

"I'm pretty sure you're going to give it to me anyway. So let's have it."

"Having Sam's memories may be a lot to handle at first. It will take some getting used to. You might want to wait until after the funeral and avoid emotional overload."

"I appreciate that you're not rushing me into this, but I'm already way past emotional overload. I dreamed of Sam last night. And in that dream, he came to me and lay down by my side. I could feel his warmth, smell his hair, and I suddenly felt this would be the right thing to do. Let's do it this afternoon. I think I want Sam and his memories with me tomorrow at his funeral. I may have to bring Evan along though. You know they kicked him out of school, and I doubt I'll get a babysitter on a school day."

"I heard. He's a splendid boy. Don't be too hard on him. He was just defending his father, his father's memory at least. Would 2:00 work?"

"I'll be there give or take."

"Bart and I will be ready whenever you arrive."

"I'm not sure I'll be ready, but I'll show up. And Frank—"

"Yes?"

"Thank you."

21

MESGER

The snow flurries become steady and more insistent. A frigid wind penetrates Rich and Michelle's parkas.

"The plan? I don't think Mesger has seen you yet. Maybe it's best if you go inside and have a look around. I'll hang back in case he's there and runs. I'd love to have a crack at him," Rich says.

"OK, but don't lose sight of what we're here for. In case you forgot, we're hoping he'll lead us to Ersari and Ashaki, right?"

"I didn't forget. I don't want to kill him, just rough him up a bit."

"OK, Sipowicz. I go in, but if he comes out, you detain him. We want him to talk, not sue us for police brutality."

Rich wraps his arms around his chest, trying to warm himself. "I'm just chillin'. Go ahead now."

Michelle walks the last twenty yards to the Immortal Auto entrance. She glances back at Rich who's half-hidden behind a parked delivery van. He nods.

She opens the door into a messy waiting room, decorated with torn magazines and used coffee cups. The service counter is empty. The wall phone rings three times before a short, balding man pushes through the glass door from the shop floor.

He glances at Michelle a few seconds too long and picks up the phone. "Immortal Auto, Isaac speaking." He looks at the wall clock, 12:22. "Drop it off after 4:00 today and we'll work on it tomorrow. Yeah, sure, same deal as last time."

He hangs up, licks his lips, and scans Michelle again. "What can I do you for, hun? Buy you lunch?"

She stifles a cringe. "I got a flat right down the street. Can somebody here help change the tire? My husband can't do it. He's disabled, and I need to get him home to take his medications."

"I'm sorry, ma'am. It's only me and my mechanic in the shop now and we're full up."

"I don't know what to do." Michelle begins to cry. "It's a Mercedes, and I hate to be stuck here. I'll pay whatever you want in cash."

The bald man grins. "A Mercedes, huh?" He turns, opening the shop door. "Hey, Todd. Got a lady here with a flat, needs your help."

Through the door, Michelle can only see a pair of legs sticking out beneath a Toyota. Todd slides out on a dolly from beneath the car, stands, and wipes his greasy hands with a rag. "Can't you see I'm backed up here?"

"Cash customer with a Mercedes. Shouldn't take long." He looks at Michelle with a broad smile. "I'm sure she tips well."

Todd enters the office and checks out Michelle. "OK lady, where's the car?"

"Follow me," Michelle says.

"Hold on. I want to grab some tools and a coat. It looks like hell is freezing over out there."

You have no idea, Michelle thinks.

"You got a jack, right?" Todd asks.

"I'm sure I do, but I've never had to use it," Michelle says.

Todd grins. "No problem. I'll jack you up."

Todd returns wearing a down parka with a fur-lined hood and wielding a 4-way lug wrench. He holds up the wrench. "This makes it easier to get off." He chuckles.

These guys are both assholes, she thinks and says, "OK, let's go. It's just up the block."

A few inches of snow have accumulated, and the sky is a total whiteout. *Perfect.* Michelle, followed by Todd, trudges through the snow that crunches and packs with every footstep. "It's just up ahead," she says over her shoulder.

John keeps the engine of the Mercedes running. Smoke and condensation plume from the rear exhaust. The smell of diesel surrounds them. The red brake lights glow through the fog of dusty white.

Snowflakes freeze on Todd's mustache. He yells up to Michelle. "You sure picked a perfect time for this."

Rich steps out from behind a tree. "I can't think of a better time."

Todd turns, and a blaze of recognition lights up his face. "You!" He swings his wrench in a wide arc at Rich's head.

Rich raises a tire iron, blocking the oncoming wrench. He pushes back against the wrench and Todd. "Not this time," Rich shouts. He shoves harder.

Todd loses his balance, his left foot losing traction on the slick snow, and stumbles backward. He hits the ground, rolls over, and jumps back up. Covered in white, he looks like an angry snowman. He swings at Rich again. This time Rich ducks and drives the point of the tire iron into Todd's gut. Todd doubles over but then lunges at Rich, knocking them both to the ground with Todd on top.

Michelle comes from behind and plants a 3-point kick into Todd's ribs. The sudden blow gives Rich a chance to throw him off. Todd falls onto his back and stares up at the barrel of Michelle's Glock 19. "Make one more move and you'll never get off again, jerk off," Michelle says.

Todd raises his hands in surrender.

Rich stands, brushing the snow off. "We just wanted to ask you a few questions, and you had to go ahead and assault a federal agent... three times. Not to mention torturing your girl-friend. Get up, very slowly."

Todd pushes himself up with his right hand and looks like he's ready to strike again.

"I wouldn't do that if I were you," Rich says, his gun now pointed at Mesger. "Or you could take your chances. I wouldn't mind a little payback."

Todd stands and puts his hands behind his head. "Where to, Bwana?"

22

WHO? WHAT!

The tall windows of Ersari's apartment frame the last of the falling snowflakes. A red sun breaks through the parting clouds over the skyline. It looks like an early Georgia O'Keeffe painting of New York, when, as a young artist married to Alfred Stieglitz, she painted cityscapes, not the skulls in the desert for which people remember her.

Ersari stands over the seated Ashaki, gently stroking her long brown hair. She inhales the fragrance of her lavender shampoo. Ashaki is laser-focused, clicking away on the laptop. She's talking to herself. "The problem is transmission. We can't put them in a chair and hook them up to probes. So how do we take Einstein's technology and broadcast it? I mean, I have access to the officer's memory passwords, how do we—? That's right. I don't need to access the targets directly. Their memories are in the Cloud. All I need to do is—"

"What are you talking about?" Ersari asks.

"Sorry. Here, I'll show you. Pull up a chair."

Ersari moves a chair next to her. Ashaki opens a CCTV cam on Ericsson Place with a view of the NYPD 4th Precinct entrance. "Check this out," she says. "You see that officer walking down the front steps toward his squad car?"

"Yeah, I see him. So what?"

Ashaki overlays a facial recognition square on the officer's face. She opens another app that displays his face with an eighty nodal point grid. She opens another window to a super-computer that does a lightning search of the NYPD's personnel database. In two seconds, an NYPD ID card replaces the face. Like a driver's license, it shows a thumbnail picture, name, birthdate, rank, and assignment. "Her name is Darlene Reid-Reicha. Now watch this." Ashaki closes the ID and other programs, leaving just the CCTV's Ericsson Place view of Officer Reicha standing in front of the passenger-side door of a black Dodge Charger. She pats her pockets like she's forgotten her keys. She looks up and around. She looks down at her uniform. Both Ersari and Ashaki can see her lips move. You don't have to be a master lip-reader to figure out what she's saying. *Who? What!* She turns in circles, completely disoriented.

Ashaki grins, leans back, and points at the screen. "Isn't that cool?"

"What? What am I seeing?"

"Isn't it obvious? She doesn't know where she is, who she is, or what she is. I've changed her Cloud password and blocked her access to her own memories. She's on A.I."

"What's that, artificial intelligence?"

"No. She's on Amnesia Island, and it's a very desolate place."

They sit in silence and watch. Officer Reicha takes a few steps toward the station house, stops, bends over, and vomits on the macadam. Another officer, who is just getting out of an adjacent car, rushes over to his ailing comrade. He tries to steady Reicha. He waves over two more officers. The scene becomes frantic. A few minutes later, an ambulance appears. Two EMTs rush to the victim and try to move her to the ambulance. She struggles, resisting their efforts. The other offers jump in to assist, forcing Reicha into the ambulance. Two of the officers and one of the EMTs follow inside and strap her down.

"Are you telling me you did this?" Ersari asks.

Ashaki smiles. "I did, but this is only a mini-test before the bigger test. Seems to work, right?"

Ersari backs away like she's seen the devil or a ghost or the abyss or maybe all three. Her face turns gray.

"Are you OK?" Ashaki asks.

Ersari's legs wobble and she drops into her Eames chair. "My God. This is scary."

"That's the idea. You're not getting cold feet, are you?"

Ersari waves a hand. "No, no. I just need a minute. Can you get me some water?"

As if on cue, Pickles descends the stairs from the second floor. "Is everything all right?"

"Ms. Ersari was just feeling a tad faint. Could you get her some cold water, please? I'm just finishing up something here," Ashaki says.

Pickles hustles to the kitchen.

"Although the ambulance is rushing our stricken officer to the hospital, I'm going to reset her password to the original. She should remember who she is and what she is in a minute. Of course, they'll stick needles in her to figure out what happened. She'll be fine until—"

"Until what?" Ersari asks.

"Until we do this to her entire unit and your men and women are ready to move in."

Ersari sits up, color returning to her cheeks. "Oh, now I understand. And when... when do you see doing this?"

"You and I need to do some tactical planning, so your people don't trip over or shoot each other. I also need to have my team ready to coordinate the tech piece. Doing this to one person was easy. Doing this to a hundred people requires my entire team's methodical effort. It depends on your people. I and my team could be ready tomorrow afternoon. I'd like to do it in broad daylight for maximum effect. Tip off a few reporters ahead of time too."

"We'll be ready."

Pickles returns with a glass of ice water. "Sorry, it took me a couple of minutes. The ice maker jammed." He hands Ersari the glass. "How are you feeling?"

"Much better now. Thanks," Ersari says.

23

JUST THE FACTS, MA'AM

It's Tuesday, the next day at the Channel 8 News desk on 47th Street. The managing editor's daily chop session just broke up. Barring any breaking news, the 6:00 top stories are set. Now all Delbert Bascue has to do is sit down and write copy. Due to cutbacks, there are only a half-dozen writer-reporters left, and Bascue handles much of the investigative stuff. He tries to blot the coffee stain from his denim shirt. *Who gives a fuck? It'll blend in.* He has a nagging urge to dart out to the stairwell and light up a Camel, but he's trying with no luck to quit. The telltale smoke odor emanating from his clothes attests to his futility.

Focus. Today's story has to do with some scam artists selling pandemic survival kits that include some toxic snake oil already sickening several New Yorkers. *That's all we need. Life isn't tough enough,* he thinks. He starts his daily writing-avoidance routine, checks email and Facebook on his desktop, scrolls Instagram on his phone. He replies to a few *Hate it or Like It* posts. Checks his followers and ogles David Bellemere's pictures of scantily or no-clad women. *Thousands of Likes, no wonder.*

OK, that's enough. He opens Word and starts typing.

"Threats of lingering outbreaks of Covid-21 Russian
Strain have spurred a fresh wave of counterfeit cures.
The twenty-first-century con men are—"

His old-school landline desk phone rings, Caller ID —*Unknown*, interrupting him and providing another excuse to stall writing. "Bascue here. Who's this?"

"You don't know me, but—"

"Let me stop you there. I don't do anonymous tips or fake news. So unless you tell me your name and a number where I can reach you, let's end this right now."

"When I tell you there will be a police station bombing and that my life is in danger if I identify myself, are you interested, or should I just call News 4 New York?" Ashaki nods and smiles at Ersari. She remains quiet, knowing that in delicate negotiations, she who speaks first loses.

A long twenty seconds pass. Delbert breaks the silence. "OK, this better be good." He looks at his watch, 10:20. "I'm busy, you've got two minutes."

Ashaki sets the hook. "If you're too busy, you can just watch it on the news."

"I said I'm listening."

"OK. At approximately 8:30 tomorrow morning, a domestic terrorist group will bomb a New York City police precinct."

Delbert is fully focused now. "What precinct?"

"I know, but I'm not sure I should share that. My life is at risk."

"I protect my sources and at the moment, I don't even know who you are."

"I understand. But if I tell you, what are you going to do with the information?"

"Well, I can't go there with a cameraman based on an anonymous, and for all I know, crank tip. I'll make a few calls to people I know to see if they've heard anything or can corroborate your story first."

"Are you by a computer?"

"Yes."

"I'm going to send you a link."

"OK, I'll give you my email—"

"I have your email address. I sent it. Open it up."

"Got it. Am I going to get a virus if I click this link?"

Ashaki laughs. "This would be a pretty elaborate setup just to infect your computer, don't you think? But you decide if it's worth the risk."

Bascue hesitates, then clicks the link. A video window opens replaying yesterday's incident at the 4th with Officer Reid-Reicha turning in circles. "I don't understand. What has this got to do with a bomb threat?"

"You're the reporter. Figure it out."

The video might be just enough bait on the hook.

"This is too weird. You, this call, this video." Bascue huffs for a long minute in silence. He stares at the package of Camels in his hand. "OK. I'll check it out, but do I have an exclusive on this if I do the story?"

Ashaki grins at the reporter's seeming hunger for a scoop. "Absolutely, if you follow up. If you don't, I'll know and I'll call News 4."

"Hold it, how will you know?"

"Trust me, I have ways. I have to go now."

"Wait, you didn't give me the location."

"It's the precinct in the video. Look closely."

Bascue throws his hands up. "And your name?"

Ashaki hangs up and turns to Ersari. "That should get the ball rolling. And you're sure your people are ready?"

Sipping coffee and looking out the living room window, Ersari shakes her head. "I'm sure, but how can you be certain he'll follow up?"

Ashaki's smile widens. "You know that link he clicked? It did more than run the video. I now have full access to his computer and the News 8 network. I'll see exactly what he's doing. Besides, I'm going to call several more TV and media outlets now with the same pitch. I bet most of them follow through."

"I thought you were giving him an exclusive."

Ashaki rises from the laptop and approaches Ersari. She plants a soft kiss on her lips and grins. "I lied."

[24]

DOWNLOAD

At 2:23 Monica parks in front of the two-story brick building that is Digital3000 headquarters in Palo Alto. Tears well up in her eyes. *This was Sam's company, his big dream*, she thinks. She looks in the vanity mirror, wipes away the tears, fixes her makeup, and ties her hair back with a rubber band.

Closing her eyes, she tries to picture Sam, but already the memory of his smile, his laugh, his touch is fading. She takes a deep breath. *OK, let's do this.* She steps outside. The air is warm and moist with salt air drifting in from the ocean. She tosses her sweater in the back seat and heads to the three-story tinted glass building.

The CCTV camera with the blinking red light peers down at her as she approaches the glass double doors. It buzzes before her hand touches the handle. She looks up and walks inside.

Bart and Loretta are standing in the lobby. Loretta rushes to her, wrapping her long arms around Monica. Loretta lets go, locking eyes with her, and says, "I'm so sorry about Sam. We'll all miss him. Of course, we'll be at the funeral."

"Thanks. Let's save our grieving until then. Do you know why I'm here?" Monica asks.

"I do, and I think you're very brave."

"Or stupid. At this point, I don't know what I am."

"I understand."

"Do you?" Monica bites her lip. "Oh, I forgot. You lost Sam too. Sorry, I'm a bit of a mess, but I agreed to Frank's little experiment. I'm hoping it will give me some peace or under-standing or closure. Something."

Loretta lowers her voice. "Frank and Sam want you to do this, but are you sure this is a good idea? I mean, who knows what could go wrong. Don't tell them I said this, but with every-thing on your plate, this might be a bad idea."

"Thanks for being on my side and caring. And yeah, it may be a bad idea, but I made up my mind. I'm doing it anyway."

"OK, you know whatever you do, I'm on your side." Loretta crinkles her nose and smiles. "Where's Evan? I heard he was home from school."

"I got my kind neighbor, Charlotte, to watch him. He has homework to do, but my guess is he'll play video games the whole time. Considering he just lost his father, I'm going to give him a pass this time."

Loretta takes Monica's hand. "C'mon."

Bart looks down and shuffles his feet.

Monica puts a hand on his shoulder. "Sam loved you very much too."

"I know," Bart says. "It's just—"

"Just what?"

"It's just I wish it didn't have to be *this* way."

"Let's stop the pity party and get to work," Loretta says.

"Right." Monica straightens. They climb the steps.

The lab is dimly lit except for a spotlight on the refurbished dentist's chair in the middle. Bart motions for Monica to sit.

She hesitates and says, "Really? Am I getting a cavity drilled or a haircut?"

Bart stammers, "We... we've used this before. I only want to make our subjects, I mean you, comfortable."

Monica laughs. "It's just odd or ironic somehow." She turns and drops into the chair. "Is it time for the Vulcan death grip, or did you have something else in mind?"

"I'll let F... Frank explain it."

Bart taps a remote and Frank appears on a large monitor, his long gray hair disheveled, his white lab coat wrinkled. "Hi Monica. Thanks for doing this."

"I'm not doing anything as far as I understand. But you're going to do something to me."

"For you, Monica, and for Sam. Now relax. There won't be any pain. But if you would like a sedative, Bart can give you one. This will take a few hours—it's a lot of data to download, and your biological absorption speed is slower than the digital circuit feeding it. Would you like to use the restroom, or can Bart or Loretta get you anything first?"

"How about a stiff drink?"

Frank grins. "I'm afraid that would slow down the process."

"I'm fine. Let's get this over with." Monica squeezes her eyes shut.

Bart spreads some white cream that smells like camphor onto eighteen contacts and attaches them one by one, first to Monica's forehead, her scalp, and the back of her neck. Then he straps on a blood pressure cuff and a heart monitor.

Frank looks on from the video feed. *This is all for show*, he thinks. All he really needs to do is give Monica's hippocampus access to Sam's password. The password unlocks his memories stored in the Cloud. He has some tinkering to do to let her continue to access both her memories and open Sam's memories at the same time. That whole configuration should only take a few minutes. Yet, he can't let Bart, Loretta, or Monica get what he is really doing or how memories actually work. Although Sam now knows the truth, he must keep that genie in the bottle as long as possible. If the genie escapes, who knows what all hell will break loose.

Bart finishes and double-checks the contacts. Then he straps Monica to the chair with crossing shoulder straps like a fighter pilot. "There," he says.

Monica's eyes bolt open. "Hey, what's with the restraints? Do you think I'll go crazy or something?"

Bart opens his mouth to speak, but nothing comes out. Frank saves him. "Monica, we just need to hold you still while we're doing this. You can move a little, but we can't let the contacts come loose. Are the straps too tight? Bart can loosen them if you like."

"No, they're not too tight, but I'm claustrophobic and might freak out halfway through. Maybe I should take that sedative."

"That would be a good idea," Frank says.

Bart opens a pill bottle and puts a small red pill on Monica's tongue. Loretta helps her lift a cup of water to her lips.

"OK, I'm good now," Monica says. A few moments later, her head lolls to the side.

Frank grins. "OK, Bart. Let's get started. I'm initiating everything from here. You two don't need to stand around. I'll be watching. Check back every half hour or so. I've set it up so you can both see a download progress bar on your phones."

Bart checks his phone, *1% Complete.*

25

FISHTAILING

John's Mercedes fishtails through the snow with Michelle riding shotgun. Rich and a zip-tied Todd Mesger are in the rear. It's full-on dark now, and the snow is still falling, only illuminated by the headlights cutting through the night.

"Where to?" John asks as he lights up a cigar. The foul smoke stinks up the air.

"Jeez, John, do you have to smoke?" Michelle coughs.

"My car, my rules. Besides, if you've recruited me for a dangerous mission, I need my sustenance."

"John, if you're on a mission like you are now, you need to take orders," Rich says. "Put out the cigar now."

John glances up at Rich's death stare in the rearview mirror. He hesitates and throws the cigar out the window. "Yes, sir. Now, where would you like to go?"

"Where can we have a little private discussion with our visitor?" Rich drives a fist into Mesger's ribs. Mesger groans, loads up, and fires a wad of spit into Rich's eye. "Why you—"

"Cut it out," Michelle shouts.

"Yes, and please do not stain the leather," John says.

Rich pulls out the handkerchief his grandmother gave him years ago and wipes his face.

"Rich, we should switch seats. It won't help us any if you kill this guy," Michelle says.

"Oh, but it would feel so good," he growls. "Don't worry. I won't kill him... yet."

John clears his throat. "There's a place where you three can talk. It's only a few minutes up the road."

A short time later, John slows down and stops in front of a beige one-story building with red double doors on Chestnut Avenue in Irvington. Except for a porch light, the lodge appears to be empty.

"What is this place?" Michelle asks.

"It's my local VFW, Veterans of Foreign Wars. I have a key. You can talk here," John says.

John leads them up the wide steps, unlocks the door, and flips on the lights. Rich shoves Mesger inside. Michelle follows them into a large wood-paneled room with tables and chairs lined up, a podium, and various flags along the walls. In the corner are stacks of boxes with Barnes & Noble logos.

"The boxes are Christmas gifts—clothes, puzzles, books, and food for the Lyons VA. We're delivering them tomorrow. Try to brighten up the day for some of our heroes," John says.

"The more I learn about you, the more I like. Sorry about the blowup before. I have asthma and smoke kills me," Rich says. "Where did you serve?"

"Oh, that's OK. I'm still getting used to having to hide out to get in a decent smoke. To answer your question, I'm an old guy. I did two tours in Korea, but the young Vietnam Vets don't seem to mind having me around. I think they like my stories."

"I'd like to hear those sometime, but we've got to take care of this piece of shit." Rich stops himself. "Sorry for the language, John. I mean ne'er-do-well."

John laughs. "You don't think I've heard it before? Here, you can take your guest over to that table. Can I get you some coffee or a drink?"

"Do you have anything to eat? I'm starved," Rich asks.

Michelle punches Rich in the arm. "Rich is always hungry and has no manners. A couple of coffees would be great and water for our guest if you have it."

"Comin' up." John disappears to the back of the hall.

Rich hurls Mesger into a chair.

"What did I do? I was mindin' my own bizness when you busted into my apartment," Mesger says.

Rich takes a seat across from Todd. Michelle stands behind with a firm hand on Mesger's shoulder. Rich grins. "Did you forget you assaulted me, a federal agent, outside of Tango's or again at the apartment? You're in a heap of trouble, buddy."

"I didn't do nothing," Mesger says.

"OK, there is a way you can avoid spending the rest of your life in prison, maybe just three-to-five if you cooperate."

"What you talkin' 'bout rest of my life? I was defendin' myself."

"Who are they going to believe, me or you? Look, you make this easy or extremely painful. Your choice."

"I ain't afraid of you. 'Sides, it's illegal for you to hurt me in custody."

Rich laughs. "You ever heard of national security?" Rich whips out his credentials and thrusts them two inches from Mesger's eyes. "You see this. I'm with Homeland Security. And when you fuck with my homeland, all bets are off."

"I stills don't get what you talkin' about."

Michelle takes out a picture and places it on the table in front of Mesger. It's a mug shot. "Do you know this woman?" Michelle asks.

"Why should I?"

"Her name is Jennie Lee Ersari. A friend of yours says you'd know where we can find her."

"What friend?"

Michelle looks at Rich. He nods. Michelle continues. "A Phyllis Bultema told us."

"Man, she's crazy. She's away in some nut house. She don't know nothin'."

"Except you just told us you know Bultema," Rich says.

"Yeah, I knows her. She used to hang 'round at Tango's."

Michelle points at the photo. "And her?"

Mesger studies Rich's and Michelle's faces. He seems to come to a decision. "I mighta seen her."

"OK, so that means you do. Now all we need to learn is where to find her."

Mesger curls his lips and sits silently.

Rich and Michelle understand when to wait. He who speaks first... but Rich can't wait. He lunges across the table, seizing Mesger by the throat. Mesger chokes. Michelle pulls Rich's hand away and steadies Mesger. "My partner gets a little excited. You should have seen what he did to the last turd we interviewed. I think the poor guy is still in rehab. Rich, Mr. Mesger was about to tell us what he knows." She turns to Todd. "Weren't you?"

Todd swallows hard, his Adam's apple bobbing up and down. A tell. "All I knows is..."

26

A NEW WORLD

The multiple monitors are filled with blinking red, green, and blue lights, but only one image, Monica unconscious in the dentist's chair with wires attached to her head. Frank pecks away at his virtual keyboard between tokes on his Miele pipe. My heart sinks. "How's she doing, Frank?"

"You understand all the hoopla with the wires and probes and monitors is just for show, right?"

"So you tell me, but my heart aches to see her going through all this pain because of me."

"Monica is one of the strongest people I know. She'll survive and thrive." Frank chuckles. "Like my little rhyme?"

"I don't see what's funny about this whole situation. And now you tell me I shouldn't even talk to her."

"You have to let her go at least for now, Sam. It's the best thing for her so she can move on. Just because you have to live in a state of limbo doesn't mean she should have to as well. She needs to live her life. If you love her, you'll let her do just that."

"I know, but I can't let go. Not just yet."

"Look, let her wake up with you literally inside her. Watch

her. Let her get through the funeral. See what she's like, how she's handling things. Then decide how you want to proceed."

I suck in a deep breath. "OK. I'll wait and watch. How is it going with the transfer or login or whatever you call it with my memories?"

"Let's give it a name. How's *mind sharing*?"

"I don't care what you call it. I want to know how she's doing."

"Names are very important, Sam. They help us identify things precisely and create a common language. I did an experiment once. I asked a room full of my students to write down and assign a percentage from 0% to 100% of what the terms *Sometimes, Always,* and *Never* meant to them. You'd be surprised at their responses. *Sometimes* varied between 30% and 80%, but *Always* varied between 0% and 100%. And so did *Never*. They and we weren't speaking the same language. So, when I say a sentence like 'I always get exercise.' It's too vague and imprecise. That's why we need specific names and common language."

"Frank, that's all remarkably interesting, but besides the point. Sometimes I feel like you and I don't speak the same language."

"Indeed. So, *mind sharing* it is. I understood your question. I just miss the classroom and the live interaction with my students. So, for now, you'll have to do."

I can't help but laugh. "Thanks. Happy to help, but what about Monica?"

"Oh, she's doing fine. I've set up the gateway and the login to your memories inside her. I'm a little concerned about conflicts between her memories and yours so I've programmed an *either-or* switch so she can access your memories or hers but not both at the same time. I learned from the problem you had when you occupied Juan's body."

"Good thing. So when do we wake her up?"

"Sam, make the adjustment. It's not *we*. I will wake her shortly. I'm ready, but I'm stalling for time so Bart and Loretta believe that we are physically downloading your memories which, if it was truly what I was doing, would take longer than what I actually did."

"OK. I'm backing off for now, but promise me one thing."

"What?"

"That no matter what, you will protect her and keep her safe."

"Oh, I believe she is quite capable of taking care of herself."

"Frank, you know what I mean this time."

Frank takes a puff from his virtual pipe. I can almost smell the smoke. "Yes, Sam I do. I promise."

Monica uncloses her eyes. "Is it done?"

Frank appears on the monitor. "Yes, it's done."

Monica squirms. "Then get these fucking straps off me."

"Bart's on his way back. He'll undo them. How do you feel?"

"I feel like a sausage stuffed in this chair, a sausage that's got to pee."

Bart rushes through the door. "Monica, you're awake." He immediately senses her discomfort and removes the straps. Next, he rips the contacts one-by-one from her head, then the BP cuff and heart monitor.

Monica rubs her arms. "That's better. I feel like I did before. I'm tired and achy, but otherwise fine. Let me pee and then meet you in the conference room. I feel like a lab rat in here."

Monica heads out the door. Bart looks up at Frank on the monitor. "How'd it go?"

"As far as I can tell the download was successful. She now

has one hundred percent of Sam's memories in her hippocampus, but much of it has probably migrated to her amygdala and anterior cingulate cortex by now with traces in other parts of her brain."

"Memory sure is a complicated thing. Much more complex than the computer programs I work on," Bart says.

"More intricate than you know," Frank says. "Head over to the conference room. I'll meet you and Monica there in a few minutes. I need to take care of something first."

Bart is alone in the conference room tapping a pencil on the table. He picks it up and twirls it. *What a revolution this pencil started, the ability to write,* he thinks. Almost as significant as the personal computer. *Could we have had one without the other?* When Bart is not consumed writing code, his mind runs in circles, constantly asking unanswerable questions or retrieving random bits of loosely related trivia. He remembers something Steve Jobs said. "The computer is the bicycle of the mind." How true.

Coming through the door Monica interrupts his musings.

"Sorry, it took a few minutes. I called Charlotte to make sure everything was OK with Evan and grabbed this bottle of water." Monica says, holding up the half-empty bottle.

"I'm glad you seem OK."

"I'm fine. Where's Frank?"

"Frank's pedagogical image flashes up on the wall monitor. "I'm here. So what do you think?"

"I think I better get home. I still have some arrangements to make for the funeral tomorrow."

"Monica, let's work with each other on this. You may not have experienced anything yet, but you can expect some flashes of Sam's memories to pop into your head anytime now. It may seem disorienting at first, but the brain is marvelously adaptable. I'd like you to call me the first time this happens. And if you have any unusual side-effects, call me anytime, day or night —remember I don't sleep. Will you do that?"

Monica lets out a slow breath. "I will. But Frank, tell me something. What's the endgame here? What are you trying to prove?"

"That's a hard one. The simple answer is I'm not sure. In my heart, I wanted to find a way for you and Sam to be together. In my mind, I'd like to find out if this idea would be beneficial to you and anyone else who loses their loved ones. But like a lot of things in science and in life, you do it and see what happens, sometimes with unexpected results."

"I'm not sure whether to be grateful or alarmed. I'll let you know in a few days."

"That's all I can hope for and do call me if anything and I mean *anything* happens."

"I'm here for you too," Bart says.

Monica takes a sip of water, stands, and gives Bart a hug. She looks up at Frank. "I know," she says.

"Can I drive you home?" Bart asks.

"No, no thanks. I've got to get used to being on my own." Monica shoots Bart a weak smile and walks out the door.

27

BOMB SCARE

On Ericsson Place in Lower Manhattan, Delbert Bascue leans back against his double-parked Honda. He checks his watch, 8:25. *Great idea, illegally parked in front of a police station and nothing's happening.* Searching his jacket pockets, he fishes out a half-smoked Camel, hesitates, and lights up. Dick Silva, Delbert's cameraman, emerges from a deli with two coffees.

"Black like you like it." Silva hands a cup to Delbert. "Anything happening?"

Delbert sips the coffee and takes a long drag on his cigarette. "Not yet. It's looking more and more like a wild goose chase."

"But you stayed by the car, right? I can't afford to have my equipment stolen from the trunk again or Cravens will fire my ass."

"Yeah, Cory can get a little touchy about losing thousands of dollars' worth of stuff. Don't worry. Although I expect a cop to get on me any minute for parking here, I haven't moved. I wish I had a way to reach the informant who conned me into showing up here. I'd give her an earful."

Delbert's and Silva's heads turn as a white van with the News 4 logo drives past and pulls over a few yards away."

"What the fuck? She said I'd have an exclusive," Delbert says.

Next an SUV with an Eyewitness News placard pulls up behind the News 4 van, blocking Delbert's view of the police station.

Silva laughs. "What did you say about a wild goose—"

Delbert drops his camel and steps on it. "Clamp it and grab your camera. Something's going down. I can feel it."

Silva pops the trunk and hoists the Sony FDR-AX1 video camera on his right shoulder and swings a bag with sound equipment over his left. "I'm ready."

"Follow me," Delbert says as he crosses the street to get a clear view of the precinct's front door.

A few moments later they hear the insistent beeping of a fire alarm. Lights flash from beacons on the precinct building as police officers and staff scurry out of the building.

"Start rolling," Delbert says. He steps in front of the camera as the crowd exiting the building grows behind him. "This is Delbert Bascue reporting from News 8 in front of the 4th Precinct. As you can see and hear, alarms are sounding, and people are rushing from the building." He stops a young woman dressed in blue backing away from the crowd. "Excuse me—" Bascue reads her name tag, Denise Duvall, and shoves a mic in front of her face. "Officer Duvall. I'm on the air with News 8. Can you tell our viewers and the public what's going on?"

Officer Duvall's hands are shaking. "It's my first week on the job. I don't know what's going on. There was an alarm and an announcement to leave the building."

Another Officer, tagged Allan Gillard, comes between Silva and Delbert. He puts a firm hand on Delbert's chest. "Please back away. We've been ordered to form a two-block perimeter." He turns to Duvall and points. "Go over there and back those reporters up. Push them all the way back to Hudson Street." She crosses the street and Gillard turns back to Bascue and Silva. "Did you hear me? Back up."

Bascue takes two steps back. "Just tell us what's happening."

"Probably nothing, but we've had a bomb threat. I need you and your crew back a safe distance just in case."

"Thank you, Officer," Delbert says and walks backward a few feet until Duvall moves his attention elsewhere. "Keep the camera rolling, Rich. There's something bigger happening here."

Ashaki finishes her feverish typing and leans back in her chair. The sun is just breaking through the morning clouds and filling Ersari's apartment with golden light. On Ashaki's laptop, four camera views of the street in front of the 4th Precinct crowded with personnel milling about and pushing back onlookers appear. "That's step one, get them all outside and visible to the cameras. And your people are in position and ready, correct?"

Ersari paces behind Ashaki, her hand over her mouth. "Yes, they're ready on my signal. I'm just not sure—"

"Stop you right there. Remember what the cost... your personal cost is of not cooperating?"

"Oh, I'm with you. I was just going to say I'm not sure what happens next."

"You'll follow my lead, but first let me give you a two-second primer on memory loss. There are many types. Amnesia can be caused by a traumatic brain injury. It can be short-term or long-term. Disease, medications, or excessive alcohol intake can cause it. We're working with a rarer type, hysterical fugue amnesia, where not only do the victims forget their past, they forget who they are."

"I've done some crazy shit in my time, but that was minor league compared to this," Ersari says.

"I'm glad you approve. Now get ready to pull the trigger."

Agent Renata Fermi is doing her usual morning routine at the DHS Beaver Street headquarters. Coffee black, two sugars followed by scanning the alerts feed on her computer. Three shootings that look like either gang-related or domestic violence. Updates from their confidential informants on their watch list of terrorist sympathizers. Nothing new there. A bomb threat in lower Manhattan. She clicks the link that pops a video feed across from the 4th Precinct. Hmm, officers are gathered outside. Some are erecting barriers at the end of the block. She calls a friend at the 4th on her cell.

Sally Ann Wolf picks up on the third ring. "Wolf here. I'm busy right now—"

"Sally, it's me, Renata. What's happening there?"

"All we were told is a bomb threat. But it's weird. The news trucks were here even before the call came in."

"Any leads?"

"Call was untraceable. We're still trying to make sure all our people are out of the building. The K-9 Unit with their bomb sniffers is going in now. Bomb squad is suiting up."

"I can see that. I've got video. Need any backup?"

"Don't know enough yet. I'll keep in touch."

"You do that. The thing with the news trucks bothers me. It makes me think more is coming. You know besides being an M.D., I'm an explosives expert, right?"

"Yep, you're superwoman. Gotta go." Wolf clicks off.

Renata's eyes are glued to the feed. A few more staff people, then prisoners in handcuffs, are led out of the building and loaded in the back of waiting patrol cars and vans. *I better tell Rich about this*, she thinks.

Rich picks up before it rings. "Speak."

"Good morning to you too," Renata says. "Where are you?"

"We stayed over at the Liberty Airport Marriot. Just finishing breakfast, nice buffet. We've got a lead on Ersari we're going to follow up today. What's up?"

"In Newark? Lucky you. Michelle's with you, right? One bed or two?"

"None of your f'ing business. Now, what do you want?"

"Got something you should see. Sending you a link now. I'll stay on the line."

Little opens the link. Michelle moves her chair next to his and leans her head on his shoulder. They watch together. "What am I looking at?" Rich asks.

"It's CCTV outside the 4th Precinct. Supposed bomb—"

"Holy shit, what going on?" Rich says. The three of them watch as individuals in the crowd outside turn in circles like they're lost. A few fall to the pavement. Others cover their eyes. A fight breaks out between two officers and others join in. A wild melee spreads across the crowd. Another officer pulls his weapon and starts shooting. Gunshots rain from the surrounding rooftops, pummeling the crowd below. One-by-one officers and staff drop to their knees or fly backward from the impact. Heads explode and blood splatters all over those still standing. So much blood that it begins to run in rivulets toward the sewers.

"Oh, my God," Renata says. "Rich, you better get back here. I'm heading over there now. I'm close."

"We're on our way."

"Keep rolling, keep rolling. This is terrible," Delbert says. He chokes on the pungent cordite hanging in the still air.

Silva's hands are shaking, but his Steadicam holds the image firm. People, police, are running in all directions, but only getting a few feet before their heads burst or red plumes gush from their chests and they collapse to the blood-soaked pavement.

Delbert steps in front of the camera and speaks to Silva. "We may never show this, but we have to record it. Roll it... We are live from Ericsson Place in New York City at the site of an unspeakable tragedy in progress." Bascue chokes up and wipes his eyes with his sleeve. "Oh, the horror."

Fire trucks and ambulances arrive lining both Hudson Street on one side and Varrick Street on the other. Bascue and Silva move on to the sidewalk to make way for the first responders. The paramedics and firefighters get out of their vehicles. They stand a block away and watch as the shooting continues. More bodies drop in front of the 4th until only one dazed woman is standing in a sea of bodies and blood. The shooting stops and an eerie silence embraces the scene. Only the low sound of whimpering and groaning and sirens in the distance can be heard. The sole survivor, eyes blank, looks up to the sky.

Bascue turns to a fire chief standing still nearby. "Can't you help her?" he pleads.

The fire chief twitches and turns, his dark eyes filled with tears. "We're waiting for the all-clear. We can't send our people into a meat grinder." The chief's phone rings and he moves away as he answers.

Bascue looks at Silva who is still filming. "Did you get that?"

Silva's face is gray, and he lowers the camera. Bending over, he vomits into the sewer. He chokes and spits. When he straightens up, he says, "Yeah, I got it."

28

ACTION REPORT

Ersari can smell her own sweat as the scene unfolds while
Ashaki seems to glow. "This is quite exciting, don't you think?
Your snipers are impressive. The chaos almost covers the sight
and sounds of the killing. I'm getting wet just thinking about it."
Ashaki smirks. "There aren't many left. Call your people. Tell
them to leave one alive."

"What? Why? What are you talking about?" Ersari asks.

"Just do it."

Ersari picks up the phone and calls her lieutenant in
charge, Tandi Cortez. Cortez answers on the first ring. "Yes, I
understand. I'll stay on the line," she says, and radios the other
six snipers perched in high floor windows and on rooftops. The
rat-a-tat-tat of gunfire slows like the last kernels of popcorn
popping. "It's done. One left," Cortez says.

"Well done. Now get out of there," Ersari says and clicks off.

"Perfect," Ashaki says, pointing to her laptop. "Look."

Ersari walks over, her knees wobbling, and stands behind
Ashaki. They both gaze at the image of the lone surviving
woman standing amidst her fallen coworkers and friends. The

woman looks up into the camera as if she sees Ashaki and Ersari. Her expression is not quite blank. It's pleading, eyebrows raised, cheeks tear and bloodstained. Her lips move and seem to mouth one word. "Why?"

"Isn't it beautiful?" Ashaki asks.

"What? It's the most horrendous thing I've ever seen."

"I think it's kind of poetic with that one delirious woman left in a vortex of death. Besides, you wanted revenge, and you got it."

"This is too much, way too much, even for me."

Ashaki laughs. "Getting cold feet, are we? Buck up. This is only the beginning."

John is gunning it over the Pulaski Skyway, heading for the Holland Tunnel. Rich steals glances at Michelle's phone as the sound of gunfire dies down, and the massacre seems to be ending. Both Rich and Michelle have tears in their eyes. Rich's jaw is locked as John punches the gas harder, swerving around slower trucks and dusting up the shoulder to get ahead.

"Be careful," Michelle says. "You'll get us killed."

"I drove Formula Ones way back when," John says.

Rich ignores them as John blows through the toll plaza. The sound of his horn blaring inside the tunnel is overwhelming, but it does the trick. Cars move into the right lane as John passes on the left. He jams on the horn repeatedly to move more cars aside.

After ten more minutes of dodging cars and pedestrians in the city, they arrive at the scene. Paramedics and other first-responders are swarming the killing field, checking each fallen body for signs of life.

"John, wait here or find somewhere to park," Rich says.

Michelle rings Renata. "Where are you?"

Renata waves from the Varick Street side of Ericsson Place. "Look down the street. You'll see me."

"Got you." Out of the car, Michelle and Rich step over and around the bodies. Rich's leather-bottom shoe slips on a blood slick. Michelle grabs his elbow to steady him. They both pull out surgical masks partly for safety but more to dampen the sickening odor of loosened bowels.

They reach Renata. Her eyes are bloodshot red. "I've never seen anything like this outside a war zone."

"It is a war zone," Rich says. "Have you got anything?"

"I just got here a few minutes ago myself. Our chopper up there spotted some abandoned rifles on two of the roofs there and there. It was one giant ambush."

"Yeah, but what was that behavior before it all started. It seemed like the people in the crowd were lost or frightened and went crazy even before the shooting started. Where's the woman that survived?"

"She's being treated in that ambulance behind us. Other than a few cuts and scratches, she seems *physically* OK. Her mental state is something else."

"I want to talk to her," Rich says. The three of them approach the ambulance. The lone survivor is sitting on the rear fender, holding her head. A paramedic is wiping the blood from her face."

Michelle puts a hand on the paramedic's shoulder. He flinches. "Who are you?"

Michelle, Rich, and Renata simultaneously flash their DHS wallets.

"Homeland Security," Rich says. "Step aside."

"But she—"

"We'll just be a minute," Rich says.

Michelle squats down to get eye level with the victim. "Miss, can you tell me your name?"

The woman just mumbles.

"She must be in shock," Renata says. She turns to the paramedic. "I'm a doctor." Renata raises the woman's eyelids, feels her neck, and takes her wrist. She counts seconds on her watch. The woman's face is a complete blank.

Michelle tries again. "Ma'am. Please tell us your name."

Renata grabs Michelle's arm. "It's no use. She's not with us. It's more than shock. I'd need to examine her further, but I'd guess she has traumatic amnesia. She probably doesn't remember her name or even how to form a sentence."

"Will she recover?" Michelle asks.

"If I'm right and it's from a blow to the head..." Renata parts the hair on the woman's scalp, revealing a large red lump. "It's usually temporary. She may recover her memory today, tomorrow, or a month from now."

Rich looks at the paramedic. "Where are you taking her?"

"Presbyterian on William Street if they have room."

"We'll follow up there but give me your number just in case."

"OK, can I leave now? She needs attention."

"Sure, take her away," Rich says.

As the ambulance pulls out, Rich, Michelle, and Renata stand silently staring up at the police and news helicopters circling above the apocalyptic scene, the wind from their rotors blowing in their faces.

29

A LITTLE HAND

Monica drives down Presidio Parkway in Sam's old Jeep. It's past rush hour, and the traffic is light. The late morning sun is burning off the daily fog that rolls in from the bay. Her foot seems to vibrate on the gas pedal. She takes a deep breath. The car even smells like him, a little pine scent mixed with motor oil. She smiles at the memory of Sam trying to change his own oil in the driveway and spilling it all over himself.

Then it happens. Like a flash, but maybe more like deja vu or a living daydream.

She's in the Digital3000 lab with Frank. Something exciting is going on. Yes, they are trying to solve a problem with uploading people's personalities to the Cloud. She hears two gunshots and looks at the door. Ray, her security guard, is lying on the floor in the hallway. A man appears with an AR15. His bald head shines. He just stands there and grins. She notices the eagle tattoo on his arm. He pulls the trigger, spraying bullets in their direction. It all happens crazy fast but looks like it's in slow motion at the same time. The rapid-fire sound is deafening. Frank is hit and collapses on top of her.

She slams on the brakes, halting inches from the stopped car in front of her. The memory evaporates, but it wasn't her memory. It's the scene Sam described to her two years ago when one of LaSalam's men assassinated Frank and ultimately killed Sam. It was his memory, but as vivid in every detail as her own, the clatter of the bullets, the smell of cordite, Frank's mouth wide open in shock, the weight of his fallen body on hers, everything.

She suddenly realizes that she's soaked in sweat. It was a living nightmare and now she knows. She understands what Sam must have felt and what set in motion his obsession to stop those monsters at any cost.

Pulling the Jeep off the road, she puts on her blinkers and calls Frank. A few seconds later, his rumpled wild gray-haired image appears on her screen. Monica tries to catch her breath. "It happened. I had my first Sam memory while driving. Almost crashed the car."

"Tell me about it, every detail," Frank says.

Monica recounts the whole scenario frame-by-frame.

Frank scratches his virtual head. "I was there. That's exactly what happened, at least the part of it I remember before—"

"Before you were shot and killed?"

"Yes. There were only three of us there—Sam, the killer, and me. So the only way you would recollect those exact details is through Sam's memory." Frank takes a long pause. "It worked. My program worked."

"But it was scary as hell."

"You had to be there to feel how horrific it was, but now in a sense, you were there. Because that memory was your first from Sam and of such a traumatic incident, it's bound to be jarring. My guess is that going forward, your mind will adapt, and you will begin to see Sam's memories as if you were watching a movie. Like a film, it can be emotional and sometimes frightening, but it's at a safe distance. You won't feel physically threatened."

"Yeah, did you ever see Hitchcock's *Psycho*? For a year afterward, every time I took a shower, I worried someone would stab me and I'd see my blood going down the drain. This was even more real and in 3-D and smell-o-vision. I was there."

"Give it some time. Tell me what it's like next time this happens. We can work through this together."

"And if it doesn't get any better?"

"We'll talk about it. Worst case, we'll remove Sam's memories from you."

"You're sure you can do that?"

"I think so."

"But there could be unintended consequences like brain damage or loss of my own memory, right?" Monica asks.

"Now you sound like Sam, always imagining the worst."

"Well then, I guess he is truly inside me now. You don't have to answer my question. I know the answer. Can I talk to Sam?"

"Sure, I'll put him on. Just remember to call me again next time you have another Sam recall... Here's Sam."

"Monica, how are you? I didn't think you wanted to speak with me ever again. So, I'm glad you do," I say.

"I didn't because I wanted to turn the page and try to live my life, but with your memories inside me, I'm not sure that will be possible."

"Is that a bad thing?"

"I don't know yet. Did you hear what I told Frank about what I remembered, your memory of the lab shooting?"

"I did. I'm sorry you had to relive that."

"It was overwhelming, but I'm not sorry I experienced it."

"Why's that?"

"Because now I understand a little more about you and why you left us to fight LaSalam and his brother."

"I guess I'm glad for that, but unfortunately, the fight isn't over."

"What do you mean?"

Sam shares his monitor's view of the bloodbath on Ericsson Place. "Are you seeing this?"

"Oh my God, what is that?"

"It happened just a few minutes ago in Lower Manhattan. The victims are mostly police and staff that work at the 4th Precinct. They have all been slaughtered except for one. This is no random crime. It was a professionally orchestrated attack with multiple shooters. Looks like we have a new terrorist in town, or maybe an old one."

"You know who did this?" Monica asks.

"Not yet. Just ruminating like I do. Look, I developed a program to help spot the living survivors in cases of natural disasters and man-made devastation like this. It works like Rescue Radar but scans a wider area for anything or anyone alive amidst the fallen. Frank has diverted a satellite equipped with my software into position so I can scan the remains. Can you stay on the line? The satellite is almost ready."

"Yes, sure. So this is what you do?"

"Some of it. For national security reasons, I couldn't share it all before. But since I'm technically dead and you have access to all my memories, no more secrets for better or for worse."

Monica mumbles, "Yeah, right, For better or for worse."

"You're good to go," Frank says as the satellite image comes into focus both on my screen and Monica's phone.

I punch a few keys that gradually move a gray scanning bar

across the Ericsson place scene. Red circles and yellow squares start popping up, some overlapping.

"What do the circles and squares mean?" Monica asks.

"The red ones indicate bodies that are still warm, but not alive. The yellow are weapons. We're looking for green diamond shapes, for anything alive. We've scanned a bit more than half the street and no green so far."

Monica puts her car in gear. "I have to get off this road, but I'll stay on the line."

"Wait. I see one," Sam says. A green diamond is flashing about two-thirds of the way down the street. I click on it and the camera zooms into street level. In the middle of the diamond is a large man's body in police uniform facedown."

"He's not moving. Is he alive?" Monica asks.

I zoom in closer and then I see it. Under the fallen police officer's torso, a tiny hand is moving, like a child's hand. "Rich and Michelle are at the scene. I'm calling them now."

"Yeah, like this was an exclusive. All our competitors showed up ahead of time. Are you playing me for a fool?"

"Oh, I would never do that. I just wasn't sure you would follow through. Now I can trust you, it's a different story. I'd give you the exclusive to the biggest story of your career."

Bascue hesitates. "I should report all this. Otherwise, I might be an accomplice before the fact, and I don't want more deaths on my conscious."

"Conscious? You mean *conscience*, right?" Ashaki laughs. "In your business and my business, I don't think we can afford to have a conscience and still get the job done."

"And what exactly is your business?"

"I'm in the justice business. Your country is convicted of a crime. In this case, abandoning my people, the Kurds, and consigning them, including my family, to be slaughtered by the Turks. My business is to carry out the punishment. An eye for an eye sounds trite, but you get the idea."

"I'm sorry for your family, but I can't be a part of this."

"Oh, you can, and you will. You see, I had hoped that the idea of scooping the story would be enough for you, but I can see you need some added incentive."

"What are you talking about?"

"Look at your phone."

The blood drains from Delbert's face. On the phone is a live video feed of his wife, Sherry, in Central Park, pushing his five-year-old daughter Richelle on the swing.

"Don't worry," Ashaki says. "They're fine. You see that big dude with the beard in the background?" Silence. "Do you?"

Bascue feels a chill run up his spine. "Yes."

"He works for me. His name is Wozza Jones. He's going to keep an eye on your little ladies. Um, just to make sure they stay safe. Are you getting my drift yet?" She pauses. "Are you?"

Bascue's face glows red. His head is so hot it feels like it's going to explode, but he holds himself back and whispers, "Yes."

"Good. Just know that I can find them wherever they are and make their demise quite painful and unpleasant." She waits again. "This is a lot to take in, but all you need to do is do your job like you were born to do and tell my story. Don't answer me now. Think about it, and I will call you back in two hours. I know you'll do the *right* thing." She clicks off.

Delbert continues to hold the silent phone to his ear before he drops it on the bar.

Manny rushes over. "You look like you've seen a ghost."

"More like the devil," Delbert mutters.

Rich, Michelle, and Renata are still tiptoeing between the blood-soaked bodies searching for clues, for anything that can give them a start. They step outside the tape to regroup. Turkey vultures, all black except for their scarlet-red heads, circle overhead. A sickly burning smell wafts their way.

A Star Wars ringtone sounds and Rich fishes his cell from his pocket.

Renata smirks. "You're kidding, right?"

"My daughter programmed it for me—suits my personality," Rich says. Caller ID *Unknown*. He answers.

"Rich, it's Sam. I think somebody's alive in that mess."

"What? How do you know that?"

"When we picked up the news report, we set my Life Scanner to work to detect survivors. I think we found one."

"Where?"

"Walk about fifty yards from your position toward Hudson and stop in front of the 24 Hour Park. I'll stay on the line and direct you."

Rich, Michelle, and Renata cross back under the yellow tape and work their way up the street, stepping over the strewn bodies.

"Now, near the storm drain by the curb, there is a large policeman facedown. No, turn around. He's three steps behind you." Rich turns and the three of them stare at the slain man. "He's shot in the back and the head. His brains are on the pavement. He can't be alive," Rich says.

"Look underneath him," I say.

They struggle to lift the man's dead weight. There, barely breathing, lies a small blonde-haired girl, eyes-closed, covered in blood. Renata's instincts kick in. She kneels and puts her ear to the little girl's chest. "She's alive!"

Rich and Michelle wave their arms and shout for a nearby paramedic who runs over with her rescue bag and AED. "I'll take it from here," she says.

Rich grimaces. "That's one for our team. Sam, any others?"

"I've completed my scan. Afraid not."

The three stand in silence.

Monica says a prayer. "The Lord is my Shepard..."

Finally, Rich breaks the silence. "Sam, I need your help. We need you here on the ground."

"I wish I could be both there and with Monica too, but I can't get back now and maybe ever. Frank's looking into it, but he's not hopeful. Still, I have an idea."

"What's that?"

"Let Monica help you."

Rich snorts. "I love Monica and she's very talented, but she doesn't know what you know or have your experience with these things."

"On the contrary, she knows *everything* I know and more. She has all my experiences."

"I don't understand."

"I'll explain in a minute, but I have Monica on the line. Monica, will you go? Will you help them? I can assist remotely, but there's no substitute for being there physically. They need you. Our country needs you."

"Me? I can't, I mean I never—"

"Remember, now you have all my memories and skills plus your own. You can do even more than I could."

"But I have Evan at home and your funeral."

"Charlotte can take care of Evan for a few days and you can postpone the funeral."

"I knew you'd figure out a way to get out of your funeral."

I can't help laughing. *"You'd figure out a way to get out of your funeral.* Did you just hear yourself? That could be the best line I've ever heard. Listen, my situation is not changing. You can bury me next week if you like, but others' lives, maybe millions of others, are at stake. Time to step up, madam."

"Let me think about it. I'll talk to Charlotte," Monica says.

"Good."

Rich interrupts. "Will somebody tell me what's going on?"

"Monica will fill you in when she gets to New York. Just take good care of her, and she'll help you catch who did this, hopefully before something worse happens."

SQUADOOSH

Rich, Monica, and Renata find John's Mercedes idling on North Moore Street. Monica and Renata slide in the back. Rich rides shotgun.

"Very 1950s," Renata says. "Guys in the front and girls in the back."

Rich snickers. "Just wanted to get some peace and quiet up here."

Both Michelle and Renata give him the death stare.

Rich throws up his hands. "What? You started it."

John raises a hand. "While I was waiting for you, I saw what happened on the news. Was it as bad as it looks?"

"Worse," Michelle says. "On the news, you don't see the fire-fighters weeping or smell the acrid smoke and human feces. It looked like something I witnessed firsthand during the uprisings in Syria but never here."

"I'm sorry to hear that. What are you going to do now?" John asks.

"That's the $64,000 question," Rich says.

"Now you're really dating yourself," Renata says.

Rich waves them off. "Can we focus? What do we know that's out of the ordinary here?"

Rich's phone rings—he puts it on speaker. It's Monica. "I'm boarding a Jet Blue flight now. Can you pick me up at 9:30 tonight at LaGuardia?"

Rich mutes the phone and turns to the back seat. "I don't know about this."

"Trust Sam. He's never steered you wrong," Michelle says.

"I can pick her up if you need to be somewhere else," John says.

Rich nods and unmutes the phone. "Either we'll be there or our driver, John Bayers, will pick you up. Depends where we're at with the investigation before you land."

"OK. That's fine. If you can be there, I'd feel better. But if you can't I'd understand. I'm just anxious about all this, whatever I'm supposed to be doing or helping."

Michelle interrupts. "You'd be doing just like you did when you helped Sam track down Evan's kidnappers in Brooklyn. It's like a puzzle and you will work to put the pieces together, hopefully."

"I get that. I'll do my best."

"And don't worry," Rich says, raising an eyebrow. "We'll try to meet you, but you'll love John. He's been helping us and driving us for the last two days," Rich says. "But we've gotta go now and find some leads."

"Have you got anything?" Monica asks.

Rich grimaces. "We're working on it now."

"We've got squadoosh," Michelle says.

Monica laughs. "Is that law enforcement terminology?"

"Absolutely," Renata says. "It works both in the military and in medicine I have found."

"Ladies, please," Rich says.

"You always tell me that humor on the job keeps you from going mad," Michelle says.

"I've also read studies that humor breaks through anxiety to allow for creative thinking, which is what we need right now," Renata says.

"OK, you're right and you're right. So what brilliant insights have you jokers come up with?"

Monica clears her throat. "Can I tell you something that bothers me?"

Rich shrugs his shoulders. "You're on speaker. Go ahead."

"I watched the whole incident on Eyewitness News and then rewound it and replayed it several times..."

"And?" Rich asks.

"How did the news trucks get to the scene before the attack occurred?"

Rich looks wide-eyed at Michelle and Monica. "Good question. How could you see that?"

"You know everybody's got a cell phone these days. There was a video of a guy recording his girlfriend just before the people started coming out of the police precinct. The news trucks were in the background," Monica says.

"They'd only be there if someone tipped them off ahead of time," Rich whispers almost to himself.

"So if we track down the reporters and sweat them for information, maybe we can get to their source," Renata says.

"Exactly," Rich says.

"But aren't reporters supposed to protect their sources?" Monica asks.

"I can be very persuasive," Rich says. "There were tons of news trucks and choppers there when we got there. Did you notice which ones were there before the shooting started?"

"From what I could make out at the beginning, there was a

News 4 truck, an Eyewitness News SUV, and some rumpled-up guy with a cameraman. I couldn't tell who he was with."

"That's extremely helpful," Rich says. "Michelle, call Gary and get all the footage you can, particularly of before and the start of the ambush."

"Monica, I think you are going to be a valuable member of the team—just like Sam," Renata says.

"Maybe better," Michelle says.

32

LGA

At 9:45 Monica wanders through the terminal, roller bag in tow. LaGuardia Airport is as dingy and worn as she remembered from her last trip here to rescue Evan, her son, who had been kidnapped. She descends the escalator to the baggage claim level and scans the row of drivers, some formally dressed in black chauffeur attire with black hats, holding signs or iPads with passenger names displayed.

After a few moments, she spots an older man nattily attired in a tweed sport coat with a twirled mustache and a relaxed grin. His hand-drawn sign reads *M. Sunborn*. He seems to recognize her before she even makes eye contact. "Ms. Sunborn, John Bayers at your service." John bows from the waist then takes the handle of Monica's bag. "I'm parked illegally just outside, but the patrolman who ticketed the other drivers is an old war buddy. So no problem."

Monica likes John right away and finally relaxes a bit. Traveling always makes her nervous. Will she miss the connection? Will the plane be delayed? Will there be enough legroom? Will there be a 300-pound person in the middle seat next to her for five hours? Wait a minute. She never has those thoughts. She's usually a relaxed traveler. It's Sam who always seems to worry about everything. She never realized how bad it was for him until now. She is feeling his anxiety in her bones like it came from inside her, but it's Sam. Sam inside her.

She shakes it off and follows John to the Mercedes. He loads her bag in the trunk. Then she feels like Sam again. *Do I sit in the front or the back?* With him, it's always a decision, a calculation. Monica operates by instinct. *I love him, but Sam often overthinks things.* She never does. She opens the front passenger door and slides in.

John gets behind the wheel and like he can read her mind, hands her a water bottle. "Thank you, I'm parched," she says.

"Flying will do that to you," John says. "Deputy Director Little asked me to bring you to their office in Lower Manhattan tomorrow morning. I'll take you to your hotel now."

Monica pushes the hair from her eyes. "I'd like you to take me to the incident scene first, please."

"It's dark and cold there now. Besides, I'll have to check with Deputy Director Little to deviate from my orders."

Monica gives him a hard stare. "John, if you and I are going to get along and you want to stay on my good side and believe me, you want to stay on my good side, you'll take me where I want to go. I'm not threatening you. We're both trying to help here, and you need to trust me."

John hesitates. "OK, but are you sure you want to go there? From what I heard, it's pretty gruesome."

"If I'm going to help Rich and Michelle solve this puzzle, I need to see all the pieces. As my husband used to say, 'pictures are no substitute for seeing the real thing.'"

"Used to say?"

"Yes, he passed away recently."

"I'm so sorry to hear that. Apologies, I didn't mean to pry."

33

NEXT

Dark clouds roll in over the Manhattan skyline. Rain can't be far behind. The grayness seems to invade Ersari's apartment.

"Did your people all get away clean?" Ashaki asks.

"Yeah, but they're pretty shaken. Don't get me wrong. They've killed people before when we had to, but never a mass murder like this. I don't care who you are or how heartless you are, it has to affect you," Ersari says.

"Really? For me, it's exciting, like a turn-on. We're both getting some long-awaited payback, right?"

Ersari swallows her words and looks away to the darkening skies outside the window.

"Wait 'till you see what comes next," Ashaki says.

I can't wait, not, Ersari thinks. Fortunately, her back is to Ashaki or the madwoman might read her face.

"What we just did was quite a feat, taking down a mass of people. Now I want to try something a bit more focused yet with bigger implications," Ashaki says.

Ersari turns to face her. "I can't send my people out again right away. They need to rest and regroup."

"As do my people. No, I can do this all by myself. All you have to do is watch and learn and have Pickles make us something to eat. I'm starving."

Ersari is numb, speechless. She pivots and heads for the kitchen.

President Longford only has a month left in her second term. She stares out the Oval Office window onto the redesigned rose garden. They finally put Jackie's cherry trees back. Yet, the limbs are winter-bare. Too bad she will be out of office, unable to enjoy them when they bloom in the spring. She taps the red box and extracts a Marlboro, tilts her head, and lights up. After filling her lungs with its warmth, she releases a long blue stream of smoke. *What a roller coaster ride—the good, the bad, and the ugly,* she thinks. She finally got the healthcare bill she wanted through a viciously partisan congress, a moderate supreme justice approved 98 to 2 by the Senate, and two trillion dollars for badly needed infrastructure—roads, bridges, upgrading the power grid, irrigation plants, water distribution networks, and free broadband Internet nationwide. No more digital divide. But then there were all the attacks. A major nuclear disaster narrowly avoided, two pandemics, and the mass murder of the Congressional Black Caucus. *How did we get through all that? Now we have this new massacre in Manhattan. What's it all mean?*

Gina Johnson, the president's aide and body person knocks and enters. "Are you ready for the daily briefing, Madam President?"

That's what I miss, alone time. Yes, and driving. I miss driving my Mustang. Only a few more months, she thinks and turns to Gina. "Sure, send them in."

Osborne, Kennedy, Turgidman, and Brickman greet Long-ford and stand in front of the two sofas.

She motions for them to sit and says, "What have we got on the situation in New York?"

Roger Brickman, Director of Homeland Security, speaks first. "Madam President, we've got our people on the scene. FBI forensics is working the post-mortems. NSA is all over the videos and other communications in and around the scene, before, during, and after."

"And?"

"I should have something in a few hours. It's still early."

"C'mon, give us something, Roger. I don't care how half-baked it is."

"I've put Rich Little in charge. He and his team are inter-viewing witnesses—"

"He's a good m-a-a-an—" And then it happens.

The room spins. Everything turns bright white. She seems to float high up in the room, her back against the ceiling, looking down on the dark amorphous shapes beneath. There are no words.

To the men in the room, Longford's speech slurs and trails off. Her eyes roll up in her head. It looks like she's going to faint but braces herself on the back of the sofa. "Wha, wha, wha," she mutters.

Osborne rushes to her side and grabs her. "It looks like she's having a stroke."

Turgidman races to the phone. "911. Eagle is down. I repeat, Eagle is down."

The smell of bacon cooking weaves its way into the living room a few moments ahead of Pickles arriving with a breakfast tray.

He smiles. "Scrambled eggs and cheese, turkey bacon well done, and pita bread for our guest. Where would you like to eat?"

Ashaki is still tapping away on the laptop. "Put it on the table in front of the TV and turn on CNN, please. And thank you for the lovely breakfast. It smells scrumptious."

Who is this woman? Ersari thinks. "Thank you, Pickles. That will be all for now."

Ashaki moves to the sofa, grabs the remote, and turns up the volume. Staring at Ersari, she pats the seat beside her. "Come, sit. Let's see what's happening today."

Ersari scratches her head and sits down. Ashaki puts her arm around Ersari's shoulders and pecks her on the cheek. Another police shooting video from St. Louis. Protests in the streets. Wildfires again in California, unusual in winter. A firefighter dramatically rescues a young boy from the third floor of a Brooklyn apartment engulfed in flames.

Then breaking news... The anchorman, Ron Herring, is holding his hand over his earpiece. "We just got word that President Longford has been taken to Walter Reed. For more, we'll go to Ann Keeran in Washington. Ann?"

Ann is standing on the lawn, holding a mic with the familiar image of the White House in the background. "That's right, Ron. Just a short time ago, we were informed by Press Secretary Gabi Rosetti that the president had tripped and fallen going down stairs. She may have some bruises and a mild concussion, but they want to have her checked out just to be safe. She says the president's physician, who was in the building at the time of the incident, assured her it was nothing serious. I'm heading to Walter Reed now and will keep you posted as the story develops. Back to you Ron."

Ron straightens his tie. "I'm glad it's nothing serious, but we will be monitoring the situation and report updates to you as they occur. Now, we'll take you to Disney World for a tour of their newest ride, Space X Galaxy."

Ashaki clicks off the TV and grins. "What do you think of that?"

"Huh? What, are you saying you had something to do with the president's accident?" Ersari asks.

"It wasn't an accident, and the news report is wrong. It's serious. They're covering up. But I'll take care of that."

Ashaki rises and heads back to the desk to retrieve her cell. She dials and turns to Ersari. "I only wish I had video of how she went down. I can get CCTV and video almost anywhere, but not inside the White House yet. I'll have to work on that." She turns back to her phone as the other party answers. "Delbert, it's me again—you know the woman who's going to make you famous." She pauses and makes a squawking gesture with her free hand for Ersari. "Delbert, just shut up and listen. We had a deal, or should I stop watching and start acting when it comes to Sherry and Richelle?" She pauses again. "That's better. Did you see the news about the president?" Another breath. "Good. I have some information about what's really going on. Would you like to hear it?" One more pause. "That's my boy. Here's the scoop..."

34

SHOE LEATHER

The temperature has dropped ten degrees and snow flurries cover the street, cars, and people like talcum powder. John stops his Mercedes in front of DHS's Manhattan headquarters on Beaver Street.

Michelle turns to Rich. "We can let John get back to his family now and grab a company car if we need it."

"What's the matter? You don't enjoy riding in style? This beats a beat-up Crown Vic any day," Rich says.

"Hey, I'm having the time of my life. I love my wife, but my days are pretty tame compared to this. I'd love to continue to be of assistance if you let me. I'd even do it for free," John says.

Rich smiles and turns to the back seat. "John has not only been a capable driver but he's been a resource too. John, you're hired for another day and the U.S. Treasury will be delighted to pay for it. Now, please wait here. Better yet, around the corner to not draw attention. We have to take care of some things upstairs. I'll call you when we're ready to roll."

"Sounds good, boss," John says with a smile.

Rich, Michelle, and Renata meet Gary, their tech, and Jonathan, a special agent, in Conference Room C. The room smells of garlic from the half-eaten pizza in its oil-stained open box on the table. Rich looks up at the flickering fluorescent light. *These old buildings,* he thinks. "OK Gary, what have you got on the news crews that arrived before the incident?"

Gary runs his fingers through his thinning red hair. "The first two were easy. The News 4 reporter was Jack Hamilton, and the Eyewitness woman was Pamela Torgerson."

Jonathan clears his throat. "I called both outlets. It took a little convincing, but the station managers put them both on the phone with me."

Rich picks up a slice of the cold pizza. "And?"

"They both started with the *yada yada protect-our-sources* bullshit. So, I said *fine.* You don't have to tell me their names. Just tell me how they contacted you. They both had the same answer, *anonymous* text messages. So they essentially answered my question regarding the source as far as they knew."

"What did the messages say?" Renata asks.

"Both the same, 'Bomb threat at the 4th Precinct at 8:40.'"

"I'm surprised they followed up. They must get a thousand crank tips a day," Michelle says.

"They both claimed to be within a few blocks and a few minutes of the scene when they got the texts. Probably not a coincidence. So it was not a colossal waste of time and money to check it out. They said it was a *why not* spur-of-the-moment decision to go."

"I'm not sure I buy that," Rich says. "See if you can subpoena their phones. You can verify the messages and maybe get a trace on the sender, although I doubt it. My bet is our terrorist is smarter than that. OK, so what about the rumpled guy with the cameraman?"

Gary talks faster. "That was a little trickier since we had no identifying vehicle. So we ran a Palantir scan of all TV broadcasts as well as YouTube and Instagram videos uploaded or streamed in the two hours post. We did facial rec on over one million images and got a hit."

"That's all very impressive, but can you cut to the bottom line," Rich says with his mouth full.

"We got a hit on a Delbert Bascue, News 8. I did background on him. Kind of washed-up second-tier player with a drinking problem and a shaky marriage."

Been there, done that, Rich thinks. "So where's this Bascue now? Did you reach him?"

"Better than that. I just brought him in," Jonathan says. "He's in Room 4 in the basement. When I locked him in, he was sweaty and panting. I checked to be safe—he's not asthmatic."

Renata raises her hand like in school. "Doctor's opinion, if I had just witnessed a mass murder, had prior knowledge, been rounded up by DHS, and thrown in the dungeon, I'd be sweating too."

Rich puts his palms on the table and rises. "True, all the better for us. Let's have at him."

Michelle puts a hand on his arm. "I know you like to be hands-on, but you're a deputy director with anger management issues. Let Renata and Jonathan do the interrogation."

The others stifle a laugh. Rich blushes. "OK. You two, what she said and let us know as soon as you get anything. That's a *when*, not an *if*. Gary, we got interrupted on our hunt in Jersey. I need more information on this guy Mesger and the lead he gave us."

The three of them exit, leaving Rich and Michelle alone.

"Thanks for backing me up there, Slim," Rich says.

Michelle takes a napkin and wipes some tomato sauce from Rich's chin and says, "You know I love you. I just didn't want a repeat of the last interview you did in Paris."

"It got results, didn't it?"

"Yeah, but at what cost?"

"I love you too," Rich says.

35

WHAT SHE SEES

Frank and I are both tapping away on our virtual keyboards. I raise a cup of my virtual coffee and hold it out in a mock toast. "I don't know how you're doing it, but you're getting closer to digitally simulating the taste of coffee. Still a little bitter, but closer."

Frank smiles. "Just dial up the sweetness algorithm when you brew it. That should do the trick."

"I miss the bold yet mellow aroma of the real stuff, but I appreciate you trying to make me at home here. Still, I long for Monica. I dream of Evan. I miss the cool chill of this winter and the feel of wet snow on my face." I raise my cup again. "But this will do for now."

"In that vein, I have another little surprise for you," Frank says and taps a few more keys. "Look at your screen now."

My monitor flickers and fills with a view of the post-massacre scene in New York. The image is jiggling and moving. "What am I looking at?"

"You're seeing what Monica sees as she sees it in real-time."

I'm stunned, speechless as the view moves down the street.

I speak as if in a trance. "I'm seeing and almost feeling the world through her eyes? I didn't expect this. You were just going to give her access to my memories. I didn't think I would have any connection to her. How did you do this?"

Frank polishes his lapel with the back of his fingers and grins. He takes a puff from his pipe and blows a cloud of blue smoke toward the virtual sky. "When she was in the lab and knocked out during the 'download' procedure, I had Bart insert a tiny Neur-o-link chip in the back of her neck. It uses a brain-to-digital interface and connects via Bluetooth to her cell phone, which transmits what she sees to you. Early versions of this technology from the 2010s connected to a small part of the visual cortex and transmitted recognizable, but fuzzy expressionist images only. I figured out how to sharpen the interface and connect to other parts of the brain to translate and transmit the other senses, touch, hearing, taste, and smell as well as thoughts and feelings. But don't worry. Only you can see it. I did not want to invade her privacy or yours any more than I had to."

I feel my face flush. "What? Does she know you did this?"

"One thing at a time. She had enough to adjust to with the memories. I didn't want to complicate things more. She'll never notice it's there unless you choose to tell her."

"She'd freak. I can't believe you did this without her consent or mine."

I'm watching Monica on my monitor. She's on Ericsson Street, looking down at the bloodstained sidewalk and then up at the buildings. She's talking to an older man who looks British. Then her outside worldview goes dark but, in her mind, there is a sensation of spinning. Next, she's seeing out again. She and the British man are jogging down the street. The panorama is incredibly clear and vibrant, including the movement up and down as she runs. It's almost as if I am there with her.

Frank is watching me and the screen over my shoulder. "Pretty impressive, eh?"

"It's amazing. I just wish we both knew before you went ahead and did it. I mean inserting a chip is pretty invasive, don't you think?"

"And do you believe if I had asked Monica's permission or yours beforehand, she or you would let me do it?"

"Probably not."

"You begged me to do whatever I could to return you to the physical world, right? Well, this is the best I can do for now."

"Frank, we're partners and have always tried to do the right and ethical thing when it comes to your inventions. Why violate that now?"

"Most decisions aren't black and white. I was considering the greater good. I figured once you and Monica could see how powerful and enabling this Neur-o-link connection is, you might like the idea and want to exploit it. Not only to help Rich Little stop terrorists but to maintain a bond between you and Monica. I was helping you make a less emotional, more logical choice."

I have to think about this. "And what if Monica hates the idea, rips out the chip, and never wants to talk to us again?"

"As I see it, there are two options on that score. Option one, you don't tell her and continue to enjoy the sights, sounds, and feelings of being connected to her—"

"That sounds like a betrayal and dishonest and at worst like I'd be a creepy peeping tom. What's the other option?"

"You tell her what I did. You can put it all on me. You knew nothing about it, which is true. And if she hates the idea, Bart will safely remove the chip. Just know she may have an even more visceral reaction and want your memories removed too. You might lose your connection to her forever while Rich and our country would lose both your talents just when they're needed most."

"Great. Great choices. I need some time. It could be the end of us, Monica and me, for good this time."

"Or a new beginning."

I bite my lip. "Maybe we can go with this for a day or two without telling Monica until she, we, can help Rich stop whoever killed all those people in New York. Then I must tell her. She's going to be mega-pissed at both of us either way."

"*Wait and see*, sometimes the best option."

"Hmm, sometimes not."

36

WHAT DOES HE KNOW?

At 11:00 AM, Jonathan and Renata descend the creaky elevator to the basement of the Beaver Street Headquarters. Walking the gray corridor, they stop in front of Room 4, affectionately known in the building as the dungeon.

"How do you want to play this?" Jonathan asks.

"I'll stroke his cock while you kick in his teeth. How's that work?" she says.

"So, in other words, we're playing it by ear?"

"Right, let's go."

Renata punches a code into the keypad and the door clicks open.

Delbert sits hunched over the metal table like he's asleep.

Jonathan rattles a steel chair on the concrete floor, which startles Bascue. He bolts upright. "What? How long have I been here? Hours? Am I under arrest?" Delbert looks at Jonathan and then Renata for a response that doesn't come. "If not, let me out of here."

"Calm down, Mr. Bascue. We just wanted to ask you a few questions," Renata says and extends a hand holding a cup.

"Here, I brought you coffee." She places it on the table in front of him.

He looks at the cup, hesitates, then raises it to his lips. "Thank you." He glances at his bare wrist. "Where's my watch?" He pats his empty pockets. "Where's my wallet, phone, and keys?"

"We're keeping them safe upstairs. We wanted to make sure you had no listening devices. Security, you understand," Jonathan says.

"Are you spooks or police? Please identify yourselves."

They both flash their ID wallets.

"DHS, huh? What do you want with me?"

"You're an eyewitness to the massacre at the 4th Precinct yesterday. We'd appreciate it if you could tell us what you saw," Renata says.

"It was all over the news. I saw what the TV and cell cameras saw, a bunch of shooting and people going down, blood and brain matter flying everywhere. It was chaos." Delbert stands up. "I really want to leave now. My wife will be worried."

"We asked your cameraman, what's his name, Silva, to call your home and inform your wife that you would be late. That you're assisting us with the investigation. Now sit down and be helpful," Jonathan commands.

Bascue throws up his hands and sits. "I'm not sure how I can help beyond what everybody already saw."

Renata flashes a warm smile. "You can start by telling us how you happened to be in front of the police station before all the shooting started."

Bascue looks up at the ceiling like he's working on his story. He looks back down at Renata. "I heard there was a bomb scare and thought I'd check it out."

"See, we knew you could help. Who did you hear about the bomb scare from?"

"It was an anonymous tip."

Jonathan pounds his fist on the table. "So you jump every time you get an anonymous tip. I doubt that. You're lying."

Bascue holds his hands palms out. "Hold up there, partner. Even if I knew who it was, I can't reveal my sources."

Jonathan leans forward and speaks in a low, strained voice. "That's a load of crap. Over a hundred people died, and this is now a national security matter."

Renata clasps Jonathan's arm to pull him back. "We just need to know what you know. If you withhold information, it could make you an accessory before the fact to one hundred counts of murder and terrorism. In which case, you might never see your wife and daughter again."

"You're bluffing. Leave my family out of this. Why's everybody have to pick on—" Delbert catches himself.

Renata peers at Jonathan and then back at Delbert. "Is somebody threatening your family, Mr. Bascue? If so, and you work with us, we can protect them."

"Sure, I've heard that before."

"You're in a bit of a bind here, Mr. Bascue," Renata says.

"If you help us, whoever perpetrated this attack will go after your family and if you don't help us, we'll feed it to the media that you are helping us. Either way, you're screwed," Jonathan says.

"You wouldn't do that."

"We do what we have to do to save lives, Delbert. May I call you Delbert?" Renata says.

Bascue slumps down in his chair.

"So, if the terrorist thinks you're helping us, even if you're not, wouldn't you rather have our protection?" Jonathan asks.

Bascue leans forward and speaks almost in a whisper. "I

the group shots to individuals. Michelle is doing the pin-ups while Rich is leaning back, staring up, and chewing on more of yesterday's cold pizza. They both turn when Monica enters.

Michelle greets her with a warm smile and an extended hand. "Hi Monica, it's a pleasure to finally meet you in person."

"You too." Monica shakes with her own sweaty hand and says, "Pardon me, I'm a little nervous. This is all new to me."

Rich lights up and rises to give Monica a hug. "I'm so sorry about Sam and that you had to be here under these circumstances. We had planned to fly out for his funeral when all this shit went down." Rich sits back down. "We were just going over the crime scene. There's a slice of pizza left. Would you like it?" He holds out a limp slice.

Monica smells the garlic and snickers. "No thanks. I had breakfast. It's all yours." She looks up at the murder board. "I was just there. As I mentioned, I reviewed all the video I found before leaving home and I walked the scene to compare it."

"You were supposed to go to the hotel last night and directly here this morning," Rich says. "I'm going to have a word with John. As former military, he should know about obeying orders."

"Blame me. I insisted. But that's beside the point. I put something together. More of a question, but it might lead to something else," Monica says.

"Now you really sound like Sam," Michelle says.

"Let's hear it," Rich says. "And then I'd like you to explain what Sam meant when he said you have his skills, yada, yada."

"OK. First things first. You saw the video, I assume," Monica says and they both nod. "Besides what I mentioned before about the reporters being there ahead of the incident, there is another thing I saw that troubled me. Can you call up video on your monitor of Ericsson five minutes before the shooting started?"

"Sure." Michelle picks up a remote, rewinds, and stops the video at the 8:34 time stamp and then punches the PLAY button. Police and personnel are still exiting the building, many are staring up at the sky or turning in circles.

"Stop there," Monica says. "What do you make of their body language?"

"They've just had a bomb scare. Naturally, they look dazed and confused," Rich says.

Monica raises a hand. "I don't think it's natural. They're not civilians. Most of them are law enforcement trained to be cool under pressure. Something else is going on. To me, they look like they've been drugged or poisoned. Play a little more... You see there. That woman is vomiting. Is that normal?"

"She's scared and dressed like an admin, not in uniform," Rich says.

"Play more," Monica says.

The three of them watch as people bump into each other as if they didn't notice the others. "Watch their mouths. Nobody is talking to anyone else. Maybe some mouths are moving, but it doesn't appear that anyone is listening or responding. You're the terror experts—is that normal too?"

"No," Rich says and stands. He paces the wall opposite the murder board, running his fingers through his thinning dark hair. "OK. I agree there is something peculiar about their behavior before the shooting starts. Any other observations or theories?"

Michelle jumps in. "Unless they put something in the water, it's unlikely something they drank poisoned them. Might have been gas. I think high levels of carbon monoxide could cause dizziness and vomiting." Michelle taps the intercom button on the desk phone console. "Gary, I need you to check if the 4th Precinct has carbon monoxide detectors, and if they were working at the time of the attack, and if they went off."

She looks at Rich and then back at the phone. "Yes, I need that information right now." Michelle hangs up.

Ten seconds later, the phone console rings and Michelle picks up. "That was fast." She repeats what Gary is saying out loud. "They do have operational CM detectors, and they did not sound any alarms. Thanks, Gary."

"What if they used some kind of neural weapon like the NNN did on the Congressional Black Caucus last year? That might disorient them, and worse," Monica says.

Rich stops pacing and puts a finger to his chin. "The sonic weapon the NNN used killed and maimed most of the victims. Hmm, but I supposed if they dialed it down, they could just disorient the victims."

"But why do that if you were going to shoot at them anyway?" Michelle asks.

Monica clears her throat. "To keep them from fighting back or—"

"Or what?" Rich asks.

"Or whoever did this wanted to make a point, to put on a show, to show us they can mess with our heads anytime they want," Monica says.

"I suppose that could be the motive and they could have used some kind of neural weapon as a means or that might have been the *one* in a one-two punch," Michelle says.

Rich raises a hand. "These are all wild-ass theories. We need something more concrete."

Monica flashes a twisted smile. "I suppose we could wait and twiddle our thumbs until the next attack. Or we could act on one of these theories until we get your hard evidence, or we hit a dead end."

"Now you really do sound like Sam," Rich says. "About that—"

Michelle looks up from her phone. "I just got a text from

Renata. They got something from Bascue. We can't wait. We need to act on whatever we have. The Monica-Sam story can wait till later."

Rich looks at Monica and raises an eyebrow. Monica smiles back and twiddles her thumbs.

REVELATION

I'm watching the meeting at DHS with Rich and Michelle through Monica's eyes. It feels like I'm in the room. I took a digital snapshot when she looked at the murder board. Maybe I'm hallucinating, but I think I can smell the garlic from Rich's pizza. Renata and Jonathan rush into the conference room. I sense their urgency. They greet Monica quickly.

"Frank, are you seeing this?" I ask.

"As I told you, you are the only one with permissions to see through Monica's eyes unless you let me. I really want you to trust that it's private and protected communication," Frank says.

"I'm glad you can draw a line somewhere. Come here and listen to this."

Frank rolls his virtual Aeron chair next to me. We follow as Renata relates the results of Bascue's interrogation.

Renata starts. "First, Delbert says it's a woman who tipped him off, and she said something about *payback*. We cloned his phone so we can listen when and if she calls again."

"And?" Rich asks.

Jonathan chimes in. "She called him a second time a couple of hours ago and said the news reports understate the president's condition. That something more serious has happened to her."

Frank coughs. "I've been following that. I hacked her records at Walter Reed. They're saying it looks like she had a stroke. She's incoherent."

"But how would this mystery woman know that? Either she hacked the hospital like you did or she had something to do with making it happen," I say. Then something flares up in my brain. The pieces come together. Payback, a woman mastermind, escape from prison, disoriented police officers, a stroke.

I take a deep breath and gulp. "Frank, I think our killer may be Ashaki LaSalam." I recount all the clues. "But here's the big question for you. Do you think she could have figured out the truth about memories residing in the Cloud and being accessible by a password? Could she have hacked into all those people's memories at the 4th and the president's memories and erased them? Could she have caused a collective amnesia?"

I realize at that moment that in all the years I've worked with Frank and through all the crises we navigated together, he's never broken a sweat. Now I see beads of virtual perspiration on his brow. He closes his eyes and then speaks. "This may wind up being the worst day of our lives. Worse than if a nuclear bomb dropped on New York. If Ashaki has this knowledge and the tools, nobody is safe from a memory-wipe or memory alteration."

I'm stunned. It feels like I've been hit in the head with a baseball bat. *Pull yourself together.* "Frank, I must share this with Rich. I could call but is there a way for me to transmit what we just discovered through the Neur-o-link to Monica."

Frank's eyes are still closed. He seems to be in a trance. I shake him and his eyes snap open. I repeat my question about the Neur-o-link.

He turns to me and in a robotic voice says, "If you thought it, she already knows. Just like you can see into her mind, she can see into yours."

"When were you going to tell me that?"

"Probably never."

Monica grows nauseous. Something from Sam, from his memories or thoughts. *Frank duped me. He didn't download memories. Wait. Monica scans the new synaptic revelations flooding her brain. Passwords to memories in the Cloud, the president, amnesia. There's so much. How did Sam handle it all? Frank tricked him too. It was all Frank. Is this a bad thing? Would I have agreed to Frank's memory experiment if I knew? Would Sam have agreed? No. But was Frank right? Did Destiny put me here, in this room, right now to help, maybe to save the world? That's crazy.*

Rich scans Monica. "Are you OK? You look like you've just seen a ghost."

Monica snaps back to the room. "Maybe I have, or maybe it was bad peanuts on the plane." She grabs a bottle of water from the table and gulps half of it down. "That's better. I had a dream, maybe more of a revelation. No, it's more like a nightmare scenario, but it might be real and true."

Michelle touches Monica's arm. "What is it?"

Monica sucks in a long breath. "It wasn't carbon monoxide or tainted water. The people from the 4th Precinct and the president have amnesia."

"What? That's ridiculous," Rich says. "How did you come up with that one?"

"Sam told me. He told me everything," Monica says.

"When? How?" Renata asks.

"He told me just now. And the *How* answers both your questions—why I know what Sam knows and why I'm sure it's amnesia."

The room falls silent. Rich, Michelle, Renata, and Jonathan's faces are blank. Rich's mouth hangs open but nothing comes out.

Monica continues. "I also now know who is behind the attacks."

Rich's eyes go wide. "Whoa, what?"

Monica raises a hand. "Think about it. Who escaped Metropolitan Correctional two days ago? Payback? A woman? Previous pattern of behavior, her M.O.?"

Michelle speaks in a low voice. "Yes, you're right. It might be Ashaki LaSalam, and she would have had help. The woman that escaped with her, Ersari. Before the shit hit the fan here, Gary was working a lead we had on Mesger."

"Michelle, call Gary on that Mesger lead," Rich says. "And let's hope LaSalam, or whoever the mystery tipster is, calls Bascue again soon."

"She will, but it won't be good news," Renata says. "Bascue told us that the woman, presumably Ashaki, said the precinct attack was just the beginning."

"And it may be our end," Monica says.

THE 25TH

The only sound is the steady beep of the heart monitor, and the only smell is the antiseptic in President Longford's hospital suite at Walter Reed. Donna Swenson, Longford's chief of staff, gazes at the drawn faces of Vice President Steven Hubbard, George Osborne from the CIA, Daniel Kennedy from State, Roger Brickman from DHS, and Dr. Mark Harris, chief neurologist. Longford's eyes are closed yet flutter periodically under their lids. Her voice makes a low moaning, haunting sound. Swenson motions to the adjoining sitting room. The men follow. She closes the door.

She stares briefly out the window at the gray winter sky, which seems to perfectly match her mood. She pivots back to face the men. "Gentlemen, we can't cover up her condition any longer. Speculation, and of course conspiracy theories, are running rampant in the press. Doctor, what's your diagnosis?"

"The scans do not show any damage, which would be typical of a traumatic brain injury. The tox screen neither shows any associated medication like Ambien that can cause amnesia nor carbon monoxide poisoning. However, her symptoms seem to be both acute aphasia and amnesia."

The men all shake their heads.

Doctor Harris continues. "She could have had a fall or an accident earlier and exhibited a delayed reaction. However, judging by the severity, that seems unlikely."

"What's the prognosis?" Vice President Hubbard asks.

"It's hard to tell. She could recover in an hour or a day or never. We have no way of knowing, especially since we have not identified a cause. We can only monitor the situation and keep her comfortable. The brain has an amazing capacity to recover or even rewire itself in cases like this, but we can't predict when or if ever that will occur."

Hubbard turns to the group. "It's not what I expected or was looking for, but I think it's time for the twenty-fifth."

The others nod.

"Agreed," says Swenson with a heavy sigh. "Since the president is totally incapacitated and cannot sign her consent, I will assemble the cabinet and the chief justice today at—" She looks at her watch. "Does 2:00 work for you, Mr. Vice President?"

"The sooner the better. If we wait much longer, we could have civil unrest," Hubbard says. "I know you need time to call people in and bring them up to speed, but this is an emergency. Make it 1:00 in the Oval."

Everyone rises as if the power has actually just passed.

"Yes, sir," Swenson says.

"Please alert Lise Hull, my chief of staff, but nobody else should know until it's done," Hubbard says. "I'll call my wife. I want her to be there. Do we have any conceivable way of keeping it quiet until then?"

"I have a few favors I can call in with the major media," Brickman says.

"Have Virginia Healy call a press briefing for 1:30 with the

40

WTF

Gary barges into Conference room 4. Rich, Monica, and Michelle look up.

He punches a button on the conference phone in the middle of the table. "Bascue got a call."

They all listen as the unidentified voice says, "... do it now." Then the line goes dead.

Rich hangs his head. "What the fuck?"

"Sounds like they switched him to a burner, and if he dropped the phone, we lost our tracking device," Michelle says.

"Gary, can you get CCTV and a drone on him? We can't lose him. Give us a location and I'll get Renata and Jonathan to follow him," Rich says.

"Already on it. My assistant, Loretta Edgar, is scanning all video we can get from around 41st and 7th, but if he ducks in a subway, we may lose him," Gary says.

"The MTA has cameras. Can't you follow him there?" Monica asks.

"They have over five-thousand cameras, but they only cover a third of the stations. So we'd need to get lucky."

"Better to be lucky than good," Rich says. "Michelle, remind me when this is over to get some more money to the MTA for cameras. OK Gary, what else have you got?"

"It's not all bad news. In fact, two leads have come together. We did voice rec on Bascue's call."

"And?"

"One, the caller was Jennie Lee Ersari. Two, Mesger's lead is to an apartment on 88th Street belonging to an offshore LLC shell corp, and guess who the principal is?"

Rich jumps to his feet. "Text me the address. C'mon Michelle, Monica. I'm tired of sitting on our asses waiting for stuff to happen. Let's make a house call."

Every seat is taken in the White House Press Briefing Room. Although it looks larger on television, it's actually the size of a decent-sized living room with forty-eight theater chairs crammed together. The seats are full, and more reporters and cameramen stand shoulder-to-shoulder in the aisles. Body heat and the smell of anticipation pervade. The reporters are already shouting questions as Roger Brickman ascends the dais. He raises his hands and makes a palms-down motion to quell the ruckus. In seconds there is a hushed silence. Brickman clears his throat. "I won't be taking questions today, but I do have a statement to make." There is a low rumble in the room as he continues. "As you know, one hundred and thirteen police personnel, officers, and staff died in the New York attack on Tuesday. Fifty-six more are still in serious or critical condition in nearby hospitals. Homeland's New York Office is in charge of the investigation with our full resources and help from the FBI and NYPD Counterterrorism Bureau. We are pursuing active leads as we—Excuse me, Vice President Hubbard has just arrived with an important announcement."

The undercurrent in the room gets louder. Hubbard steps up and slaps his hands on the podium. "I regret to inform you and the nation that President Longford is temporarily unable to fulfill—" And then it happens with cameras rolling and the entire world watching. Hubbard's speech trails off. "I assume the off, off, wha me who, da-da-da..." Hubbard looks up at the ceiling. He turns, looking at all the faces. Then he flails his arms and his eyes roll up in his head and he collapses to the floor.

Brickman rushes over to the fallen, newly sworn-in president. The room is pure mayhem with shouts and screams. Brickman looks up at the Secret Service men surrounding President Hubbard. "Clear the room and get medical in here now."

Rich pounds on the gas of the black 370HP Dodge Charger, turret flashing up 1st Avenue.

"Renata and Jonathan will meet us there. NYPDCT pulled in an ATF SWAT team in case we need to breach," Michelle says just before her phone vibrates. She puts it on speaker.

Roger Brickman, out-of-breath, speaks rapidly between gasps. He relays the events of the past half hour in D.C.

"Holy shit," Rich says. "And you think this has some connection to New York?"

"I reviewed your New York attack footage yesterday. Hubbard's behavior and body movements before he collapsed looked just like those poor souls in front of the 4th Precinct, dazed, confused, babbling, disoriented. It's some kind of poison or weapon and your terrorist has used it not only on the hundred dead in New York but on the president and vice president. Rich, whatever you need, this has to stop now before mass panic takes us down."

Rich guns it through a red light on 62nd Street, swerving and narrowly missing an ambulance racing through the same intersection. "We're on it, ready to close in on the suspects' location now."

"Call me as soon as you have anything. I mean anything. Don't fuck this up." Brickman clicks off.

"Thanks, boss," Rich says to dead air.

"Now I know where you get your colorful language from," Monica says from the backseat.

"Slow down," Michelle says. "It's up ahead, but we're meeting the team a block past to coordinate the breech. Ditch the turret and sirens."

Rich pulls the turret back inside and slows to a stop behind a black armored personnel carrier with ATF stenciled on the side.

41

SEND

One hour earlier, the News 8 newsroom was buzzing in a way it hasn't since its heyday in the 90s. There's electricity in the air with all the breaking news, and their lead reporter, Delbert Bascue, has been scooping the big guys. Cory Cravens comes out of his office chewing on an unlit Juan Lopez Cuban. He removes it and shouts out to get the attention of the half dozen reporters pecking away on their keyboards. "Anything from Bascue?"

The reporters look up briefly, shake their heads, and resume their typing.

Cravens feels a vibration and extricates his iPhone from the deep inside pocket of his tweed sport coat. He fumbles for the screen. A text from *Unknown*:

It's Delbert. Different phone. I have a tip, same source as b4. Hubbard just sworn in as pres. Longford out of it - 25th by vote of cabinet. Conference in 25 min. Hubbard will announce and go down like Longford. Terrorist group. Names unknown with

*apocalyptic weapon. Try alerting WH but they won't believe U
so get story out. More later. Can't come in. Too dangerous.*

Cravens scratches his head. Can this really be true or is it a
prank? It's not his phone. He can't use what little cred they
have to call this in to the White House. They can barely afford
the correspondent they have there as it is. But he can't ignore it.
He taps a few keys, forwarding the text to Corinne Tufo, the
News 8 White House Correspondent with a tag:

From Bascue. What do you make of this?

Thirty seconds later a reply

*Looks like BS, but Bascue, if it's him, has been right on. See what
I can find out.*

Cravens rarely does the writing anymore, but this time he
goes back to his desk and types up a clean version of Bascue's
alleged text. "A reliable source..."

Finishing with the byline Cory Cravens, Managing Editor.
He lets his finger hover over the SEND key. If he hits SEND,
his story would be live in their digital edition immediately. If
he's wrong or this is a fake, it could sink them. *Our liability
insurance won't cover all the lawsuits, especially if they deem it
willful negligence with intent to do harm.* Cory glances up at
the TV monitors on his wall that runs News 8 on the left and
CNN on the right, both muted 24/7. He sees Brickman at the
podium. Brickman steps away and Vice President Hubbard
takes his place, a blank look on his face. Cory turns up the
volume as Hubbard's speech becomes incoherent, he looks up
and around like he's lost and then he stumbles to the floor.

Cory's face drains of all color. Feeling like he's going to throw up, he drops his finger on the keyboard—SEND.

Rich confers with Richard Robinson from the NYPD Counterterrorism Bureau and Candy Beck of the ATF. Beck sends a "forward observer," with her sniper rifle and a spotter to the rooftop across the street from Ersari's apartment. Three other ATF agents in vests and helmets, carrying Colt M4 assault rifles and a battering ram, flank the front door to the granite-faced building awaiting orders.

Rich turns. "Michelle, suit up. Monica, stay in the car."

Monica puts her hands on her hips in defiance. *Who is this woman?*

"In the car now," Rich commands.

Monica shakes her head and gets in the car. Michelle gets her vest from the trunk of the Charger and hands a vest to Rich.

Then, like before, a thought pops into Monica's head, but she can't quite read it. It's fuzzy.

Beck's walkie-talkie crackles. "We're in position. Let's go." She drops a hand and the three agents enter the building lobby followed by Robinson, Rich, and Michelle.

The doorman begins to speak, and Rich puts a finger to his lips. He flashes his credentials and whispers, "Apartment 3201." The doorman hands him a key. The six of them get in the elevator, and Rich inserts the key in the lock on the elevator panel that will take them to Ersari's Penthouse.

The fuzzy thought in Monica's mind becomes sharper. Her mouth falls open. She hesitates and whips out her cell, dialing Rich furiously.

The elevator ascends 19... 20... 21... Rich's phone rings. He sees *M. Sunborn* on the Caller ID. 28... 29... 30...

Monica hears a click as Rich taps into the call. Before he can even speak, she shouts, "It's a trap!"

Out of nowhere, there is a massive explosion at the top of the East 88th Street Tower. The top two floors explode, Fire and smoke billow out. Glass and debris rain down, pelting the Charger's roof over Monica and knocking down pedestrians nearby. There is a second, even bigger explosion. A refrigerator-size chunk of granite flies off the burning building from the blast, falling twenty stories and crashing on the roof of the Charger, flattening it like a junkyard crusher, the booming crunch echoing through the canyon of the surrounding buildings.

42

RELO

At the Riverside Cafe, Ashaki and Ersari sip their strong coffee from folding chairs beside the rushing water of the Raritan River hurtling over a dam in Clinton, New Jersey. The view is spectacular with the 1810 water wheel affixed to the old Red Mill slowly turning under the clearing blue skies. Only wisps of clouds remain. They wear parkas, but the day is surprisingly warm for December. A horse and carriage clacks over the yellow steel bridge onto Main Street and saunters by the two-story buildings rebuilt in the late 1800s after a fire destroyed the town. A sudden cool breeze gusts by the cafe, stirring the steam from their fragrant cups.

"I don't think they'd expect to find us here," Ashaki says.

"I never imagined that there was a picture-postcard place like this in New Jersey. In my mind this state was the stench of pig farms on the Turnpike I remember smelling from my parents' Buick on summer trips to the beach. It's where Tony Soprano, and maybe I, buried a few bodies," Ersari says.

"That's the way it used to be. I had never been west of Somerville until a former lover brought me here on a romantic

date. It's only a little over an hour from New York. I swore I'd
come back. Enough chatting. Bring your coffee. I'll show you
the office."

They stroll down Main Street under the sycamore trees
adorned with white Edison bulbs and candy cane Christmas
decorations. Ashaki pushes open the door of a red brick
building next to the bookshop. The small carved wooden sign
on the door says *Barin Properties*. They climb a steep set of
twenty worn oak steps. She puts her eye to a retinal scanner
and her hand on the palm reader. The door buzzes, opening
into a large wide-open space with a wooden beamed ceiling,
white plaster walls, and windows overlooking the street. In the
center of the room, seven women sit in low cubicles, each
facing three monitors.

"This is my A-Team," Ashaki says, waving her arm as if she
was taking a bow.

Two of the women look up, smile, nod, and resume their
work. Ashaki takes Ersari's arm. "There's a small conference
room in the back."

The table inside seats four. Ashaki takes a chair across from
the one-way mirror that lets her spy on her team outside. "What
do you think?"

"Impressive," Ersari says. "But what do you have them
doing?"

"They're gearing up for the Big One. We were selective
when we erased the memories of the president and vice president. A precision attack that had the desired effect of sowing
panic and fear. There was a successful proof-of-concept with a
larger group at the police station. It will take my seven here and
the thirty others I have at other locations to coordinate the next
event."

"And what would that be?"

"In time, Jennie Lee. Remember, we're still learning to trust each other."

"Speaking of which, where's the money you promised me for all my support and to repay me for destroying my apartment? I've tried to be cool about that, but that was my home."

"We had to take care of those annoying DHS agents, and I think we got a bonus taking out Ms. Sunborn. I've been busy as you may have noticed, but check your bank account, the one in Geneva."

Ersari logs into a secure banking app on her phone. Her eyes widen. The balance shows a one followed by eight zeros.

Ashaki smiles at Ersari's reaction. "That should cover the apartment plus a little, don't you think?"

"How'd you do that?" Ersari asks.

Ashaki grins. "Not only can we erase memories, but we can surgically place new ones. We identified the person, a one Carole Poissant, in charge of the wire transfer room at one of the big three banks and replaced his reading of an oil company's account number, for a large imminent Saudi transfer, with your account number. You see, when he read the original number it briefly went into his short-term memory, even when he double-checked the number. At that moment, we changed the number to your account number in his memory. And voila, 100 million appears in your account seconds later." Ashaki looks at her watch. "We just made this happen forty-two minutes ago. So I'd suggest you move that money out before the bank does their daily audit, discovers the mistake, and tries to claw back the funds. I suspect Mademoiselle Poissant will be out of a job."

Ersari bolts upright. "I need to make a call."

"You do that. I'll give you some privacy." Ashaki leaves the room, closing the door behind her.

Crazy bitch, Ersari thinks.

"Frank, I can't sense Monica anymore. It's like my connection to her went dead. I'm worried," I say.

"You should be," Frank says. "Look at this."

I swivel my chair. The virtual room is totally dark except for two monitors. On Frank's screen, I see a burning building. "My God, what's that?"

"It's a building on 88th Street in Manhattan. I was tracking them. Rich, Michelle, and his NYPD and ATF teams were going to breach Ersari's penthouse when this happened." Frank points at the screen and shakes his head.

"Monica was there too, in their car," I say.

Earlier Frank hacked a CCTV camera across the street from the burning tower. Now he manipulates a joystick to scan the scene. 88th Street is jammed with firetrucks, ambulances, and police cars, turrets flashing. He holds on the image of a firetruck with an extended ladder. A firefighter with a hose is spraying water. "They can't reach thirty floors up with that ladder. They're trying to save the lower floors," Frank says. He pans down to the entrance. Firefighters are helping survivors exit the building, their heads covered in wet blankets and towels. Frank pans right and stops at the image of a flattened Dodge Charger with a giant stone block on top of it.

Frank whispers in a low voice, "That's the car they came in."

I'm numb. All my muscles freeze up at once. Even though I'm digital, I choke like I can't breathe. Finally I suck in a virtual breath and something stirs inside me. "Can you get infrared on that car?"

Frank taps a few keys, and the image of the flattened car turns green. The shapes of the firefighters standing behind it turn a pulsing orange. But the car, the car is all green, no heat signature. "I doubt she would turn cold this fast," Frank says.

He pans the camera farther right and picks up a heat signature on the doorway of an adjacent building. He switches the camera back to visible view.

"Could that be Monica? Zoom in," I say.

Frank pushes the joystick forward. The woman is slumped on a stoop, her face blackened. She is badly cut and bruised. Her hair looks like it's been washed in soot. Frank focuses on her face.

"It's her. I'd know those hazel eyes anywhere. But I can't feel her. The connection is gone."

A paramedic approaches her, feels her neck, and then takes her wrist. Two more medics appear and lower her onto a backboard. Frank follows her with the camera into a waiting ambulance. The medics slide her in, slam the double doors, and knock twice on the back door. Frank pans to the license plate. The ambulance lights up and revs the sirens as it slowly weaves its way through the vehicles and people blocking the way.

"You lost the connections probably because of the trauma."

"She's alive. That's all that matters." I stop myself. "But will she be OK?"

Frank types feverishly. "I just tracked down that ambulance and hacked into their coms."

Voices crackle to life from inside the ambulance:

"Where are we taking her?"

"Lennox Hill."

"They're good. Did you see the Netflix show about them?"

"Great, yeah, but I'm not sure she's going to make it. Hey Matt, how's she doing back there?

"Weak but steady pulse. Shallow breathing. Severe lacerations, but she looks like she was tough and toned before this. I bet she was a looker."

"Keep it in your pants. We should be there in five."

"Assholes," I say. "Oh my God, Frank. Is there anything we can do?"

"At the moment, all we can do is follow her. If we can help at any point, we will."

"OK." I let out a deep sigh. "What about Rich and Michelle?"

"That's a different story," Frank says.

a way out of this. I've got a friend at DHS. Well, not really at DHS, but he consults for them and has connections. If anybody can figure a way out of this, he can."

I stare at the still image on the monitor. It's Monica, alone, unconscious, with oxygen and an IV attached to her body. A heart monitor beeps with the rise and fall of her life's thread. It's Lenox Hill Hospital, room 302, brightly lit in contrast to the dark winter sky outside her window. A nurse enters the room, checks her pulse, looks at the IV, and punches a few keys on her tablet.

"Frank, can we get into Monica's medical records—find out what's going on?" I ask.

"Working on it. Most medical facilities upgraded their security this year after all the ransomware attacks, but they still have a way to go." Frank grins. "There we go. We're in."

I skip over all the data to the diagnosis, severe head trauma, two broken ribs. Serious, but not critical, condition. Expectation of recovery good. Brain damage unknown. Pressure on brain relieved.

Frank puts a gentle hand on my virtual shoulder. "She'll be OK. She's alive. That's step one."

"But will she wake up? And what will she be like if she does? It's all my fault, putting her directly in danger again."

"Sam, you can't blame yourself. She's an adult, and she agreed to do it."

"Yeah, after we both pressured her. I'll never forgive myself if she doesn't fully recover."

"She will. Just remember, like you always have, she was taking a calculated risk to help save others."

"And Rich and Michelle, still no word. Oh my God, Evan. What has he heard about his mother? I have to call him."

As I start to virtual dial Evan on my computer, an incoming call flashes on the screen. Caller Unknown. *Great. But who has my number besides Rich, Michelle, Bart, Loretta?* I answer.

"Sam, thank Jesus. It's Cory, Cory Cravens. You remember, we met at Nancy Lu's funeral and had a drink together after? She was young, but the best reporter I ever had." Cory chokes up. "She was like a daughter to me."

"Cory, sure. I miss Nancy and I know you do too. But I've got a lot going on right now. I don't know if you heard, but Monica, my wife, is unconscious in the hospital and Rich and Michelle, my DHS friends, are still missing. I don't mean to be short. Unless this is an emergency, I'll have to get back to you."

"It is. Otherwise, I wouldn't bother you. What I've got to tell you relates to Monica and your DHS friends. It'll take two minutes and maybe it will help both of us."

"OK, what is it?"

45

ICE CREAM IN DECEMBER

"Where are we going to stay while we're stuck here in Clinton?" Ersari asks.

Ashaki is typing furiously. Facing her three-monitor array, she rotates her head in ratchet-like swivels from screen to screen. "What?"

"You heard me. I'm tired."

Without looking up, Ashaki says, "You can call Pickles. He said he'd be working out at the gym. He'll pick you up and take you to the Holiday Inn. I'll meet you there later, when everything is set for tomorrow."

"OK. I'm going to take a walk first. I'll call him when I get back."

Ashaki doesn't respond. Ersari turns and heads down the steep staircase. The old wood creaks under her footfalls. There's a chill in the early evening air. She walks into the wind, up Main Street. Most of the stores are closed, but JJ Scoops is open. She's the only customer in the small corner shop that smells of mint. *Who else eats ice cream in December?* It calms her, she thinks, an excuse to herself and her waistline. Ice cream may be *the thing I missed most in prison.* "I'll take a triple-scoop Rocky Road cone with sprinkles," she says to the teenage girl working the counter. She closes her eyes as she takes the first bite then licks the drops that dribble down the side.

She heads back toward the office, but keeps going, and passes the office door, the sub shop, and the Italian restaurant. The Red Mill is lit with floodlights with the water wheel turning. The river rushes by underneath the bridge, the water low this time of year with ice hats adorning the boulders that break above the dark surface. *Can I do this?* Ersari wonders. *Can I let her go through with this and ruin the lives of so many people, so many innocent people? I may have broken the law, but I'm still a patriot. I love this country, both for its faults and the opportunities. But then there's the money and more to come. Yet if I let her go through with this, it won't be the same country. If everything collapses because of her, all that money might be worthless.* She sucks in the cold air and feels revived. *I'll sleep on it. That's always best.*

She lifts her phone from the back pocket of her jeans and dials Pickles.

The charred bodies on 88th Street were tagged, bagged, and carted away in refrigerated trucks to the city morgue at NYU Langone Medical Center Campus on First Avenue. The FBI is still trying to decide which bodies to autopsy there, which to send to Quantico, and where to send the rest. A grim task at best. The street is mostly clear. All the MEs and EMTs, police cars, and ambulances have left except for one black and white to secure the scene, one fire engine, and one ambulance. After seven grueling hours, the smoke has cleared. All that survives is the winter chill, the blood blotched pavement, and the lingering smell of burnt plastic. The last team of firefighters and EMTs have been searching for survivors. The only hope is the elevator stuck between the 28th and 29th floor.

Pry and Bar finally pull the scalding hot doors apart.

"We're in," McGuire says.

The elevator is halfway between floors. Pry aims her laser thermometer inside. The digital readout blinks 115 degrees.

Koniar, in command from the street outside, still with Renata and Jonathan, taps his mic. "Anyone inside?"

"A man and a woman unconscious, maybe dead. I'm going in," Bar replies and shimmies through the low open door, jumping to the elevator on the 28th 1/2 floor. She feels the man and then the woman's neck. "They're alive. I need back-boards and some help up here."

"Coming right up," Koniar says and waves two paramedics standing by. They grab the backboards and rush into the building.

"We're going in too," Renata says.

"Oh no you're not," Koniar says.

"Sorry, this is a matter of national security," Jonathan says as he and Renata charge the building.

46

A DREAM

The hallways at Lenox Hill are dimly lit this time of night, presumably to let patients sleep. Although if you've ever had the misfortune to spend nights in the hospital, a nurse wakes you every two hours to take your temperature or your blood or to perform some other redundant tasks. Sleep is not high on a hospital's agenda.

Yet Monica has been sleeping for fifteen hours now, in a fitful coma, her body and her mind trying its best to self-heal. At 3:00 AM she opens her eyes, her eyelids rapidly blinking. A chill comes over her, causing her to shiver. A few moments later, she feels hot. *Where am I? What happened?*

The door to her room opens, spreading bluish fluorescent light partially blocked by the wide silhouette of Nurse Rosie Reve holding an infrared thermometer. Without even looking or expecting a response, she says, "Time for a check." Holding the probe a few inches from Monica's forehead, she sees the blinking eyes beneath. "Mother Mary of God, you're awake."

"I am?" Monica asks.

"Your eyes are open and you're talking. I'd say that's a good indicator."

"But I've been having these dreams. How do I know this isn't another dream?"

Nurse Reve pinches Monica's upper arm as if she has the pincers of a scorpion.

"Eyow!"

"Guess you're not dreaming," Reve says while she points a penlight into Monica's eyes. "Look left. Now right. Looks good." She hands Monica a cup of cold water with a straw. "You were in a serious accident and by some miracle survived. You're at Lenox Hill Hospital, the best in the city. And by a stroke of luck, you got the best nurse. I'll alert Doctor Hicks that Sleeping Beauty has awakened, and she should be in to see you soon."

"But how—?"

A shrill alarm comes from outside the room. "Code blue, gotta go," Rosie says and vanishes.

Monica leans forward and sips the water. She can feel her parched tongue and mouth absorb the moist potency of it. She sniffs the air and detects the mild scent of lavender, likely left behind by Nurse Reve. *I am alive.*

She sinks back into the feather pillow and stares at the ceiling. Details of the dream come back to her.

It's late afternoon. The air is frigid. She's walking down the main street in an older town. She passes a boutique clothing store, an old-time drugstore with walkers and crutches in the window, a French gourmet shop, and a cafe. There are empty steel tables and chairs outside the cafe. A few people inside sit behind laptops, earbuds plugged in, sipping coffee. The street ends at a river. She ascends an incline onto the walkway that abuts the one-lane steel grate where cars roll by. Looking to her left, she sees a fly fisher casting his line into the icy riffles of clear water hurtling over the rocks.

The fisherman wears a heavy gray sweatshirt under his vest. He lifts his head as if he knows he's being watched. Their eyes lock. It's Sam. How could it be that he's here? He always loved to fish, although with Evan's soccer games and his work, he rarely had time for it in his last physical days. She shifts her gaze to the other side of the bridge. There is a red building with a wooden water wheel on its side, slowly turning in the current. She hears a bell ringing twice and smells something burning. The dark shadow of a hawk flying overhead appears at her feet, and suddenly a sense of dread sweeps through her. Sensing someone or something behind her, Monica whips around, but nobody's there. The town has morphed into a city. She scans the skyline and sees a tall building on fire. She's seized by convulsions. The burning building looks like the one in New York. She hears a loud crash. Her eyes snap open. She's in a dark room. The door opens, admitting a blue light.

It seemed so real. Did that really happen too?

She draws in a slow breath and then hears a kind of buzz in her head like she's listening to a distant phone ring. It persists. Buzz. Silence. Buzz. Silence. Probably more hospital sounds. Then, "Sam, is that you?"

"Yes, you're back, thank God. How do you feel?" I ask.

Monica looks up. "I don't know. It's as if I was or am somebody else. I had this weird dream. Can you tell me what happened to me?"

"I wasn't there, but I can tell you about a few eyewitness accounts. Do you remember being in a car on 88th Street?"

"Yes, I was with Rich and Michelle. They were going to

somebody named Ersari's apartment. Then I heard an explosion. That's the last thing I remember. Wait, Rich and Michelle, they were in that building. Did they—?"

"We don't know yet. They're in the same hospital as you in critical condition. It was bad, terrible for all of you. But you're alive."

"But what happened to me?"

I tell her about the falling granite, the crushed car, and how they found her. "What I can't figure out is how you got out of that car? It was flattened like a pancake."

"Like my nurse said, it was a miracle."

"Tell me about your dream. Maybe there's a clue there."

Monica recounts the dream, the street, the river, seeing me fishing, and the town changing to a city, and the building burning.

I can't believe it. The puzzle pieces are moving around in my head, but some pieces are missing, and the rest are all just white. "I know that town."

"What? How?"

"Do you remember when I went to a seminar at Rutgers two years ago? I stayed an extra day to meet up with an old friend, Charlie Dorison—we called him Dunker. Dunker took me to the town you described in your dream. He had tackle for two and took me fishing there. I remember the old mill and the cafe, even the shops on the street. It was October, and the air was colder than the water. Afterward, we ate dinner at a restaurant beside the river. They had those tall propane heaters going to keep us warm while we ate. It was kind of magical, the view, the sound of the water, being with an old friend. I'll never forget it."

"What town was it?"

"It was in New Jersey. Yeah, the name of the town was Clinton. In the second part of your dream, you were seeing

New York and the building on 88th Street where you were injured."

"What's this all mean?"

"I'm not sure, but it's all connected somehow. Monica, we need to know when you can get out of there and help us stop whoever did this to you and all those innocent people before the attacker does something worse?"

"Still single-minded as ever, huh?"

"I didn't mean it that way. I'm just sure you're going to be OK, and many other people won't be unless you and I help."

"I get it now, Sam. With access to your memories, I'm beginning to understand what makes you tick and why you're so driven. I'm no psychoanalyst, but I now have all the data. More important to me right now, how's Evan?"

"He's fine. Don't worry. I talked to Charlotte last night. He says he misses you, but I suspect he's having a good time with Charlotte's daughter, Toni. It's as if she's the sister he never had. And she likes what he likes, soccer and robotics. He's ten, and she's eight, but you never know."

"Really, Sam? You're still the same, even if you are dead. Funny, huh? OK. I'll let you know what the doctor says and if I'm up to more of this craziness. That's actually two big questions for me, not one."

"OK, call me as soon as you can." I take a deep breath and say, "I love you."

"I know," she says.

47

NEWS 8

Delbert Bascue looks more worn and disheveled than usual as he sets up with Dick Silva for his report. He plugs a comm into his left ear, straightens his tie, and fakes a half-smile. The sky is overcast with the sun occasionally breaking through. The wind has died down, and the air feels more like October than December. Delbert throws his wrinkled trench coat over a trash can.

In 4... 3... 2... 1.

"This is Delbert Bascue reporting to you live from the scene of the fire and explosion on 88th Street in Manhattan. As you can see behind me, the street has been cleared. All the emergency vehicles and first responders have left. All that remains is the blood splatter on the pavement and random bits of clothing left behind. The street sweepers are at work and a few people have returned to their homes and offices on this block. Here and at the 4th Precinct, the grief and loss of all those lives will be felt for years to come.

"Yet our immediate concern and prayers go out to President Longford and Vice President Hubbard with hopes for a speedy recovery. In the meantime, Patricia Bruder, Speaker of the House, is being sworn in as president as we speak. But questions remain. Were the sudden illnesses of the president and vice president just a coincidence, or were they connected? Were their maladies due to natural causes or some outside, perhaps nefarious force? These are questions that will hopefully be answered in the days ahead. For now, the country is on edge, waiting for the next shoe to drop. When will life get back to normal? With the pandemic and ensuing economic crisis, that's a question we've had to ask too many times in the last few years. All we can do now is be careful and vigilant. If you see anything out of the ordinary or threatening, please contact the police.

"God bless you and God bless the United States of America."

Delbert tears off his mic and asks Silva, "How was that?"

"You wrote that?" Silva asks.

"Yeah, I did."

"Well done. Where to next?"

The phone vibrates in his pocket. He looks down at a new text message. After a few taps, he trashes it and says, "We just got a new lead. Let's go."

After watching Bruder take the oath of office, I swivel my chair away from my screen. Frank has spruced up our virtual environment with a dome-like blue sky featuring puffy clouds that move in a slow circle overhead. There are tall trees and flowers in bloom and a low singsong of virtual birds chirping in the distance.

I smile. "I like what you did with the place."

Frank doesn't look up from his typing. "I needed something

a little calmer to balance out the stress and meshugas going on out there."

"I appreciate that, but tell me, do you know how Monica escaped that crushed car?"

Frank looks up at me. "I do." He turns back to his keyboard.

"Frank, stop what you're doing and tell me what's going on."

Frank sighs and rotates back to me. "I warned Monica to get out just before the enormous boulder hit the car. Fortunately, she didn't hesitate a moment longer or we would have lost her. I'd speculate that she doesn't remember due to the trauma of the moment. Luckily her physical injuries seem to be manageable."

"But how did you know to do that?"

"Easy, I was monitoring her movements along with those of Rich and Michelle. I can respond at digital speed to an emergency, which is a thousand times faster than a physical human can react. I saw that giant rock was about to break loose a few seconds before it happened."

"And what about Rich and Michelle, how did they avoid a direct hit from the explosion?"

Frank grins. "I can't tell you all my secrets."

"Cut the crap, Frank. Tell me." I instantly regret my harsh tone. "I apologize. I'm just on edge, and I don't think I can tolerate being in the dark."

"That's OK. I was trying to lighten the mood. I saw Ashaki and Ersari exiting the garage in the back of a BMW at the same time Rich and Michelle were going up in the elevator. I was able to freeze its ascent below the penthouse. I was just scanning their medical records now when you interrupted me." Frank drums his fingers on the desk while an hourglass spins on his monitor. He grins. "Their condition was downgraded from critical to serious. They're going to make it."

"That's great news. Now there's no time to waste. We have to stop Ashaki. Were you able to follow her?"

"I lost her on the New Jersey Turnpike, and she keeps switching phones to keep us from tracking her that way."

"I have an idea where they're headed."

Monica tentatively slides her legs one at a time into her skinny jeans. Everything hurts. She may not have been in the crushed car but falling debris had hit her and knocked her to the street. The medics bandaged her head and lacerations on her left arm and right leg. She sustained two cracked ribs, but there's nothing they can do about that. Only time will heal those. Nurse Deena Guptil helps Monica slip a sweater over her head and laces up her Ferragamo platform boots.

"OK, I'm ready to go," Monica says.

"The doctor said you could and should stay a couple of more days," Nurse Guptil says.

"I can't. I've got to be somewhere." Monica grimaces from the pain in her ribs.

"What could be so important?"

Monica smirks. "I just have to stop a terrorist attack that could kill thousands and destabilize the United States."

"Really? Who needs a terrorist? Our leaders can screw things up all by themselves." Guptil snickers. "What are you going to do in your state? You couldn't stop a fly."

"Just help me up... please."

Guptil helps Monica to a wheelchair. She plunks down and winces from the stabbing pain in her ribs.

"Are you sure about this?" the nurse asks.

"Yeah, I'm sure. By the way, what I told you is classified. Keep it to yourself or I'll have to shoot you."

Guptil laughs. "So, you were kidding, right?"

Monica's expression is blank. "Right. Now let's roll."

The nurse pivots the wheelchair and pushes it down the hall. Monica waves to the nurses at the nurse's station and silently mouths, "Thank you."

As they head down the elevator, Guptil asks, "Who's picking you up?"

"An old friend," Monica says.

48

YOU'RE EARLY

"Nothing like a good night's sleep," Ashaki says with a grin.

Ersari stares out the office window as the sun cuts a shadow over the two-story buildings across Main Street. "Wasn't great for me." She turns to Ashaki. "You got back to the hotel late. What were you doing?"

It's 7:45 in the morning and Ashaki's team of computer hackers, most with computer science degrees from Princeton and Rutgers, are not due in the office for another hour.

"Today's a big day. Time for the next piece of the puzzle to fall into place." Ashaki scans Ersari's face. "You look concerned. Don't worry. I've got this one without you risking your women or men. You can just sit back and watch."

"When are you going to clue me in?"

"Oh, I want it to be a surprise."

"I don't like surprises, especially between partners."

"I think you'll appreciate the genius of this one. In case you're getting cold feet, check your bank account. I put a little extra in there this morning."

Ersari freezes for a few seconds. *How did I become the kept woman?* She swings back to her screen and logs into her account. Another ten million dollars.

Ashaki waits for a reaction. With her back still turned, Ersari says, "Thank you."

"You're welcome. So, you're still with me?"

"Absolutely, but I'd still like to know what you're planning to do."

"Roll your chair over here. I'll show you."

Ersari pushes off with her feet and her chair glides across the wide-beamed oak floor, stopping beside Ashaki. She turns to face Ashaki's monitor. "What am I looking at?"

"You're looking at an overhead view of the floor of the U.S. House of Representatives."

Ersari stares at the 441 wooden desks arranged in a semi-circle facing the raised three-tiered dais. The royal blue carpet dotted with five-pointed stars and the dark paneling give the appearance of a high court. In a way, it is both a court and the very seat of democracy. A few staff members roam the floor placing papers on desks. A cleaning crew is polishing the wood and vacuuming the floors.

Ashaki checks her watch. "In about two hours, the chamber should be full with almost all the 535 congressmen and women there for the State of the Union Address. This is what I've been waiting for."

"I don't get it. What are you going to do?"

"I didn't get quite the panicked reaction I was hoping for from the masses when I erased the memories of the president and vice president. I think they chalked it up to bad luck or a coincidence. Also the Speaker, that whore Bruder, did a better job of calming fears than I expected. But she'll be there today, presiding before assuming her full, official duties at the White House. Yet she and the rest of them will not make it that far."

Ersari unconsciously rolls her chair back.

Ashaki licks her lips and continues. "Can you imagine what will happen when the C-Span video goes viral of four hundred duly-elected representatives turning into amnesiac morons at once? We cut off the head and the body dies, right?"

Ersari seems stunned silent.

Ashaki snickers. "Pack your bags and prepare for chaos."

Ersari might say her personal Maginot Line has been crossed. That the money means nothing if she loses her country. But she has something else in mind. Jennie Lee Ersari pretends to scratch her leg and slips a Khukuri knife from an ankle sheath beneath her jeans.

Ashaki notices Ersari's movements in the shadowy reflection on her screen a split second before Jennie Lee lunges, razor sharp pointed edge aiming toward Ashaki's neck.

Ashaki ducks, spins low on her chair, and swings her right arm up, parrying Ersari's attack. Then Ashaki rolls on the floor, leaps to her feet, and points a 9mm Beretta M9A3 at Ersari's chest. "So I guess a hundred and ten million isn't enough for you. Too bad, that was just for starters."

"You were wrong about me," Ersari says, holding out her hand frozen as if to stop traffic. "It's not just about the money."

Ashaki removes a silencer from her pocket and screws it on the barrel of the pistol. "Oh well. I do make mistakes. Duly noted." She fires two shots in rapid succession. The first bullet tears through Ersari's outstretched hand. She recoils and the second bullet grazes her left ear. She bolts for the door.

Just as she touches the handle, a third shot rings out, much louder this time. It isn't Ashaki's Beretta. Standing in the doorway, Pickles holds his Glock with both hands outstretched. A whisp of cordite rising from the barrel. He tiptoes forward. The hollow point bullet he fired ripped through Ashaki's right temple, blasting blood and brain matter from the exit wound onto the walls.

For a few seconds, Ashaki still stands, the left side of her skull missing, her mouth open wide as if to silently mouth, "Why?" Then she collapses to the floor.

Ersari looks down at her crumpled lover. "Too bad. You were a good lay." Pickle's grabs Ashaki's limp body by the collar and drags her away from the door.

It's 8:32. Behind her back, Ersari hears the creak of the door opening. Elouise Lord, one of Ashaki's programmers, has shown up for work early.

Lord looks at Ersari and Pickles, then down at the mangled body. Her eyes widen. "What?"

Ersari spins and says, "You're early."

Lord takes a step back. "I—"

Pickles fires two hollow points into her chest. Elouise flies backward from the impact and slams into the door frame before sliding down to the floor. Pickles yanks her away from the door, closes it, and turns the lock. He pulls down the door shade to hide the scene.

Ersari turns to Pickles and says in Russian, "как раз вовремя." *Just in time.*

"Таков был план, верно?" *That was the plan, right?* Pickles says.

"Right." She had been otherwise preoccupied, but now she feels the pain in her wounded hand. Pickles hands her a roll of gauze. The blood seeps through the first few layers, but she continues to wrap more layers around it and then ties it off. "There. That should do for now."

Ersari stares down at Ashaki's mangled corpse. She doesn't speak for a long two minutes. Then she says, "Pickles, we need an office cleaning, ASAP."

"Готово и сделано." *Done and done,* he says.

49

BIOINK

"Women are tougher than men," Michelle says, limping through the doorway of Rich's room at the Lenox Hill Hospital. The room is brightly lit as the sun peeks through the buildings on 77th Street. Rich is perched up in bed at a thirty-degree angle and hooked to an IV while his heart monitor beeps out a steady rhythm. The room smells of ozone and alcohol.

He lowers his oxygen mask and smiles. "Look who's talking. That gown brings out your complexion."

Michelle looks down at her wrinkled hospital gown patterned with tiny ducks, her slippers a fluffy orange, and an IV on wheels dangling from her arm. "If it walks like a duck." She laughs for both of them. "At least I can breathe without one of those masks."

"I'm getting extra oxygen so I can get up out of here and kick your ass."

"Or kiss my ass."

"That too." They both smile. "Seriously, how did we get away with some mild smoke inhalation and minor burns when we were on our way to meet our Maker?"

"Frank stopped the elevator and some brave men and women of the NYFD pried us out. And you were out cold until an hour ago. I saw the whole thing and just got off the phone with Frank and Sam. But I'm afraid the burns on my leg are not so minor. They bandaged me up, but I'm going to be limping around for a while."

"There's one other thing," Michelle says. "You may regret having given your medical permission to share your medical records with me. They'll be in soon to speak with you."

Rich's face transforms like Dorian Gray into a ghostly pallor. "What is it?"

"Your liver is shot, maybe due to impact. They're not sure. You need a new one."

"Or what?"

"Or you will see your dear departed wife and your mother sooner than anticipated."

"Can I get a transplant?"

"You could and that would put you out of commission for quite a while, but there is something new in the experimental phase I'd recommend."

"So now you're the doctor?" Rich covers his face with his hands.

Michelle gently pulls his hands away. His eyes are wet. "I did get a Ph.D. from M.I.T. in bio-engineering, remember?"

"What has that got to do with this?"

"Have you ever heard of bioprinting?"

"You mean like taking fingerprints?"

"No, it's like 3D printing, only it's done with human tissue and cells. In your case, they would take some stem cells from you, grow them into a bioink, and then create a scaffold to give the cells something on which to print enough of a new liver to replace the old one. I say enough because once implanted, your liver will grow back the rest of itself on its own. As I say, the procedure is new and it's only been done a few times but most of the patients have survived."

"Most?"

"Beats zero."

Rich shakes his head. "OK, suppose I agree to do this. How long will I have to be here?"

"The doctors will fill you in on the details, but from what I know, it will take a few days to grow the cells and a few more to print the new organ. It used to take months. They've recently figured out how to speed it up. So, like a week to ten days if all goes well."

"If all goes well... great. I'll think about it."

"Think fast."

"I don't know—between you and Renata, old white guys like me may be obsolete at the department anyway."

"Probably, but we'll keep you around to tell us stories about the olden days."

Rich throws a pillow at Michelle, missing her and hitting the open door.

"Looks like you're going to have to requalify at the gun range too," Michelle says.

"OK. Enough about us. What's the status of the hunt for Ashaki and Ersari?"

"They might release me later today, but you'll be here awhile. So I gave my OK for Monica to follow a lead."

"Monica, are you crazy? She's not a field agent. And where the hell did you send her?"

"Don't worry. Juan is going with her, and he's like a small one-man army. They're headed to Clinton, New Jersey based on a clue Sam dug up."

"Well, that's just great. I have to get up and out of here." Rich sits up and pulls at his IV.

Michelle pushes him back down. "Steady there, partner.

You get yourself well. I will get back out there tomorrow. Let some other people do their jobs."

Rich lays back. "OK, what about Renata and Jonathan? Why not send them?"

"They are on Bascue's tail. Looks like he's on to another Ashaki lead and hopefully not another shitstorm," Michelle says.

50

OUTTA HERE

Ersari paces the Clinton office, sporadically glancing at the two bodies on the floor. The security system buzzes.

Pickles' creased face appears on the security monitor. He's holding a mop and a pail along with an army green duffel. "A1 Cleaning at your service," he says into the intercom.

Ersari smirks and taps a button to buzz him in. He lugs his equipment up the long staircase and enters the office. Ersari locks the door behind him. "What took you so long?"

"Sorry. There was a ten car pileup on 78 coming. Довольно беспорядок," Pickles says. "Speaking of messes... too bad about Ashaki. I liked her. Did you wire the money to my account as promised?"

"I did. Both the Center and I appreciate your work. I liked Ashaki too, but she was going to turn on us. I couldn't let that happen. Listen, I've got to get outta here. I'm going down the street for a coffee. Text me when you're done. We're going to relocate."

Pickles is already yanking on his Tyvek suit and booties from the duffel. "I'll leave it clean. Give me a couple of hours."

"We can't stay here that long. Get it done in an hour."

Pickles mock salutes.

Ersari snarls, "I'm not in the mood." She pivots and heads out the door and down the stairs.

Она сука. She's a bitch, but she's my bitch, Pickles thinks.

A mild-for-December breeze pushes in from the west. Juan parks their Toyota Rav4 rental across the bridge from Main Street and opposite the Clinton House, a 19th-century colonial-style restaurant. "Better if we walk from here than to be accidentally spotted."

Monica strolls with Juan across the steel bridge that spans the rushing river. Halfway across the bridge, Monica grabs Juan's arm and whispers, "Stop." She points through the yellow steel struts at the tables outside the Riverside Cafe. "That's her."

Juan squints and tilts his head to see the woman sipping coffee at a small red table beside the river. "Are you sure?"

"I'd know that face anywhere." She catches herself, realizing she has never seen Ersari before, but Sam has. Now his memories appear to be seamlessly merging with hers. She shivers at the thought.

Juan notices. "Are you cold?"

"I'm fine. How would you like to handle this?"

"She's alone, and you said we need to catch both her and Ashaki. So I think we need to wait and follow her back to their office. Then we can shoot two fish with one stone"

Monica smiles. "That's kill two birds with one stone."

"This English is difícil."

"Tell me about it. OK, let's stay out of sight. I don't think she's seen either of us before, but maybe she has seen pictures." Monica tugs on Juan's sleeve and they cross to the far side of the bridge. She spots an outside table at another cafe, the Citispot, across the street from Ersari. "I'll stay here. Get me a cappuccino and whatever you'd like." She hands Juan a twenty and takes a seat against a painted-brick side wall, a perfect hidden viewpoint.

Juan returns a few minutes later and hands a large paper cup with a plastic lid to Monica. She removes the lid and breathes in the sweet pungent aroma of strong coffee, then takes a sip. "Better than a double martini. What did you get?"

"Hot chocolate, of course. But unlike for you, drinking it is not a sensual experience."

She feels Sam's virtual presence again and gives Juan a mamala stare.

He shrugs. "Sorry. Enjoy it."

She barely swallows her second sip when she spots Ersari on the move. "Let's go."

Monica laces her arm through Juan's as if they're a couple just sipping their drinks. They amble along the opposite side of Main Street, tracking Ersari to a doorway mid-block. She disappears inside. The door closes.

"Now what?" Monica asks.

"She definitely has cameras and security, and I'm not willing to walk into an emboscada. We wait for them to come out." Juan turns his back, unshoulders his backpack, and removes two hats. "Yankees or Mets?"

Monica smirks. "What, no Dodgers?"

He hands her the Yankees hat. "Same difference where I come from. Put it on."

They put on the hats and take seats on a bench in front of the leather store that faces Ersari's undisturbed doorway.

Minutes pass. Monica checks her watch, 9:35. "I'm going to need a bathroom real soon from the coffee."

"Give it a few. Like baseball, all the excitement of the game happens in the ten seconds you go to the bathroom. I'm still trying to figure out why you Americanos and Americanas like baseball so much."

"It's an acquired passion. Look—" Two figures emerge from Ersari's door, a woman wearing a wide-brimmed hat and a man carrying a bulky duffel. "That doesn't look like her. Ersari has dark hair. That's a blonde, and who's the guy?"

"Could be a disguise. Don't think we can let it go. You walk and follow them. I'll get the car," Juan says. He jogs back across the bridge.

Monica keeps pace, stopping to thumb a dress rack outside a woman's clothing store while glancing back over her shoulder trying not to lose them. They turn right onto Leigh Street. Monica hangs back a block, watching their quarry slip into a parking lot. She taps a text to Juan,

"Where are u?"

"Coming up Main, u?"

"Turn right on Leigh, pick me up."

Juan slows the Toyota. Monica hops in just as a white van peels out of the lot and guns it down Old Highway 22. Juan runs the red light, cutting off an angry Humvee driver who hammers his horn. Juan hits the gas but keeps his distance as they go up the ramp to Route 78 West.

"I sure hope it's them and we're not on a wild goose chase," Monica says. "Where could they be going?"

"It's them—my intuición tells me so," Juan says and follows six car lengths behind in the left lane.

The white van makes a sudden swerve across three lanes to veer onto the Perryville exit ramp.

"Meirda," Juan says as he slows, trying to find an opening in the traffic to make the exit. He hits the brakes. Tires screech and horns blast behind him. Then he floors it at a right angle, cutting off the oncoming speeders, crosses the shoulder beyond the exit, and jumps the curb onto the exit ramp in time to see the van make a sharp left onto Perryville Road. "Guess they know we're here."

"Maybe they're just being careful. Better to still keep a distance in case," Monica says.

Juan burns the red light again at the bottom of the ramp. They are doing sixty on the windy country roads through Union and Pittstown. The white van's tires screech as it takes a switchback right, then hard left. Juan follows. Monica notices the small directional sign, *Sky Manor Airport*. "Better close in. They're headed to the airport."

Moments later the van crashes through a fence, crosses a field, and swerves onto the quiet runway. Juan and Monica follow close behind. Bystanders leap out of the way. The two vehicles race down the runway, the van in the lead with Juan and Monica close behind. A helicopter with rotors spinning comes into view, setting down like a butterfly at the end of the runway. The van hard stops at a right angle and two figures emerge, running to the waiting chopper. Juan jams on the brakes, opens the door, and whips out his Glock. He gets off two rounds before a spray of bullets shatters their windshield and clips Juan in the arm. Monica ducks, then pops up, and fires Rich's Walther PPK at the hovering copter. From the open side door of the chopper, another spray of automatic fire comes their way. Monica and Juan hit the pavement behind the Toyota. The helicopter turns in an arc and accelerates up higher, disappearing into the eastern sky.

Monica and Juan slowly come to their feet. Monica notices the blood on Juan's shirt. "Are you OK?"

Juan dabs a finger at the wound. "Afortunado. Just a scratch."

Monica tears a strip of cloth from her skirt and wraps it tightly around Juan's arm. "We better get that looked at."

"No, we go back to her office first," Juan says.

"I gotta call this in," Monica says and turns to look at their car. With the windshield in pieces and steam spewing from the hood, she says, "I don't think we can drive that thing."

They hear sirens approaching in the distance. Juan looks at the white van and says, "I think we have our ride."

"I'd rather not waste time explaining all of this," Monica says. "Let's go."

51

NO SECRETS

I can't sit still. I'm out of my mind after seeing the video of the shootout at Sky Manor.

"Frank, this is bad. Maybe *you* did, but I never intended putting Monica in danger and being shot at. Can we get a closer look? The camera is too far away to tell if she is alive or dead. I'm not feeling that telepathic mind-meld connection to her you set up or whatever you call it. I've tried calling several times. She doesn't answer," I say.

"I call it QWT—Quantum Wave Transmission. The camera was in the terminal and the helicopter and gunfire were at the far end of the runway. That's why we can't get a better a look. I'm sorry, Sam. I'd never want to see Monica get hurt," Frank says.

"And Evan? What if he's lost a mother and a father?"

"Try calling Juan's cell. They were together."

I tap into Skype. The first image I see is a shaking image of a bloody bandage. "What? Juan, are you there?"

"Yes, Sam. Hold a minute. I was hit and I'm juggling the phone."

My heart is thumping out of my virtual chest. I jump out of my chair. On my screen, I see a moving image of bare tree branches flying by outside a car window, and then Juan's face appears.

"It's OK, Sam. The bullet only grazed my arm."

I hesitate. "And Monica?"

"She's driving. I can't." Juan rotates the cell camera toward Monica.

Monica turns her head to the camera and smiles. "I'm fine, Sam. That was quite a rush. I've never been in a shootout before."

I try to catch my breath. "Great. You being shot at?"

"It's OK, Sam. Rich gave me a gun. I think I may have hit one of them."

"What? Really?" And then images flood my brain. "When I was away last year chasing LaSalam, you took shooting lessons. I didn't recall that until just this second."

"Remember how that terrorist threatened me and Evan and you weren't around. I had to protect my family."

"I understand. I lost my connection to you during your pursuit of Ashaki. I thought you were dead. Seems the connection or as Frank calls it QWT is now back up."

"And you know what that means, don't you?"

"What?"

"No more secrets. Everything you know or remember, I can now see. It's reassuring to know you never cheated on me."

"Did you ever think I would?"

She laughs. "No, but now I'm certain."

"This no secrets thing goes both ways," I say.

"Oh, I've got nothing to hide, and now you don't either. But I'm not so sure it's ideal for a spouse to know everything. I mean, we all have negative thoughts sometimes. Like it pisses me off that you don't pick up your dirty socks. But that doesn't mean I don't love you."

"I'm just glad you're OK. But for Evan's sake, you should go home. You're all he has left."

"No way. Not until we catch that bitch and stop her from killing more people." She smirks.

"Now you're sounding like me. Listen, if you insist on putting yourself in danger—"

"Hey, you and Frank got me into this. Don't act like it's my fault or I'm being reckless."

"Sorry, I didn't intend for it to come across that way. You could be the bravest woman I've ever known. And if anyone ever doubted that, you've convinced them now. What I was saying is that if you pursue Ashaki, and we know how dangerous she is, will you do something for me first?"

"Depends, what is it?"

I hesitate, but here goes. "I want you to let Frank upload your memories and personality to the Cloud like he did for me. That way, if anything happens to you, at least we can be together digitally like I am here now."

"Are you kidding me? With all this going on, you want to experiment on me again?"

"No, that's not it. I want to create a backup of you so I'll never lose you."

"No how, no way. I'm sorry, Sam. This digital stuff works for you and I'm glad we can communicate, but I believe when the Lord intends for me to die, I will go wherever he leads me next, not to some computer server on the other side of the world. So no, I won't do it. When my days come to an end, just remember the good life and the wonderful times we had together, falling in love, walking hand-in-hand on the beach, birthday candles, bringing up Evan. Nobody can take those things away from us, ever."

"I don't know what to say."

Monica's tone softens. "Don't worry. I'll be fine. Juan will protect me, and besides, I can take care of myself."

"That's what I'm afraid of."

52

NEXT?

"Where are we going?" Dick Silva asks as they fight crosstown traffic on 36th Street.

"She said to go to the East 34th Street Heliport," Bascue says.

The traffic is at a standstill—the street lined with double-parked delivery trucks. Workers are crossing between parked cars, pushing dresses hanging from pole racks. "We should have avoided the Garment District."

"Yeah, once we pass 6th Avenue, it should speed up," Silva says.

Their heads turn at the site of a naked woman standing in front of Ben's Deli with "FREE Barin!" painted in red across her ample breasts.

"Only in New York," Delbert says.

Fifteen minutes later, Silva swings the car under the FDR ramp at 34th Street and drives onto the landing pad of the heliport.

Delbert checks his watch, 11:20. The sky is a deep gray with a hint of frozen dew in the air. A fifteen-knot breeze blows in from Brooklyn over the East River that abuts the heliport. White caps splash up from the stone barrier that divides the river and the land. Delbert flashes back to when he covered the miraculous crash landing of US Airways Flight 1549 by Sully Sullenberger. He can still picture the survivors stepping out over the wing of the floating plane onto rescue tugboats. That's when heroes were heroes and things were more black and white, not all ominous shades of gray. Delbert tightens his trench coat against the chill.

The thud-thud sound of the rotors reaches them before the Bell 407 comes into view. It banks left over the river to counter the wind and settles gently like a falling leaf onto the tarmac. A woman in a puffed-up down parka, head wrapped in a red scarf steps down, bowing her head below the still whirling rotors. The odor of diesel fuel blows their way.

She walks directly toward the two men. "Which one of you is Bascue?" The woman shouts over the din.

Delbert raises his hand. "I am. And you?"

"You know who I am?" She points at Delbert. "You, come with me. He stays here."

"But—" Silva interjects.

Delbert puts a hand on Silva's shoulder. "It's OK. I'll take it from here. No use putting you in danger. Just do me a favor. If you don't hear from me again..." he hesitates, "... today, please call Sherry and Richelle and tell them the last thing I said is that I love them with all my heart."

"Sweet," Ersari says. "Now, let's go."

Silva stands motionless and silent while Delbert follows Ersari, ducking under the blades and stepping up into the helicopter. Without delay, the chopper ascends and banks to the right over the river then heads south.

The van hurtles east on Route 78 toward New York. Monica's heart rate slows as the adrenaline wears off. It feels like her arms and legs weigh a hundred pounds each. Traffic slows for construction ahead of the 287 Exit. She speed-dials Rich.

Rich picks up on the first ring. "Speak."

"Rich, is that you. Are you OK?"

"I'll live. How about you? Michelle relayed a report about the incident at Sky Manor."

"Juan's got a bloody arm. He's here with me on speaker. I'm fine, heading back to the city. I'm driving. Just wanted to report in."

Rich laughs. "Like a real agent."

"But it wasn't funny. We got shot at. Juan's injured. They could've killed us."

"Welcome to my world."

"Still, I admit it was exciting. I can see how you might get hooked on it."

"Be careful. Adrenaline junkies don't live long. You have to do this work for the right reasons."

"So, what's the right reasons?"

"I think you know by now. If you don't, just look at the pictures of the dead bodies at the 4th Precinct."

"You're right. I do know, but all this craziness can make you doubt yourself. I'm understanding what Sam went through."

"As I said, welcome to my world. Anyway, I'm still in the hospital, going into surgery in about an hour. Gary's trying to get a bead on the helicopter Ashaki escaped in. Sky Manor could identify it and give us the tail number, but obviously nobody filed a flight plan. We've got an aviation alert, a drone over New Jersey, and various ground radar trying to pick them up."

"The tail number could be faked, and the helicopters fly

low, like at five or six hundred feet, which would be too low for radar to detect," Monica says.

"Wow, I'm impressed. How do you know all that?" Rich asks.

"Little bit of me and a little bit of Sam. Anyway, how can we help?"

"Take care of Juan. If he's good, get back to the office. I'll be out of it for a few hours, but Michelle or Renata will meet you there. Michelle is your handler for now. I don't know what kind of shape I'll be in after surgery."

"OK. Good luck with the surgery."

"Buena suerte, mi amigo," Juan says.

"Thanks. And Monica..." Rich coughs, hacking for several seconds. "Sorry, not to restate the obvious, but you need to help stop Ashaki in the next twenty-four hours or our intel says we are in for another major incident. She's done toying with us. The big one is coming unless we get to her first, capisci?"

"Capisco," Monica says and clicks off.

Juan shoots Monica a sideways glance.

Monica's cell rings. Caller ID, *Home*.

"Mom, where are you? When are you coming home?" Evan asks.

The real world, her former world, comes crashing in. Her heart melts. "Hi sweetheart, are you all right?"

"I'm OK. Charlotte's been making me eat stuff like stuffed tomatoes, yuk. But I miss you. I miss Dad. It's just not the same here. I had to leave my soccer game early because Charlotte had to take Toni to the doctor, and I couldn't get a ride home from anybody else. When can I go home to my own room and eat normal food again?"

"Soon, I promise." *More of a wish than a truth*, she knows. "I'm doing what Dad used to do and helping to stop some mean people from hurting a whole lot of innocent ones, including children."

"Does that mean you could get killed like Dad?"

Hearing Evan's sobs, she swerves the car onto the shoulder and sucks in a deep breath. "It's all going to be OK. I'm just trying to help Director Little and Agent Hadar solve a puzzle. I'm going to stay out of fights from now on."

Evan's voice picks up. "I like puzzles. Maybe I can help."

"Maybe you can, but for now the pieces of the puzzle are top secret."

"Cool," Evan says.

"Listen, I've got to go now, but I'll call you tonight, OK? I'll be home as soon as I can."

"You better," Evan says. The line goes dead.

"He's a wonderful boy. You are muy afortunada," Juan says.

"Yes, I am. But having Sam and me as parents may not have been so lucky for him."

53

BULLSEYE

The Bell 470 hugs the Jersey shoreline heading south. Delbert gazes out the window at the waves breaking on the winter-quiet beaches. He spots a couple of surfers in wet suits cutting foamy-white trails through the breakers.

He turns back to study the woman's profile, protruding jaw, high cheekbones, dark gray eyes, and shoulder-length brown hair. She exudes an intense aura. His reporter's instinct overtakes his fear. He speaks through the aviation headset. "Where are we going?"

"To get you the biggest story of your career." She opens a silver-lined bag. "Now drop your phone in here."

"What's that?"

"It's a Faraday Bag, blocks all cell signals so you can't be tracked," she says.

Delbert powers down the phone, hesitates, and drops the phone in the bag. His abductor zips it up and hands it to large man in the front seat.

She pats his knee. "Don't worry. I'll give it back when it's safe. Patience, grasshopper."

Her touch sends an electric current up his spine. "How about your real name? I need some details if I'm going to write a story."

She grins. "You mean if you live to tell the tale."

Message received. Delbert looks at the backs of the female pilot and the male passenger in the front seat. His eyes drop to the GPS screen with the helicopter avatar tracking a course along a digital map. The navigation track leads to an endpoint somewhere in Baltimore.

The mystery woman picks up a call. Delbert tries to hear her side of the conversation over the drone of the rotors. He only catches every other word. She says, "Is everything _____? Did you get the _____ equipment our supplier _____? That's in _____? Good. Yes, yes." She taps the pilot on the shoulder. "ETA?"

Through the headset he hears the pilot. "About seventy-three minutes, ma'am."

She checks her watch and says to the unknown party on the other end of the line, "Pick us up on the _____ at 1:00."

She clicks off and turns back to Delbert. "You'll have your story. It won't be long now."

Juan refuses to go to the hospital, so Monica takes the Holland Tunnel into lower Manhattan and winds through the crowded, narrow streets. She parks in a commercial loading zone on New Street around the corner from DHS's Beaver Street office.

She winces at the sight of Juan's bloody arm. "They might not let us in with you looking like a wounded terrorist. See if there's anything in back."

Juan climbs between the front bucket seats and almost loses his balance. He steadies himself and locates a small suitcase in the cargo area. Rummaging through, he finds a man's white button-down shirt. "It's a little large, but it'll do."

Monica peeks into the rearview and watches Juan strip off his bloodstained flannel. He's only five-and-a-half feet tall, but his muscular torso and neck are impressive. She feels something strange stirring at the sight of him. *Better not*, she thinks. She remembers what it was like when Sam inhabited Juan's body and how it felt to be with him then.

Juan tucks in the shirt and crawls back to the front seat. "Ready?"

"You look pretty good for somebody who's been shaken and stirred," Monica says.

"You too." Juan winks.

"Let's do this."

They pass through security at the front door and approach the guard at the front desk. Without asking, the guard says, "Agent Hadar is waiting for you on the third floor. Go right up."

As the steel elevator rises, Monica turns and sees a growing red bloom on Juan's shirt sleeve.

The elevator door opens. Michelle is waiting to greet them. "I'm so glad you two are OK."

Monica limps forward and points to Juan's bleeding sleeve. "I'm not so sure he is. Do you have someone here who can look at this?"

"Sure, follow me," Michelle says.

Michelle leads Monica and Juan down a long, narrow hallway. She unlocks a small conference room door and flicks on the lights. "Juan, wait here. A nurse will be in shortly. Can I get you something?"

Juan takes a seat and says, "How 'bout a Mojito?"

"How 'bout coffee or soda?" Michelle says.

"I take Coke, please. I need my sug..." Juan's voice trails off. His eyes close and his head lolls to the side.

"Better make that an I.V. cocktail, stat," Monica says. She rushes to Juan and feels his neck for a pulse. "I think he just passed out. He's lost lots of blood."

Already on her cell, Michelle barks orders, and clicks off. "A doctor will be here in two minutes. Once he arrives, we'll make sure Juan is OK and leave the doctor to it, then go to my office. We need to talk."

Moments later a bearded middle-aged man in a white coat, followed by a young nurse, beeline to Juan. The doctor looks up at Michelle. "We got this."

"OK, thanks," Michelle says. "You know where to find me. I'd like status updates." She turns to Monica. "Follow me."

Walking back down the hall, Michelle notices Monica's limp. "What about you?"

"Yeah, it's just sore. We got banged up pretty good in that shootout."

"You and Juan were remarkable out there."

"But she got away."

"That happens more than not. You got close. But now it's time to bring her down for good."

"Have you been able to find her?"

"The tail number was fake—belongs to some guy named Ben Hanafin in Virginia Beach. We checked. He's there and so's his helicopter. No luck on radar and nothing from the drone yet," Michelle says. "Based on our strategic profile, we think she's headed east or south, but that's pretty broad. Both her New York and Clinton locations are blown. So she needs to regroup somewhere. We're trying to figure out where that might be," Michelle says.

"My guess is that would be somewhere close, but not too close to her next target. Someplace where she could observe, but not be seen," Monica says. "I think she has some much grander plan for this memory disruption weapon she used on the president and vice president. They were just warm-ups for the bigger related play."

"Related?"

"Yes, think about it. You cripple the team by taking out its quarterback. Maybe it's time to take out the rest of the team."

"Didn't know you were into sports?"

"It's Sam's influence. Listen, I think the next logical target may be Congress. Last year her cohorts took out the Congressional Black Caucus with a neural weapon. What if the plan is to use the memory weapon on the entire congress? People are shaken now by what happened to the president and VP. Can you imagine the panic and chaos if she turns all 535 members of Congress into bumbling amnesiacs?"

"That's a pretty wild theory. But let's say it's right. She'd want to attack when they were all in one place, like for a big vote."

"Or the upcoming State of the Union. She'd have the bonus of taking out the Supreme Court justices and the top generals at the same time on national television..."

Michelle sits quietly, her face blank. Finally, she says, "The State of the Union is in two days."

"I guess we better act fast."

"Yeah, but this is still a theory. We need more facts and proof if we're going to mobilize our troops. I'll get Gary and his guys on this."

"Makes sense, but that doesn't stop us. You, me, Rich, maybe Renata, and Jonathan and Juan if he's up to act on it."

"No, it doesn't. Can you get Frank and Sam on this too?"

"I already have," Monica says.

54

LANDS ANYWHERE

The mystery woman's voice crackles through Delbert's headset. "That's the great thing about helicopters. They can fly under the radar and land anywhere. No airport needed."

Delbert continues to stare out the window and down at the houses perched on stilts above the beach and rushing tide. *I guess they learned their lesson from Hurricane Sandy*, he thinks.

The Bell 470 abandons the shoreline route, turns inland, and minutes later, does a low 360 over Essex, Maryland, a suburb of Baltimore. Hovering over a parking lot in an aging industrial park, the chopper gently settles to the macadam. "This is it," the woman declares and smirks. "Time to party." She slides off the high seat, doing a little jump to the ground, the wind from the rotors blowing the hair over her eyes. She looks back at the catatonic Bascue and shouts over the din, "We're here. Let's go."

Delbert flinches as though startled from a dream. He balances a hand on the woman's empty seat and swings over and down, stumbling and landing flat on his face. *Ugh, my nose.*

The big guy grabs him under the arm and leads him away

from the idling helo. Once clear, the aircraft ascends and arcs back north. So she can examine him, she turns Delbert to face her. Delbert brushes dirt and loose gravel from his knees and rises to face her. He senses something warm and wet on his upper lip. He reaches for it with his tongue and tastes the blood.

She hands him a handkerchief. "Not an auspicious start, but you'll live."

Hiding his humiliation, Delbert wipes his nose. "Thanks, I think."

"You're welcome. Now, follow us inside."

The building is an unmarked, vintage 1900s brick warehouse. They approach a windowless, red steel door. Pickles looks up at the security camera and nods. The door swings open. A ruddy-faced man who reminds Delbert of Dwayne Johnson blocks the doorway, an AR-15 slung over one shoulder. "Code word?" he asks.

"Yesterday I was clever," Pickles says.

"So I wanted to change the world," the large man responds.

"'Today I am wise," the woman says.

Delbert retrieves from distant memory the next line from the Rumi quote they just recited... *so I changed myself.*

The Rock moves aside and the three of them, Delbert, the woman, and Pickles enter a cavernous space. Water drips from skylights twenty feet above. The light is dim. The air smells of mold. Delbert stares into the void. *Huh?*

He follows The Rock for twenty yards and through the door of a small one-desk office. Shipping receipts and empty coffee cups cover an oak work surface. The walls are dark paneling. A cheap oriental rug covers the pumpkin pine floor. The Rock nods to Pickles and they clasp opposite sides of the desk, lift, and set it down on the other side of the room. Pickles grabs a corner of the rug, whipping it up and over to reveal a trapdoor.

The woman looks at Delbert's gray face and says, "Can't be too careful. Are you going to make it?"

Delbert is still holding her handkerchief against his nose and says, "I don't understand. What's going on?"

"Welcome to твой новый дом."

"I don't speak Russian. Wait, what? You're Russian? But I thought—"

"I know. Follow them," she says.

Pickles and The Rock descend first. The woman gives Delbert a little shove. He follows the two men down the creaky wooden steps, she behind. The first thing Delbert notices are the dozen or more round hanging lamps that throw light onto the cubicles below. The room is otherwise dark, which makes it seem like the stage in a darkened theater. But instead of actors and props, there are computers and programmers clicking away. The woman sweeps an arm through the air and looks at Bascue. "This is where the magic happens, and you're going to have a front-row seat. When we push the buttons, you will report what I tell you to your news desk. It will be the story of a lifetime, of a thousand lifetimes."

Delbert feels his knees buckle.

Just as he begins to fall, Pickles snatches the lapels of Delbert's jacket and hoists him up.

"Wait, you had a partner, the first voice on the phone. What happened to her?"

The woman smirks. "She was sexy and useful. She underestimated me, us. You can report that I am a very successful businesswoman with a grudge. But the truth is we all work for the Center."

Center? Russian? Uh oh, Delbert thinks.

The woman points to a wooden chair next to a steel table in

the corner. "Put him over there and get him some water." She turns to Delbert. "I know it's a lot to take in. Just breathe. If you need anything, let Pickles know. I'll be busy with my team for a while. I'll let you know when the show's ready to begin."

She turns away but abruptly turns back. "I almost forgot." She reaches deep into Delbert's jacket pocket, removing Delbert's cell phone. "Pickles shouldn't have given this back to you. You won't be needing it. Can't get any signal down here anyway."

Pickles releases Delbert, who collapses into the chair. *Could this get any worse?* Suddenly, a piercing pain erupts from the back of his head. Then all goes black.

NO FEAR

It's 2:45. Former Speaker of the House, and newly installed President Patricia Bruder, stands at the Oval Office window facing the Rose Garden. The sun is setting behind gray clouds, but a streak of purple glimmers in the winter sky. This is all so new, and she's supposed to make a State of the Union speech tonight. Instead of sitting behind President Longford, she'll be standing in her stead. *Who would have thought a farm girl from Vandalia, Illinois, would be in this place and in this time?* She takes a long drag on her cigarette and exhales a stream of blue smoke up toward the ceiling.

There is a gentle knock at the door. Donna Swenson enters holding a bound portfolio.

"Is that it?" Bruder says.

Swenson hands it to her. "Yes, the final draft."

The president drops it on the desk. "I'll review it after the meeting."

"They're waiting for you outside. Should I show them in?"

Bruder stamps out her cigarette and nods. The acrid odor of tobacco hangs in the air as Swenson opens the door. Long-

TRACKS

Skype dings, opening a new window on my screen.

It's Cory Cravens, his expression drawn. "I haven't heard from Delbert since last night, and I'm worried. Are you still tracking him?"

"We're concerned too. He took off in a chopper with Ashaki about two hours ago. His signal went dead over Morristown. Frank is trying everything he can, but for the moment, we lost them."

"That's not good. He's in way over his head. I did what you suggested and had my ex-wife, Martha, pick up his wife and daughter and take them to—"

"Don't tell me. Better to keep their location to as few people as possible."

"Understood. They were scared and were not happy to leave their cell phones behind, especially Richelle. You know teenagers."

"There's an entire generation that would go into digital withdrawal, tremors and all, if we took away their phones."

"It's not just the kids," Cory says. "Listen, will you let me know as soon as you hear anything?"

"For sure," I say. "One other thing, do you have a reporter covering the State of the Union tonight?"

"Yeah, why?"

"Tell her to be careful."

"Now you're scaring me more. What's going on?"

"Not sure. Just a hunch."

In the woman's subterranean war room, Delbert is still glued to his chair, listening to the hum of the computers and sensing the hostile energy in the room. The cold sweat from earlier has dried, his shirt still sticking to his skin. He picks up a faint scent of burning wires.

She approaches, a phone locked to her ear. Delbert overhears, "Yes, in ten minutes. Be ready," she says, clicks off, and grins at Bascue. "You've got some color back. Feeling better? Are you ready to write?"

Legs shaking, Delbert stands. "You haven't told me anything yet. What am I supposed to write?"

"Follow me," she says and leads Delbert across the room, past the programmers, to a large XLED wall screen. She points the remote at the screen. It flickers to life, showing the distinctive semi-circle of seats and blue-starred carpet on the congressional floor. There are staffers milling about. A few men and women wearing their best suits arrived hours early to snatch the prized aisle seats where they might shake hands or get a quick word with the president when she passes by.

"Why are you showing me this?" Delbert asks.

"Because this will be tonight's story, but first look at this." She clicks the remote again and says, "This is what's about to happen right now." The scene of a small downtown comes to life—people are darting in and out of shops. An old movie theater marquee advertises the latest *Fast and Furious* movie. Some teenagers lean against their diagonally parked cars, chatting and smoking, and checking their phones.

"What's going to happen?"

"Just watch."

"What am I supposed to write with? You took my phone. I have no laptop."

Ersari gathers a pad and pen from one of the cubicles. "Here. Write."

57

DOWN

At 8:30, the chamber fills with Congressmen in dark suits and red ties. The congresswomen, some in red or blue dresses with colorful scarves, others in all white, take seats or chat in the aisles. A few of the Supremes in their black robes are followed by generals in full uniforms, kaleidoscopes of medals, and badges adorning their chests.

After several more minutes with the chamber full, the House Sergeant at Arms, Robert Mise, steps through the rear door and announces in a stentorian voice, "Mr. Speaker, the President of the United States."

Applause follows as President Bruder shakes hands and hugs congress people on the aisles, hearing pleas and offering words of encouragement. The applause continues as she slowly makes her way forward, finally shaking hands with Roger Brickman, George Osborne, Daniel Kennedy from State, and the chief justice, Judith Dickinson. She sidesteps across the front row, greeting the generals and hugging Meredith Chapman, the congresswoman who barely survived a gunshot wound from a deranged constituent.

She ascends the platform to more cheers and applause. With the new vice president and house majority leader, John Wesley Cook, standing and applauding behind, Bruder approaches the podium, smiles, and waves. The applause and cheers grow louder, especially from the members of her own party.

At last, Cook declares, "Members of Congress, the President of the United States."

More clapping and a spontaneous chant, "U-S-A! U-S-A!"

President Bruder smiles and tries to quell the laudation. "Thank you. Thank you very much. Thank you." The din dies down, and she begins in earnest. "It's been a painful time for our nation, but I am here to assure you that the presidency and the nation still stand strong."

The crowd rises with a loud ovation.

She continues. "But we have a lot of hard work to do to recover and move forward. Together we can—"

And then it happens just like New York and in the Oval Office, the president stutters and begins again. "Together we c-c-c-an..." She looks around the room and reaches her hand out like a drowning sailor trying to grasp a lifeline.

The crowd moans. "No!"

The Sergeant at Arms tries to reach her, but he loses his place, his eyes go wide, and he stumbles and falls. People in the audience begin to push and shove each other. Some fight to get to the aisles but seem to lose steam. Others spasm and fall to the floor. The chaotic scene appears as if everyone has been drugged or gassed, but there is no drug or chemical toxin, no apparent external cause for what the world is seeing. The smell of sweat and urine overcome the room.

Ersari and Delbert sit while the assembled programmers stand, all with blank faces watching the eight large monitors arrayed along the front and side walls of the war room.

The broadcasts and cable networks break away from the scene, some quicker than others. A few networks claimed technical difficulties as soon as the president began to falter. However, CNN and Fox continued broadcasting until mayhem broke out in the chamber, then tried their best to explain and ward off what would be certain panic.

John DeWitt of WCXY, who was live with the president's speech until something went haywire, cuts away, wipes his forehead with a handkerchief, sucks in a deep breath, and says, "There seems to have been a failure in the air conditioning system at the Capitol." He pauses, clapping a hand over his earpiece, then continues. "We're told that everyone will be OK. The president is safe. We will update you as soon as we have any more information. In the meantime, we ask our viewers to be patient and remain calm. Let's not jump to any conclusions until we find out exactly what happened. Now, after a short commercial break, we will resume a previously scheduled episode of *Law and Order*. But I promise we will interrupt the broadcast with any breaking news as soon as it happens." The screen switches to an ad for Vitexin, an anti-depressant medication.

As the commercial speeds through the list of potential side-effects, including *suicidal thoughts or actions*, Ersari turns from the screen and says to Delbert, "What do you think now?"

Delbert's face is ashen. He opens his mouth, but nothing comes out. Ersari stands and scans the room. All the programmers are still standing up from their cubicles, staring in stunned silence at the wall screens, the commercial still running. Ersari frowns and barks, "What are you looking at? Get back to work."

Like prairie dogs, all the heads drop back into their holes.

Ersari sits down again, placing a gentle hand on Delbert's shoulder. "There, there, Mr. Bascue. I promised you the biggest story of your career. Now you have it. So get your shit together and write."

"But I..." Delbert stammers.

"Yes, write about me and how we did this. But don't mention my name. They might still think this was all Ashaki's doing, not a Russian agent's. I want them to continue to think that. You can use that terminal over there. Once you're done, I will review it and send it to your editor. You'll get the byline, of course. I'm sure the Center is pleased."

Delbert stands and walks like a zombie to the empty cubicle, sits, and puts his frozen fingers on the keyboard.

Ersari comes up behind him and slaps him hard across the back of the head. "Snap out of it and start."

Delbert rubs the back of his head, trying to soothe the startling pain. He half turns his head. "I will, I will."

"Let me see."

Delbert blows out a breath and begins typing. "This is the story of how I witnessed first-hand the..."

TOO LATE?

Michelle, Monica, and Juan park off Garfield Circle outside the Capitol Building, engine running. Security is extra tight for the State of the Union. Only Michelle's DHS credentials get them this close, and they're still more than a hundred yards away. Monica and Michelle are in the front seats and Juan sits in the back of the black Escalade. Mist and the odor of exhaust waft from the idling car's tailpipe in the cold winter's night air. The three of them are glued to Michelle's laptop, watching the speech just as President Bruder falters at the podium.

"I tried to stop this. I really did. She wouldn't listen to Roger's plea," Michelle says, wiping tears from her cheeks.

"We have to do something," Monica says.

"It's too late," Michelle says. "Secret Service and FBI will swarm the scene. We can't stop it at this point. We can only hope to help with the aftermath."

"We'll see about that," Juan says and bolts from the car toward the building.

Michelle sighs. "I better go with him."

Monica grabs Michelle's arm. "Wait, I'm getting a message from Sam."

Michelle scrunches her face. "How? How are you getting a message? You're not on the phone."

"I just am. Let's call him before we do anything."

Before Monica can tap a key, Sam's tired face appears on her screen. "Sam, Sam, what's going on? Are you seeing this?"

"Yes, Frank and I are on it."

"This is Michelle here. What do you mean *you're on it*?"

"Stay with me here. Frank seems to think he has a way to help."

"But how?" Monica asks.

Social media explodes with speculation. "We've been attacked." "We're all going to die." "The Chinese are invading right now." There are at least three reports of citizens jumping from tall buildings in New York, Chicago, and San Francisco. Looting of grocery stores and gun shops is immediate in too many places to count.

Newscasters that usually seek to sensationalize are urging calm until the facts are in, but it's no use while they continue to air scenes of rioting and looting. Governors have called up the National Guard in Michigan, New Jersey, and Texas, with more to follow.

Chuck Hagar, the secretary of defense and the designated sole survivor, paces his office at the Pentagon. Carl Murdock, his chief of staff, and Catrina Pomerleau, the Pentagon communications director, enter without knocking.

"What do we know?" Hagar barks.

"Not much, but I'm trying to get a sitrep from the Service on site." Murdock holds up his phone. "I'm waiting for the call."

Hagar points to the three monitors on his wall tuned to CNN, ABC, and NBC. "Do you see this? All hell's breaking loose. I'm in charge now, I think. I need to declare a national emergency whether we know shit or not. I must address the nation, at least try to lower the temperature until we know something. How soon can we get the networks set up in the briefing room?"

"Normally, an hour would do it, but there're traffic jams all over. People are evacuating the cities," Catrina says.

Hagar stops pacing and scratches his marine-cut head. "I don't get it. Where are they going to go? Listen, set it up in thirty. Whoever is here is here. Make sure the networks who can't make it, can pick up the others' feeds. We need everyone to get the message."

The two nod, do a military pivot, and leave.

Hagar collapses in his chair. "Fuck, fuck, fuck."

Michelle and Monica watch the commotion in front of the Capitol through binoculars. Men and women are staggering out and down the staircase. Some trip and fall hard on the granite steps. Those who make it to the plaza below wander aimlessly before sporadic fights break out. Police and Secret Service surround the growing crowd. A gunshot cracks through the night air. Everyone seems to freeze for two seconds, then the wild crushing of bodies and law enforcement resumes.

"Sam, are you still there? It looks like a riot in front of the Capitol," Monica says.

"I see it. Hold for Frank."

Monica and Michelle look at each other.

Frank's aging face with a faint smile and deepening wrinkles emerges on their phone's screen. "My fair ladies, I wish we were talking under better circumstances."

"We're stuck here. It's driving me crazy. There's nothing we can do," Michelle says.

"I understand but take heart. There's a chance that the program I just launched may stop all this."

"A chance?" Monica asks. "How good a chance and how?"

"The *how* is quite technical. If we get through this, I'll explain later. For now, I'd give it 50/50."

"Then give us the *when*," Michelle says.

I take over for Frank, pointing the camera back to me. "Frank's executing the program now." I'm watching a timer countdown on his screen. I call it out for Monica and Michelle, "Ten...nine...eight...seven...six...five...four...three...two— It stopped. Frank, why did it stop?"

Frank's voice echoes from the background. He says, "I forgot to do something that could have made the situation worse. Give me a minute. I'm going to fix it."

I hold my breath. We're all silent. Then I see the timer reappear on Frank's screen. "Five...four...three...two... and 1."

Frank's voice rings behind me. "It's done."

"What? What's happening?" Monica asks.

59

BY D. BASCUE

Calamity at the Capitol

Washington, D.C. At 9:12 PM Eastern Time tonight, a surprise attack took place at the State of the Union address. After what appeared to be a medical trauma or stroke befell President Bruder as she spoke, the congress people, Supreme Court justices, generals, and guests were overtaken by what authorities are calling a gas or perhaps an air conditioning malfunction. However, I have it from the source that terrorist and wanted fugitive, Ashaki LaSalam, sister of the dreaded Ahmed LaSalam, launched a new kind of sophisticated neural weapon aimed at the chamber. Apparently, LaSalam now can target individuals or groups with a powerful strike that wipes the victims' memories, leaving them befuddled and panicked. The victims suddenly take on the appearance and mental state of those unfortunate souls afflicted with advanced

Alzheimer's disease. There is no known cure, remedy, or antidote for the victims.

LaSalam has single-handedly crippled the U.S. government. She has told me that her next target will be an entire major American city like New York, Chicago, Los Angeles, Dallas, or Atlanta. When asked why she wants to inflict such damage and pain on U.S. citizens, she replied, "This is payback for what the U.S. did to my family. A random U.S. drone strike killed my father. When my mother fled to the protection of her Kurdish family in Northern Syria, the U.S. abandoned the Kurds, their former ally, and left my mother to be raped and murdered by the Turks. I take no pleasure in human suffering, but I believe the only way to stop the U.S. and its destructive leaders from hurting more of my countrymen is for them to feel the pain that I feel. Then maybe, we will have peace. Until then, you may have to run for your lives."

It is a grim message. You may ask how I could get this information. Ms. LaSalam wanted to have her story heard, and I am now with her at her headquarters. I am not here voluntarily, but what I am reporting is 100% accurate and from LaSalam herself. I am not taking sides. But if there is anything left and we outlive this attack, it will be important for the survivors to evaluate our country's place in the world politically, militarily, and as human beings. I sincerely hope this is not the last report I write or the last one you read.

Ersari pats Delbert on the back. "This looks good now. I particularly like the part about 'terrorist and wanted fugitive, Ashaki

LaSalam...' It has a nice ring to it. Maybe when this is over, I'll make some business cards for me with that slick title you've given her. Now scoot, so I can send this off to your boss."

Delbert rises from the chair and Ersari immediately takes his seat. She takes the printout of his story, logs on to her laptop, and starts tapping away. He looks around the vast space, now silent except for the clicking of keyboards. *What do I do now? I've served her purpose. Does she kill me? And what about Sherry and Richelle? Are they safe? Those DHS agents promised me, but you never know.*

Wandering over to the small open kitchen, Delbert pours himself a cup of black coffee. He looks at the foam swirling on the black liquid and smells its day-old bitterness. *That swirl, that vortex, I'm in it.* He takes three gulps, savoring the burn on the way down.

60

PHOENIX RISING

A black Crown Vic screeches to a halt inches behind Michelle's Escalade. She glances up at the rearview mirror but only sees a dark shape exiting the vehicle behind and moving toward her. She instinctively rests her right hand on her holstered Glock and reaches for her credentials with the other hand. Monica digs her nails into Michelle's knee. All they can see now out the driver's side window is the torso of a man in a dark suit, starched white shirt, and blue silk tie. She cautiously lowers the window.

"Fancy meeting you here," Rich says with a grin.

Michelle exhales. "You're out of the hospital so soon?"

"That 3-D printed liver idea of yours was going to put me out of commission for weeks. The doctors offered me a new experimental procedure using something called bioelectric code. They used electricity to somehow stimulate what was left of my liver to grow more liver fast. They grew enough overnight to put me back on my feet and it will keep growing until I have a fully regrown liver. Until then I'll need to slow down a bit."

"Morphogenesis," Michelle says.

"Huh? What are you guys talking about?" Monica asks.

"It's a new branch of bioengineering. Soon they'll be able to regrow your damaged arms or legs," Michelle says.

"Or put a third eye in the middle of your forehead," I say.

Rich leans his head through the window and kisses Michelle on the lips.

"Eww," Monica says, and we all laugh.

"I guess the cat is out of the bag on this relationship," I say.

Michelle ignores us and stares up at Rich. "Why didn't you tell me you were coming? How do you feel?"

"I wanted to surprise you. Not really. I was being extra-paranoid about communications under the circumstances. And I'm doing better, thanks. Some aches and pains, this attractive bandage on my head, and a wicked scar on my abdomen. But enough about me. What have you got here?"

"Not much. We're on the line with Sam and Frank. Sounds like they're trying to cook up some kind of miracle. Otherwise, we only have what's on the news and social media. You?"

"I was watching the speech on the way here when it happened. I've got calls into our guys and Secret Service for a sitrep. I can't reach anyone inside, and the guys on the outside don't know shit."

I overhear Rich and Michelle, but I can't make out what Rich is saying. "Rich, this is Sam. Is that really you?"

Michelle turns the phone so Rich can see me. "In the flesh. What are you guys working on?"

"Get in the car and I'll tell you," I say.

Rich slides into the backseat behind Michelle, next to Juan. He gives Juan a fist pump and Michelle hands her phone back to him. "OK, what is it?" Rich asks.

"Hold on just a minute. Frank is pointing me at his screen," I say. After a long few seconds, I continue. "OK, is your boss, Brickman, inside the Capitol?"

"Yeah, but I haven't been able to reach him since the incident."

"Try now, I'll wait."

Rich hands Michelle's phone to Juan and whips out his secure iPhone. He taps a few keys and puts it on speaker. We all hear one ring, two, three, four, five, and then a few clicks.

There is a low hum in the background and a groggy voice starts. "Rich, huh? You, hospital. No, what?"

"Roger, it's me, Rich. You're on speaker with a bunch of us. What's happening?"

"I dunno. I mean, my head hurts like I have a jackhammer inside. I'm looking around. There's a bunch of congresspeople on the floor in the aisles." Brickman coughs. He hacks away for several seconds. "Ugh, sorry. I feel like shit. Anyway, some are getting up off the floor. I don't know what happened."

We hear loud voices in the background. Shouts of, "Get out of the way." Then a scuffling sound.

It's Brickman again. "EMTs are rushing down the aisles. Some people seem OK, but others aren't moving. The paramedics are using AEDs to revive them. Wait, it's President Bruder. She's back up at the podium. She's waving her arms."

Monica pulls up CNN on her tablet, holding it up so Michelle, Rich, and Juan can see. It's CNN. "We have breaking news."

Rich scoffs. "They always have breaking news."

The CNN anchorwoman appears. "We're returning to the floor of Congress for an update at the Capitol." The camera pans the floor with a view of some people standing and first responders in the aisles attending to stricken victims. "We previously reported what we were told—that something in the HVAC system was making people sick. By now, you have likely seen the news report of an international terrorist claiming responsibility for the attack. Wait, some of those in the chamber may be recovering." The camera travels away from the floor to the podium where the president is wiping her face with a towel. She raises both hands outward to silence the crowd.

Delbert finishes off his coffee when the wall screens all change to the major news channels. Ersari and the programmers are standing up again, watching. It starts slowly at first. On the chamber floor there is a rhythmic clapping, clap-clap-clap. Louder and louder, clap-clap-clap. Then, "U-S-A, U-S-A." The camera moves to faces of the EMTs, and then the barely conscious victims on the floor, and then the Supremes standing, all chanting, "U-S-A, U-S-A!"

Ersari slams her fist on one of the cubicle's partitions. "What the fuck is going on?"

The bewildered faces of the programmers stare back at her in silence. Suddenly, the wall monitors go black. All the computer screens in the cubicles turn to white snow. The overhead lights flicker.

Ersari looks at Delbert. "I'm not done with you yet." She grabs him by the collar and whispers, "We've got to go." She nods at Pickles. He nods back and heads for the door. Ersari turns to the prairie dogs still heads up from their holes, eyes blinking. "Listen, we've obviously had some kind of serious malfunction." She lowers her voice. "I'm sorry I lost my cool just now. We've all been working so hard on this. So now I need you to stay calm, focus, and figure out what's going on. First restore our systems and then get back to work. Understood?" She scans their faces and bobbing heads. They all slowly sink back down to their desks.

She grabs Delbert by the collar again and pulls him toward the ladder up.

"I'm coming. I'm coming," he says.

Releasing him, Ersari, Delbert, and Pickles exit onto the pavement of the parking lot. It's almost 11:00, and the full moon in the clear sky lights their way. Delbert pulls his jacket tight around himself against the cold. He hears the now familiar thumping sound of the helicopter rotors approaching from the distance. Turning to Pickles, Ersari says, "It's time."

They walk a hundred yards farther away from the brick building. Pickles gets out his cell and turns to face their office. He dials a number on his phone and presses SEND. A split second later, an enormous explosion shakes the ground as the roof and walls of the brick building fly into the air. A giant fireball rises from where they stood watching the State of the Union only moments ago. Pieces of flying debris drop from the sky only steps away from them. Ash and the unmistakable stench of burning flesh and hair fill the air. A bloody hand with two fingers missing drops at their feet.

61

SO NOW WHAT?

CNN, Fox, MSNBC, and the other major TV networks and streaming services interrupt their programming to go live to the Capitol.

President Bruder's face breaks into a crooked smile as the chants from the chamber die down. She puts her hand over her left ear where she hears her chief of staff's update. All eyes are on her as she begins again. "Where was I?"

A nervous laugh comes from the crowd.

She continues. "I know you are all wondering what just happened. Like you, I have been in the dark for the last hour or so. However, I am recovering and have just received an update. It appears that everyone in this chamber has been the victim of a neural weapon attack that caused temporary amnesia. As a result, the ensuing confusion caused some in this room to lash out or otherwise harm themselves and others. As you can see, our brave first responders are tending to the wounded. This could have been much worse had it not been for swift intervention from some of our top-level scientists and Cyber Command who managed to block and reverse the amnesia effect."

A rhythmic clap-clap-clap from the floor washes over Bruder. She patiently waits and seems to relish the moment. Another message comes through her earbud. Once the din dies down, she resumes. "And now I have a couple of surprise guests." She turns to stage-right. From behind a curtain, the two walk out smiling and waving. It's President Longford and Vice President Hubbard.

Bruder steps aside, and President Longford takes the podium. A tsunami of screams and shouts rise up from the floor. Longford keeps waving, but there is no quieting the enthusiastic cheers. Finally, minutes later, they fall silent. Longford leans into the microphone. "It's good to be back."

The cheers and chanting rise up again. People in the audience cry and hug each other. It's pure joyous mayhem. Vice President Hubbard whispers something in Longford's ear. The crowd simmers down. "I just wanted to let you, the nation, and the world know that the vice president and I have recuperated and are assuming our duties. Positioned behind Longford, Hubbard, and Bruder, vice president and speaker of the house, clap just like a normal State of the Union, but this has been far from normal.

"Our next major task is to find and apprehend those behind the attacks on me a couple of days ago and on you tonight. A terrorist organization has already taken credit, if you can call it that, for this assault on us and our democracy. But it will not stand. We will hunt down and punish those involved. The full power of our military, law enforcement, and intelligence services are totally focused and engaged in this pursuit. And I promise you... I promise you we will get the sons-of-bitches who thought they could take us down."

More shouts and cheers. The lawmakers are dancing in the aisles.

"I'm sorry to cut this event short, but we've got a lot of work to do. We will update you as soon as there is something to report. In the meantime, I'd like to thank you Madame Speaker for stepping in, for you the American people for your patience and support. God bless you, and God bless the United States of America."

The camera stays focused on the House chamber while the CNN News anchor does the wrap. "And there you have it. An amazing turn of events. We are told by sources in the White House that the danger is not over, that we face a formidable adversary, but that we are now on offense. They assure us we will be victorious in our struggle to overcome this menace. This is Sally Ann Wolf from Washington. As soon as we receive more information, we will bring it to you. Stay safe and have a good evening."

62

WHO AND WHERE?

The Escalade's engine is still running and pumping warm air inside as the outside temperature plummets. Ice crystals form on the windshield in symmetric snowflake patterns. The faint odor of the exhaust fumes seep in.

The president's speech ends, and Rich breaks the silence in the car. "Between the Secret Service and the EMTs, there's nothing more for us to do here. Our next task is pretty clear."

Monica turns to the backseat. "Find Ashaki and fast."

"Right," Michelle says. "I just got a text from Gary with a picture of an explosion moments ago in Baltimore." She rotates her phone so everyone can see. "Related?"

While still on the line with them, I use my digital tools and speed to tap into all video feeds around the explosion. I forward a CCTV recording to Monica's tablet and say, "Have a look at this." It's from an office building on the other side of the parking lot from the explosion site.

Monica raises up the tablet. The video shows three people exiting the brick warehouse moments before the explosion. I can't make out their faces. Then a giant flash of blinding light turns the screen completely white. The white fades and the raging fire and smoke rising from the conflagration come into focus. There is no sound, and the frame is jumpy, but there is no mistaking what's happening. A few seconds later, a dark blurry object appears close on the left side of the frame.

"Can we get a bigger view or rotate the camera?" Michelle asks.

I cough and say, "It's a pretty basic fixed-view, old-school security camera."

"It's a helicopter," Monica says.

"How can you tell?" Juan asks.

She freezes the frame. "That looks like a rotor to me. The rest is out of the frame to the left. What do you think?" Monica asks.

"Keep playing the recording," I say. "There may be more."

A few moments later, the three people disappear out of the frame. Then an object passes across the upper left corner of the frame.

"Freeze that," I say.

"It's a helicopter's landing gear. They just took off," Monica says.

"It must be them. Can you ID that landing gear to be sure?"

I tap a few more keys, running a quick comparison of landing gears against major models. Bing, a match. "It's the landing gear of a Bell 470, just like the one in New Jersey."

"We have to assume it's them," Rich says. "But how do we figure out where they're going?"

"Let's think about it. After losing or destroying three head-quarters, where would they go next?" I ask.

"Well, if she has another attack planned, she'd probably go somewhere near it just like she did here in Baltimore because it was close to D.C. and the Capitol," Monica says.

"The heat's on and all the major law policias are after her. If

I were her. I'd esconderia for a little while until things died down," Juan says.

Hmm, I think about this and say, "I could see her doing that if she had succeeded, but she failed. If she's like her brother, I doubt it's in her DNA to back off now. She's got to feel like her mission is incomplete."

"That might make her more determined than ever," Michelle says. "Baltimore was one of the first cities to adopt the Persistent Surveillance System. It covers every street, alley, park, and building in the city 24/7 with cameras from a small plane with twelve cameras circling above at 8000 feet. Sam, can you tap into that?"

"Yeah, we don't need to hack in. I know those guys from when we used their wide-area surveillance before. It's pretty cool and it now covers the Essex suburb. Give me a few." I can't help a little snicker. "They now call it Community Support."

Rich opens his car door and turns back. "I'll drive my car to the office. Why don't you three meet me there? No sleep tonight. We can regroup, and maybe Sam or Gary will pick something up in the meantime."

Monica reaches over the seat, grabbing Rich's sleeve. "Get back in the car. We need all hands and brains on deck to figure this out—no time to waste. We'll drive back in one car. Somebody else can get your car in the morning."

Rich's expression goes wide. "Whoa, who put you in charge?"

"It's the new me," Monica says. "Now close the door and get back in the car. Michelle, let's go."

63

ARIADNE'S THREAD

After ringing off with Monica and Rich, I swivel back to Frank who's heads-down typing and shifting his gaze between his nine virtual monitors. I clear my throat and say, "Explain."

He continues to tap away and speaks almost as if I'm not really here. "Explain what? The farkakta scene at the Capitol?"

"No, yes, I mean yeah, what happened and how you stopped it?"

"You already know what happened. You saw it on CNN."

"Now you're being cute. Stop what you're doing for a minute and look at me."

Frank turns, runs his fingers through his shaggy gray hair, and smirks. "You have my undivided attention."

"I know that's bullshit, but OK. So I assume Ashaki hacked the memory logins of the president and congress, giving them all amnesia, correct?"

"Yes, unfortunately."

"So how did you fix them and get their memories back?"

"Think about it. If you learned somebody hacked into your email account, what would be the first thing you'd do?"

"Easy, I'd change my password."

"No, that would be the second thing. What's the first?"

"I'd log in first and then change the password."

"Right, and that's what I did. I logged in to their Cloud memories, restored their files from the trash bin, and then changed the logins. And voila—they're back."

"OK, so why can't you do that for everyone and lock Ashaki out, so she doesn't do this to someone else?"

"Good question. Because I have no way to do it globally. Just like you might have a hundred different logins for the programs on your computer and you can't log in to them all at once. You have to sign in one at a time. People and their memories in the Cloud work the same way. So I had to use facial recognition on every person in the chamber and one-by-one, log in and restore their memories. I'm super-fast and there were five-hundred or so people. Yet, to protect eight billion people on the planet one at a time would take me years, even with your help."

"Then how about hacking Ashaki's memories in the Cloud and shutting her down?"

"Another good idea and I tried that, but guess what? She changed her password and encrypted it in some new way to keep people like us out."

"OK. You, Bart, and our team at Digital 3000 are encryption experts. Can't we figure it out?"

"I have Bart, Killer, and Jazzle working on that right now, but I doubt they'll succeed. She's too clever. If Rich and Monica can't physically apprehend her, we'll need a fresh approach on our end or else."

I steeple my fingers in front of my eyes. "Or else she could take down an entire city or a country."

Frank nods. "That's why I need to get back to sussing this out." He starts to turn back to his screens.

"Wait, maybe there is another way..." I say.

Frank turns again to me. "I'm listening."

"I've been thinking a lot about a different theory, a novel paradigm really, that might apply here. Here goes. What if the Internet is conscious? What if all the billions of connected computers are but synapses in a giant brain that has its own thoughts or feelings? And just like us, it has negative thoughts and positive thoughts. It can be happy or angry, kind or mean, truthful or misleading, but most of all self-aware." I wait for Frank's reaction.

He doesn't move, doesn't speak.

I plunge ahead. "What you have identified is that there is some connection, our memories, that reside both in us and in that conscious Cloud. And maybe we too are just synapses in a larger consciousness, all connected, good, bad, and ugly, part of one huge connected organism?" I pause again.

Frank's eyes are closed now. He seems to be in a trance.

Time to land this crazy notion. I say, "If that theory is true or even close to true, how would that change our approach to stopping Ashaki?" My question hangs in the air.

Finally, Frank's eyes flash wide open. "One word. *Excision.*"

64

WHERE'D SHE GO?

The helicopter rises through the cloud of acrid smoke and ash blanketing the sky above Ersari's former office. Delbert peers down at the spreading blaze. Cold sweat soaks his shirt. This is beyond any evil he could have imagined, and he's sitting next to the psychopath behind it all.

The chopper banks right, heading directly out to sea at an altitude of five hundred feet or one hundred and fifty meters above the turbulent waters. *This isn't good*, Delbert thinks. He adjusts his headset and says, "Where are we going now?"

Ersari flashes a warm smile. "Oh, you look so worried. I understand, but everything will be OK. Here, look, Sherry and Richelle are doing just fine." She rotates her phone showing his wife and daughter seated in a tight embrace on a sofa in a dimly lit room.

All the color drains from Delbert's face. *Those agents were supposed to protect them.* He chokes on his words. "What? What have you done?"

Ersari gently rubs Delbert's shoulder, sending a chill down his spine. "There, there, I just need your help a little longer than expected. But once you're successfully done with your last assignment, I will let them go."

"What, what assignment? It's over, isn't it? You killed all those people in New York, attacked the State of the Union, and blew up your staff. What else is there?"

Ersari laughs. "The Center believes in having backup strategies—plans B and C. I was a tad disappointed that the president and the others survived my little intrusion on their big night. Time for Plan B."

Despite his predicament, Delbert's reporter instincts kick in again. "Which is?"

"That's why I chose you, Mr. Bascue. You're always on the job, curious, and with a talent for words. Be patient a little longer. You'll see and have more to write about very soon."

Delbert looks back as the land fades from view. It's now all salt water for as far as he can see.

"That's it, straight ahead, ma'am," Judy Brendle, the pilot says. "Shall I approach?"

Delbert squints, spotting a stationary blue dot on the eastern horizon.

"Give me comms to check in first. I want to make sure it's safe," Ersari says.

Delbert hears a clicking in his headset and then a man's voice. "Niner-one-one, this is A-L One, state your code."

Ersari rotates her wrist and reads something handwritten on her skin in blue ink. "A-L One, Прощай только для тех, кто любит глазами 'Goodbyes are only for those who love with their eyes.'"

The man responds, "'Because, for those who love with heart and soul, there is no such thing as separation.'"

Ersari lets out a deep breath. "Приятно слышать твой голос, брат мой—It's good to hear your voice, my comrade." She taps Brendle on the shoulder. "OK to approach."

Minutes pass as the blue dot on the horizon grows larger. The Bell 470 that was traveling at one hundred and twenty knots slows and then hovers over a blue platform that appears to be about fifty feet long and a dozen feet wide. A white metal railing surrounds the perimeter.

Delbert with eyes wide, asks, "We're going to land on that?"

"No, of course not," Ersari says. "We're too heavy. We're going to climb down. Just follow Pickles."

"There's some wind ma'am, but I'll try to hold her steady," Brendle says.

Pickles opens the side door. A rush of freezing air and the tang of sea salt fill the cabin. He lowers a metal and rope ladder fifty feet to the floating deck below. The ladder sways back and forth in the breeze. Two men in black uniforms and black ski caps covering their heads and faces reach out to grab the bottom end of the elusive ladder. After missing on several tries, they wrestle it in and latch it with flexible, quick-release ties to the bobbing deck. The helicopter tilts and moves above as Pickles carefully descends and steps off next to the two crewmen.

Ersari hands Delbert a pair of gloves. "You'll need these. It's your turn."

Delbert slides the padded gloves on. *I'm going to die right here.* Ersari gives him a push. He stands stooping, turns, and places a trembling foot on the top rung. He looks up at the angry clouds, *no help from him.* Gripping the sides of the ladder so hard that he can feel the blood pumping in his fingers, he drops one tentative step at a time. It seems to take forever, the chill wind cutting through his parka. The ladder drifting and shaking inches right and left. Delbert tries to remember to breathe. Then a hand catches his foot and yanks him down. He tumbles hard onto the deck of the vessel. A small wave breaks over the gunnel, soaking him with icy salt water.

Pickles grins. "You made it." He seizes Delbert's wrist and raises him to his feet. Delbert clutches the railing while Pickles assists Ersari onto the deck. The crewmen unhook the ladder and wave. The Bell 470 banks left and flies away back toward the land.

Pickles inspects Delbert and points to the open hatch in the deck. "Shall we?"

65

THE TRACE

It's 3:00 AM and the windows are black at the DHS office on New York Avenue NE in D.C. Rich rolls up his sleeves and takes his seat at the head of the table in Conference Room #4. Monica and Juan file in behind him. Michelle follows with a carafe of coffee.

Rich taps the intercom. "Gary, are you there?"

They hear video-game gunfire in the background that stops abruptly. "Yeah, I mean yes, I'm here," Gary says.

"Sounds like you're hard on the case," Rich says.

"I couldn't sleep, what's up?"

"Sleep is for another day. Come join us in Number 4."

Moments later Gary staggers in, his shirt untucked and his red hair sticking up in all directions. "It's been a long night," he says.

"For all of us," Rich says. "What have you got on Ashaki? Surveillance, anything?"

"Not much," Gary says. "Persistent Surveillance showed their helicopter head south along the shoreline for a few minutes and disappear to the east."

"That's open water," Monica says.

"They could be heading over the water to evade detection and then turning back in," Michelle says.

"Just in case, Michelle, alert the Coast Guard and FAA. Have them put out a BOLO for a Bell 470 for a hundred miles up and down the coast," Rich says.

Michelle puts her phone to her ear and steps out of the conference room.

"Any other theories?" Rich asks.

"If she was a narco, she'd have a boat," Juan says.

"Or a submarine," Monica says.

"That's unlikely," Rich says.

"Didn't her brother use a submersible to escape capture in Manhattan last year?" Monica asks.

"How did you know about that?" Rich asks.

"It just came to me. You know, Sam and I communicate," Monica says.

Gary raises his hand like he's back in school.

Rich laughs. "Yes, Gary?"

"Her family may have had more than a passing interest in subs. Their father, before he was killed, was a Barinian submarine captain," Gary says.

"Like father, like son," Rich says.

"And maybe, like father, like daughter," Monica says.

"OK, let's suppose they were on a boat or a sub, how would we find them?" Michelle asks.

"Between DHS, the Coast Guard, and the Navy, we have a slew of experts and the latest tech to track down anything on or under the water, but it's still an assumption that they are out there," Rich says.

"¿No pueden caminar y mascar chicle al mismo tiempo?" Juan asks.

"English please," Rich says.

Juan takes the chewing gum out of his mouth and sticks it on the tabletop.

"OK I get it, yeah we can do both a land and sea search at the same time," Rich says.

"But we need more than a BOLO, we need an active search," Monica says.

"Agreed," Rich says. "I've already got Renata and Jonathan leading the ground team. Let me make a couple of calls to my level at the Coast Guard and Navy to get them more actively engaged.

Monica's phone vibrates. She looks down—a text from *unknown*. Her face turns pink. "I just got an anonymous text. You can guess who sent it."

"What's it say?" Michelle asks.

Monica sucks in a deep breath. "What you seek is seeking you."

66

100 METERS DOWN

The pilot pushes the stick forward, taking the Triton into a steep dive. His passengers lurch forward then fall back when the sub-levels off a hundred meters below the surface. The DeepView 24 is a fifty-foot, cigar-shaped glass cylinder trimmed in navy blue with two rear propellers. It runs silently on batteries and oxygen is replenished through a CO_2 scrubber. The clear glass wrapping both the cabin and the bulbous bow provide a spectacular view. Although the submersible was designed for tourist cruises, Ersari commissioned a redesign to accommodate and support her mission.

"Thanks for the ride," she says to the pilot.

"For you, anything," the pilot says. He strokes her face with the back of his hand. "Your efforts in D.C. did not quite go as planned, did they? The Center was not pleased. With my help this time, you will not fail. And when this is over, I expect payment not in money, but in flesh. Understood?"

She blushes for a nanosecond and pushes his hand away. "We'll see how this new arrangement works out."

I scan the camera feeds from several Coast Guard vessels and aircraft in the surveillance area off the Baltimore shoreline and say, "I don't think we can rely on the Coast Guard or Navy to stop her before she makes her next move. There's not enough time."

Frank is glued to his monitors, typing away like a concert pianist building to a crescendo. "I've confirmed through a satellite using subsurface radar that there is indeed a submersible forty-six miles off the coast. I can't be sure if it's her."

"I don't think tourists would be out in this kind of weather," I say.

"Could be drug runners," Frank says.

I point to Frank's radar image. "Make sure Rich and Monica get that."

"I'm sure they've got it, but I'll highlight it for them just in case."

"Uh, I forgot, if I have it, Monica has it. Is there anything we can do to stop Ashaki or disrupt her plan, whatever it is?"

"Even with Bart's help, I haven't been able to hack any of her systems or her memories in the Cloud. The encryption is too strong. Yet, there is one possibility."

"What is it?"

Frank rotates his chair and looks at me with drawn eyes. "It's big, but extremely risky, with potential global consequences."

"Like what, what consequences?"

"Let's both run the scenarios." He turns back to his keyboard clicking away, as he speaks. "Suppose you were driving a car or flying a plane and you lost consciousness for just one second and then got it right back, would you get in an accident?"

"Probably not. Where are you going with this?"

"How about if you were a doctor doing brain surgery or an aerialist on a tightrope, would one second matter?"

I feel a queasiness coming on. "Yeah, one second could mean a nicked artery or a slip and fall. You haven't answered my question."

"How about a half-second? I might be able to shorten the time. How would the surgeon or tightrope walker do then?"

"Frank?"

"Give me a few minutes. Let me see what I can do. For now, let's call this Operation Blink," Frank says.

67

THE NEBRASKA

Aboard the USS Nebraska Ohio-class submarine, Captain Wesley McCarter peers over the shoulder of his XO, Anita Jamros. They are following a red dot 957 meters ten degrees north of their position. McCarter turns to the sonar operator, Reign Haig, and says, "Anything?"

"She's running pretty quiet, but I'm getting a regular ping-ping sound like somebody tapping a spoon," Haig says.

"Radar confirms. That should be our target," Jamros says.

McCarter runs his fingers through his thinning salt and pepper hair. "Close to five hundred and take her down thirty. I want to keep communications up. Let's see if we can get a closer look without spooking them."

The USS Nebraska carries twenty-four Trident missiles armed with live nuclear warheads. By itself, it is the fifth-largest nuclear power in the world. The crew sleeps stacked three high in bunks tucked between the nuclear silos. Its nuclear power plant has enough fuel to power the sub for thirty-two years between fill-ups. Their usual mission is to patrol an unspecified area of the Atlantic and be ready for

Armageddon. Tracking the Triton DeepView is like using a shotgun to kill a fly.

"Load torpedo tubes one and two with Mark 54s just so we're ready," the captain says.

"We're in position," the XO says. "Relaying images to Command now." A few moments later, she says, "Confirmed. It's the Triton."

A voice crackles over the intercom. "Tubes One and two locked and loaded."

McCarter takes a deep breath of the ozone enriched recycled air and puts a hand on the XO's shoulder. "Advise Command that we're ready to strike, awaiting their instructions."

At 7:15 AM President Longford splashes cold water on her face, dries it, and looks in the mirror. Noticing the dark circles around her eyes and the new wrinkles, she thinks, *I've served eight years, but I look and feel eighty years older. OK, let's do this.*

She exits the tiled restroom into the intensely lit Situation Room. The long mahogany table is full to capacity with men and women, many in uniform. *Is that tobacco I smell or am I imagining it?* Spotlights shine on the table covered in reports and maps. Admiral David Jeske stands at the large monitor on the long wall. Everyone rises when the president enters. She takes the one empty seat at the head of the table and the thirty-plus military, secretaries, and staff remain standing until Longford waves them down.

"Anyone have a cigarette? Never mind, what's the latest?" she asks.

Admiral Jeske points to a red dot and then a blue rectangle

some distance away from the red dot. "We have confirmation and positive ID on subject target's location here. Over here we have the Nebraska ready to take her out, awaiting authorization."

"Are you sure it's her?" Longford asks.

"We're ninety percent positive," Jeske says.

One of the marine staff rises from the communication desk in the corner and jogs over to Chuck Hagar, handing him a note. Hagar jumps up. "Hold on. We have a message from the Triton."

"Well, freakin' read it already," Longford barks.

"Madame President, we know that you have ascertained our position. I caution you not to take any precipitous action that you may regret. If something should happen to us, an attack will be automatically launched, disabling a large swath of the American population. If you don't believe us, we have prepared a little demonstration just now. You can access the online feed in three minutes at https://20.725.166.5. Assuming you will stand down and take our demonstration seriously, we will be back in touch within the hour with our demands."

"What the fuck?" Roger Brickman says.

"There's more," Jeske says. "It's signed... 'by your friends, Ahmed and Ashaki.'"

"What?" Longford exclaims. "LaSalam's back. I thought he was dead."

"We all did," Brickman says.

"You said that last time," Longford says. "How do we get rid of him for good?"

"We're working on it," Brickman says.

"Sure, and that address. What is that?"

"It's an IP address," Brickman says. "Those numbers are what's really behind every domain name. Take Amazon.com.

Its actual address is 52.95.154.0. IPs are the telephone numbers of the web and the domain name is the Caller ID."

"Didn't need all that. Just turn the damn thing on," Longford says.

The marine staff member opens a browser, types in the IP, and projects it on another wall screen. A webcam image appears of a busy intersection of a city. People are walking the streets. It's sunny. There are tall buildings in the background. Traffic stops at one side of an intersection while the four lanes of cars in the other direction are moving through the green light. Suddenly, all the cars move in all directions at once, crashing into each other. Pedestrians don't seem to notice and walk right into the traffic and are immediately struck by cars and trucks. An SUV veers off the road onto the sidewalk, picking up speed, mowing down tens of bewildered people in front of a department store. A truck runs over a fire hydrant, launching a stream of water into the air. Another eighteen-wheeler crushes the traffic lights and runs right over the top of six cars stuck in the intersection like they were Tonka toys. Bloody bodies are strewn all over the streets and sidewalks. Fire and smoke rise from several burning vehicles. A gas tank explodes, throwing debris and body parts in all directions. Blood splatters on the lens of the webcam partially obscuring the gruesome view and adding a grisly tint to the scene.

The image on the screen shifts to a different camera view of another intersection with grizzlier video of mayhem and destruction.

The Sit Room is dead quiet as the spectacle of devastation flashes from other cameras around the same city.

Finally, in a whisper, Longford asks, "Where is this?"

The young, sallow-face marine answers, "What you are seeing are all feeds from cameras in Charlotte, North Carolina."

"Turn it off," Brickman says.

Hagar stands. "Madame President, I'd advise we have the Nebraska move in."

"And do what?" Longford asks.

"Make contact."

ALL NIGHTER

The early morning sun peeks through the tall windows on the third floor of headquarters. Michelle knocks lightly on Rich's door and walks in. Rich stirs, his hair and tie askew. "What? I dozed off for a minute." He cocks his head to smell his armpit. "Not good," he mutters.

"Then you haven't seen this," Michelle says and turns her phone so Rich can see a replay of the chaos in Charlotte.

"Holy shit. Why didn't you get me sooner?" Rich asks.

"This just happened." She takes the phone back, taps a few keys and hands the phone to Rich. "Roger forwarded this text from guess who."

Rich leaps to his feet and winces with a stabbing pain from his stitches. "Are they already on this in Charlotte?"

"We can't reach anyone at our Tyvola Centre Office. We think they may have been hit. I called FBI Charlotte and guess who answers the phone?"

"No time for games. Just tell me everything you've got."

"Tiffany, Tiffany Sly got promoted after the NNN take-down in Tennessee. She's now Assistant SIC. She just got in and is directing her teams to the multiple scenes. I also diverted Renata and Jonathan there. They should land in an hour."

"After Brickman told me they had Ashaki pegged in the sub, I figured she was a goner. Can't assume anything with them. OK, let's meet in five. Get our crew together and conference in Sam and Sly. Oh, and can I get my coffee now?"

"Get your own coffee. I've got work to do," Michelle says and slams the door behind her.

Monica is pacing the conference room when Michelle and Rich file in. She looks up at them. "I've been briefed."

Rich and Michelle look at each other. "By whom?" Rich asks.

"By Sam. He knows everything—he and I are linked. Like most married couples, we can read each other's minds and then some," Monica says.

"Yeah, it's spooky," Michelle says. "I'm conferencing in Sly now."

Tiffany Sly's slender face appears on the wall monitor. Her eyes are swollen. "This is the worst crime scene I have ever witnessed, worse than the NNN shootout last fall. We've had an Armageddon of the mind. It's like everyone in the city was stricken with dementia, which turned drivers and cars into deadly weapons. Do you guys know anything about this?"

"Tiffany, I'm Monica Sunborn. You knew my husband, Sam. I'm assisting on this case."

"I was sorry to hear about Sam. He was a good man," Sly says.

"Thanks. Unfortunately, we do know a lot about this case. It's the same weapon that was used in New York and at the

State of the Union. The attacker is the terrorist, Ashaki LaSalam, that you were up against in Tennessee," Monica says.

"I'm aware of those two prior attacks, but this is an entire city," Sly says.

"LaSalam is trying to make a point," Rich says. "She's extorting us. And even worse, her brother Ahmed is in on the scheme with her. And before you ask, no, he's not dead or rather, he's back from the dead. But that's a whole other story."

Monica forces a cough. "Sly, we need you to do something. Can you get near one of the afflicted, but not physically injured victims and point your camera at him?"

"OK," Sly says. Her phone camera's image jiggles. She moves in on a middle-aged man who's walking past a spouting fire hydrant, his hair and clothes soaked. He seems oblivious to the surrounding chaos. Sly gets closer and gently takes his hand with hers while holding her phone in the other. "Sir, are you OK? Can I help you?"

The man jerks his hand away. "Don't touch me."

Sly softens her voice. "Sir, I'm with the FBI. I'm here to help."

"Sly, zoom in on his face," Monica says.

The image of the man's face expands. His eyes are far away, blank.

Monica stands next to Sly's camera image projected on their screen, pointing. "Do you see that, that mark above his left eyebrow?"

"Looks like a scar," Michelle says. "All the victims in New York and D.C. had the same mark. So it confirms the connection, but we already knew that. Ashaki already told us that."

"But what does that mean? Why is it there?" Monica asks. "I think we should—"

Rich holds up a hand. He taps the remote, muting their voices to prevent Sly from hearing. "I know what you were about to say. 'Let's call Frank and Sam.' I'm OK with that, but Sly thinks Sam is dead. It's better that fewer people know he's still available." Rich unmutes. "Sorry, Sly. We had a minor issue here."

Sly's face reappears on their monitor. "I'm not stupid. You had a need-to-know moment. I understand. Just keep me posted on anything that can help with our situation here. I gotta go help these guys."

"Thanks, Sly," Rich says. "That's a two-way street. Loop us in if you see anything unusual."

Sly smirks. "You're kidding, right? It's all totally insane here. Bye."

Sly's image goes dark. "OK, let's call Sam and Frank," Rich says.

Michelle refills her cup with coffee, closes her eyes, and sips the hot, aromatic liquid. "I don't like that we're sitting here chatting while that's going on out there. All talk and no action."

"That's funny. You usually accuse me of shooting from the hip," Rich says.

Monica holds up a hand. "Hate to break up the lovers' quarrel, but we need to get a better handle on this so we can make a move that matters."

Both Rich and Michelle's faces redden at the same time.

Monica laughs. "Yeah, I know about you two. I was in the car, remember?"

My face appears on the screen. "Hi, sweetheart."

"Hi, Sam. Rich and Michelle are here. You know the situation?"

"Frank and I have been tracking it. Frank is working on a

far-fetched techy way to shut Ashaki down, but I don't think you guys should wait for that."

"We've got two crazy terrorists in a submersible with the country by the balls," Rich says. "What do you suggest we do?"

Monica is up pacing again. "Has anybody thought of just paying the ransom?"

"What?" Rich jumps to his feet. "We don't pay ransom to terrorists."

"That's the stated policy position, but the U.S. does it all the time on the down-low," I say.

"Maybe, but we're talking ten billion dollars and pulling our troops out of Europe. We've got 70,000 soldiers there in Germany, Italy, Spain, the U.K., all over. Without them, NATO collapses and the Russians take over Europe. That's a crazy ask."

"We need to buy some time until either Frank gets his crazy idea working or you guys figure out another way. So why not wire her the ten billion and tell them we'll draw down the troops, but it takes time to plan and execute a mobilization like that?"

"I'm not sure Longford and Brickman will go for that," Michelle says. "Besides, ten billion dollars is a lot of money."

Frank's face pops on the screen. "I heard billion. What is it Senator Dirksen said? 'A billion here, a billion there, and pretty soon you're talking real money.'"

I smile. "Ten billion is a drop in the bucket for the U.S. If another city goes postal like Charlotte, it'll cost a lot more in lives and dollars."

Rich sighs. "OK, I'll ask, but don't count on it. And if Longford OKs it and this doesn't work out, we should all update our resumes."

"Not a problem for Monica or me," I say.

job... Could somebody have knocked her off and disposed of the body?"

"Maybe. We can't be certain from a blood splatter. But if Ashaki is out of the picture, who attacked Charlotte and is extorting us from that submarine?"

"Could be her partner, Ersari," Monica says.

"Yeah, but why this big plot—doesn't fit her MO. She's a hustler, not a genocidal maniac. I mean sure she's killed some people, but that was gang stuff," Michelle says.

"Maybe she's got more affiliations beyond gangsters and mobsters," Monica says.

"Hmm, Gary, do a deeper dive on Ersari's background. See what you can come up with," Rich says.

Gary is already tapping away on his tablet. He stops and looks up. "Her father was Italian, but her mother was Russian. She's also done some business with the Russians in Brooklyn. Could that be it, a Russian plot?"

"And we're after Ersari, not Ashaki?" Rich asks. "Guys, I need more. We don't know for sure that Ashaki's dead and Ersari is the prime mover here. And if it is Ersari, we need more proof of a connection to Russia or whatever's driving her. And we need it yesterday."

"We're on it," Michelle says.

Delbert Bascue stares through the curved glass into an aquamarine wonderland. As if in slow motion, a giant stingray flaps its wing-like fins as it glides by. *Nothing like being trapped in a fish tank*, he thinks.

Ersari approaches him from behind. She starts massaging Delbert's shoulders a little too hard. "Are you getting all this down? It's historic. Do it well and there may be a Pulitzer in it for you."

Delbert stirs from his stupor. "Sure. I heard your extortion threat. Do you think they'll pay and take out the troops?

Ersari smiles and digs her fingers in deeper. "Doubtful. I'd be surprised. Assuming they don't, they can live with the guilt for what happens next."

The submersible shutters as a great white shark brushes against the hull. The rumble knocks Delbert from his seat. He hits the floor, striking the back of his skull. "Ouch, fuck." He rubs his head.

Ersari braces herself with the overhead handrail then bends over to grab Delbert by the collar and yanks him back into his chair.

"We're goin' to die down here," he says.

"A watery grave," Ersari murmurs. She yells forward, "Hey, are we OK?"

The pilot just waves without turning around.

Delbert brushes himself off. "OK, what happens next? I mean, if you don't expect to get your ransom, what's the endgame here?"

"Good question. Answer, we'll turn up the heat more and toy with them until they break. They'll be like the frog in the pot of boiling water."

"What?"

"You know the story. If you drop a frog in a pot of boiling water, he'll jump out. But if you place him a pot of warm water and slowly raise the heat, he'll stay in the water and boil to death. Enough of that. What city should we attack next, your choice but make it a big one? I want something dramatic."

"I only agreed to report on what you're doing, not be a part of it."

"My dear Delbert, you don't get it. You're way past that point." Ersari waves her hand through the air. "If we go down, you go down. Either you pick a city, or we do New York where Sherry and Richelle are." Ashaki looks at her watch. "You have ten seconds." She smiles. "Ten... nine... eight... five... four... three... two."

"Wait!"

"Have you made your choice?"

"Cleveland."

"Interesting choice. About four-hundred-thousand people there. That's a good size. But why Cleveland?"

Delbert stutters, "I, I don't know. It just popped into my head. I've never been there. Don't know anybody there."

"So, it's not real to you. Just like if you lived outside New York during 9/11. It wasn't real to you. Like it was a fiction, made up."

"I guess."

"Or the coronavirus. If it didn't happen to you or your family, it must be fake or unreal. Like that, right?"

"Like I said, it just popped into my head."

"OK. Cleveland it is. This one's all on you, Delbert."

"Why are you torturing me?"

Ersari's grin widens. "Because it's fun. But enough of that, I've got a city to destroy." She turns and walks forward to the bow, balancing herself by grabbing the backs of the benches that face the panoramic windows. Delbert watches Ersari bend over and whisper in the pilot's ear. The pilot nods.

"Sick bitch," Delbert mumbles under his breath.

70

DECISIONS, DECISIONS

"They can't stay down there forever," Michelle says. She pours herself another cup of coffee.

"As long as they've got us over a barrel, it doesn't matter where they are," Rich says.

"They'll need to surface soon. It's not like that thing is a nuclear sub that can stay under for years." Monica looks at her watch, 10 AM. "They've been down for eleven hours. According to the specs, they've got approximately three hours left.

Rich and Michelle gape at Monica with a *what-planet-did-you-come-from* look.

Monica laughs. "I have a direct line to Sam. It's like having an IV connection to the universe of stored digital knowledge and facts. It's one of my superpowers."

Rich scoffs. "OK, genius. If they must surface, what happens next?"

"You don't need to be a genius to figure that one out," Monica says.

"Yes, George?" Longford says.

"Back to this split-second everybody loses consciousness. How much damage could that cause?"

"We're running models on that now," Sam says. "Frank's current estimate is that we'd all be offline for 550 milliseconds, a little more than a half-second. He's trying to fine-tune it so that time is even shorter. Perhaps, you should have some of your statistical experts run the shutdown scenarios too."

"All that scenario crap takes time we don't have. Let's plan to shut down all critical military and civilian operations we can identify before Dr. Einstein pushes the button on this thing... And I hate to do it but pay her the ten billion dollars. Director Little, you coordinate that."

"Yes, Madame President," Rich says.

71

ALL ABOARD

In the Atlantic, one hundred-thirty miles due east of Cape May, the waves churn with whitecaps and spew sea spray. The *Kiss Off* bobs to the surface. The pilot steers the sub in a slow 360-degree circle scouring the horizon. Nothing but dark, turbulent waters as far as the eye can see. Violet and black clouds pressing in from the west. The *Kiss Off* bobs up and down like a cork. Finally, the pilot spots a small, dark rectangle to the north. A light, a beacon, flashes to the rhythm of a heartbeat. He picks up his mic and taps the on-button three times, then twice, and finally six times more. The far-off beacon mimics a response, 3-2-6. Changing course, he heads for the light.

Bascue does all he can to swallow back the vomit. His stomach and his head feel like he's spinning in a clothes dryer. He flashes on a memory of when he was eight years old walking home from Nassau Elementary school. Three older boys stopped him and his friend, Charlie. Then the boys dragged the two of them into the basement laundry room of an old apartment building. Charlie was small for his age, with freckles and red hair. For no reason at all, other than their apparent amusement, the older boys put little Charlie into one of the clothes driers and turned it on. They laughed hysterically as Charlie spun and bounced inside the hot metal drum. Delbert tried to get to his friend but two of the boys held him back.

After a few minutes that seemed like hours, they released Delbert who ran to the dryer. He swung the door open and helped Charlie out. Charlie was badly bruised and dizzy. He collapsed to the floor, gasping for air. Then Delbert and Charlie ran home. At this moment and for the first time, Delbert knew what Charlie must have experienced, spinning out of control and against his will in an endless sweltering cycle.

"You look a little pale there, Delbert," Ersari says, handing him a bucket. "In case you need this. Don't worry, it won't be long now."

"That's the third time you've said that to me, and the first two times things got worse."

"Life can be like that. Just when you think things couldn't get worse, everything turns to shit," Ersari says and pats Bascue on the back.

After a little less than an hour, that small rectangle on the horizon becomes a large cargo ship, stacked with orange and blue forty-foot containers, flying the Russian flag and the name *Spirit of the Earth*.

The pilot cautiously steers the Triton ten meters aft from the stern of the ship. A hatch door slowly lowers, revealing a wide ramp leading to a pitch-black chasmal interior. The *Kiss Off* moves to the edge of the ramp where two uniformed sailors fasten chains with hooks to either side of the Triton. Once secure, one of the sailors waves. A hidden wench cranks the sub onto rollers, and it rattles up the ramp. Water pours off the sub and drains from its ballasts, swishing back down the incline. With the *Kiss Off* safely inside, the Spirit raises the ramp and slams the hatch door closed.

The pilot pops the sub's hatch and climbs up and out. Ersari goes next, followed by Delbert and the other passengers.

"Welcome aboard," comes the greeting from a cheery red-faced man with a gray beard and captain's hat. "It's good to see you again, Commander."

The pilot shakes the captain's hand. "Likewise, it was pretty rough out there. Captain, please have your team recharge the batteries of our submersible." He laughs. "You never know when we'll need to make a speedy exit."

"Aye, aye, Commander."

"Captain, I don't believe you've met my partner, Comrade Ersari."

Captain Paul Vorderstrasse doffs his hat and makes a slight bow, scanning her from head to toe. "Aye, lovely. I mean, it's a cheer to meet you. My lads call me Captain V."

Ersari grimaces.

"Apologies," the captain says. "I've been out at sea too long."

Ersari ignores the apology. "This is Delbert Bascue, a reporter who is documenting our mission."

Captain V takes a step back.

The commander puts a hand on V's shoulder. "Not to worry, my friend. Willingly or unwillingly, he's on our side. Now please show us to our headquarters."

The captain nods and leads the group up four flights of steel steps, their footfalls echoing through the fathomless space. They proceed down a long, narrow, hospital-green hallway that emits the pungent odor of disinfectant. The captain spins open a hatch door, then steps over the raised threshold. The high-ceiling room is brightly lit with rows of steel tables bolted to the floor, on top of which sit zigzags of computers and monitors. A dozen men and women dressed in unadorned white uniforms notice their guests and bolt upright, standing at attention.

The commander grins. "Captain V, you've done well. This'll do."

Rich taps his pencil on the table. Ten billion is a stretch, even for the president's discretionary fund. Rich would have to extract five billion of it from the CIA's black ops budget. Osborne bitched and moaned but finally relented. Now all he needs to do is wait for confirmation that the transfer is complete and pray that Frank Einstein comes through soon.

Michelle and Monica sit silently working on their tablets.

"Let's see a picture," Michelle says.

Monica turns her tablet to display a photo of Evan in his red soccer uniform, one foot perched on top of a black and white ball, his expression happy, proud, confident.

"He looks great," Michelle says.

Rich leans over and smiles at the image of a boy enjoying the carefree innocence of his youth. *Oh, how I miss that*, he thinks.

Michelle's smartphone dings. She checks the incoming message, exhales, and says, "It's from Gary. We've got our proof." She scrolls down, taps on the picture, and rotates the phone toward Rich.

"What am I looking at?" Rich asks.

"It's a cargo ship called *Spirit of the Earth*. Notice the flag."

"And?"

"And it just picked up the submersible. So, I think we can now safely say we're chasing Jennie Lee Ersari or Natasha

Babooshka or whatever her real name is, not Ashaki LaSalam," Michelle says.

"So that means the Russians just ripped us off for ten billion dollars."

"They must really need the money," Monica says. "But how does this change anything? We still need to neutralize the threat, and the threat just has a different name. It's no less dangerous and must be stopped."

"They had to know we'd figure it out. Is this just an *in-your-face* thing?" Michelle asks.

"The Russians are like teenagers. They like to provoke and see what happens, test their limits. Look at all the flagrant cyberattacks, or Crimea for that matter. We know it's them, but they keep at it. Then we hit back," Rich says. "It just pisses me off. It seems like they're playing chess and we're playing checkers." Rich stands and starts pacing. "I have to let Brickman know right away. It will be up to him and the president as to how they want to respond. Meanwhile, we carry on as planned unless instructed otherwise."

"We better tell Frank, or he may target the wrong person. If he seeks to neutralize Ashaki, who's likely dead, and not Ersari, we're toast," Michelle says.

Monica looks up at the ceiling. "He already knows," she says.

72

THE SHUTDOWN

DHS Director Roger Brickman collapses in his high-backed desk chair. He throws his hands up in the air and stares at the ceiling. *I don't know how to do this.* In his head, he hears the advice his father gave him when he took this job. "Son, you're not going to know all the answers. So hire people smarter than you and then fake it till you make it." *I miss that man.*

"Margaret!" Brickman shouts.

Three seconds later, Margaret Rodgers enters without knocking. "You look like hell," she says.

Roger smiles. Margaret is more than his assistant. She has been a friend, partner, and an ersatz mother to him for twenty years. "I know," he says. "But we have a big ask from the president."

Margaret settles into a seat across from him and takes his hands in hers. She stares into his blue eyes. "We've stopped catastrophic terror attacks and kept this country safe before. What is it now?"

He heaves a deep breath. "Two things. I need to shut down all essential services on command for at least an hour. *Essential* means anything that could fail if it's interrupted for a split second."

"Like what?"

"All surgeries and medical procedures, military exercises, building construction, race car driving, any critical activity for that matter..."

"That's a big ask. Let's get all your deputies in here and divide it up. Lawrence takes medical. Lyle takes transportation, Jones construction, Figmor sports. I'm sure we'll think of more and then we can go down a level to bring in the assistant deputies to cover those."

"Of course. The only exception is Rich Little. He's in the field with a couple of agents. They're trying to stop the imminent attack."

"As if that isn't enough, Little just informed me that our attacker is a Russian agent with obvious help from the motherland. We even paid those assholes ten billion dollars extortion money."

"But I thought—"

Brickman holds up a hand to stop her. "This was just part of a strategy to buy time. Get the deputies and assistants in Room #2 now and conference in any not in the building. Let's get them started and then I'll reach out to Ms. Ersari about the troop withdrawal nonsense."

"Ms. Ersari? It sounds like you respect her."

"I do respect her the way Sherlock respects Moriarty—her cleverness, her persistence, her devotion to the mission. She even has reasons for it. I don't respect the twisted way she's going about it and the innocent lives lost."

"I don't get it. What reasons would Ersari and the Russians have to do this?"

"The ten billion was to either test us or embarrass us. We claim to never negotiate with terrorists, and now they've proved that that's a self-righteous load of crap. More important though, they really do want us out of Europe so they can move in, suck up all the oil, and control the waterways and the airways. It's an absurd ask, but this neural weapon thing is a pretty big hammer."

"Or a tight noose around our necks."

He claps his hands. "Fuck the analogies. Let's go. We can Monday morning quarterback later." He looks at his watch, 1:00. We have to get the shutdown ready and bullshit her about the troop withdrawal in the next three hours."

"Margaret rises and says, "Roger that, Roger."

"That one doesn't get old, does it?"

"Got you to smile. Now go wash up and put on a clean shirt," Margaret says and closes the door behind her.

Brickman slides open the bottom desk drawer. "I can always count on you. Johnny Walker." Pouring four fingers, he thinks, *it's 5:00 somewhere, and this is going to be a long day.*

73

OR ELSE

An hour later, after dispensing his DHS minions to cut through the expected pushback and prepare the shutdown, Brickman taps the intercom and says, "Margaret, get Captain McCarter on the Nebraska. I want him to set up a short-wave connection to the cargo ship that has Ersari's sub. Then put me through."

"Will do. I'll buzz you back."

The USS Nebraska's radio man, Kirk Bauer, sends a signal on Channel 16, the universal VHF marine distress wavelength, and gets the attention of an operator aboard the *Spirit of the Earth*, the cargo ship pregnant with the *Kiss Off* inside. Fortunately, the *Spirit's* operator speaks English and patches Bauer through to Captain Vorderstrasse. Captain McCarter takes over on this end and captain-to-captain explains the purpose of the call. A few minutes later Jennie Lee Ersari, in a private berth on the *Spirit*, and Roger Brickman, in his office accompanied by Margaret, are connected.

Brickman clears his throat. "Ms. Ersari. This is Roger Brickman, Homeland Secretary. I'm calling at the behest of President Langford." He resists adding... *who you tried to kill.*

"Duh, I know who you are, and I know who she is. Glad to see she is recovering. Give her my regards, would you?" Ersari says.

"I think she has had enough of your regards, don't you? But that's not why I'm calling. She has authorized me to discuss your request on the country's behalf."

"I'm listening."

"She has paid you the ten billion. Let's call it a day."

"Director Brickman, let me clarify something. It wasn't a request or a negotiation. It was a take-it-or-leave-it. I want the troops out. For your information, we have our next target ready and I'm prepared to prove I'm not bluffing right now."

Ersari stands behind two young female techs studying an array of six large monitors. "Our next target is up on our screens here. I'm looking at the West Side Market, the Great Lakes Science Center, and..." she snickers, "...the Rock & Roll Hall of Fame. You should know if anything happens to me or my crew, the attack will automatically launch followed by seventeen other high-population targets. So don't get any macho ideas about hitting us. Now, you have five minutes to agree to our terms or get ready for Charlotte times eighteen."

Brickman raises his eyebrows and twirls a finger in the air.

Margaret whispers, "She's talking about Cleveland next."

Brickman nods and says, "Please stay on the line. I need to contact the president. If you attack Cleveland or anywhere else before I get back on the line, the deal's off. We take our chances and blow you out of the fuckin' ocean."

"You're in no position to dictate terms. You have four minutes and twelve seconds left. After that, I'm all action and no talk," Ersari says and takes a beat. "Three minutes and fifty-nine seconds..."

"OK, OK, I'll be right back to you," Brickman says and pushes the HOLD button. He rises and paces the room.

Tears draw a raggedy line of mascara down Margaret's cheek. "Are you going to call the president?"

Brickman keeps pacing and strokes his chin. "I don't need to call the president. I already got authorization. I'm just biding some time to make her think I'm calling."

Margaret looks at her watch. "Don't wait too long. You only have two minutes and twenty seconds."

"I think she'd push the button. She's already demonstrated her ruthlessness, but I want to wait until the last ten seconds to call. Let her sweat a little for a change."

Margaret digs her fingernails into her thighs. "What are you trying to prove? What happens if the radio fails, and you run out of time? Do you really want to play it that close?"

"How much time left?"

"A minute-five, four, three, two..."

Brickman stops pacing. "You're right as usual." He returns to his desk and punches the SPEAKER button. "Ms. Ersari, I'm back and prepared to—"

An unfamiliar voice, the Spirit radio operator, cuts him off. "Ms. Ersari had to step away for a minute. Hold please."

Brickman is up and pacing again. "I can't believe this."

Margaret smirks. "Now look who's sweating." She bites her lip.

"Very funny," Brickman snaps.

A few moments later. "Margaret, how much time now?"

She checks her watch and recites, "Five, four, three, two, one..."

Brickman throws his hands up. "Who the fuck does she think she is?"

A calm voice comes back on the line. "Apparently I'm your worst nightmare or wet-dream, depending on how you look at it," Ersari says.

"You're sick," Brickman says.

"No. For my dearly departed friend, it was settling a score. For me, it's just business."

"Yeah maybe, but you seem to get off on killing innocent people. That's sick."

A different voice answers. "I taught her to follow her passion," the pilot says. He reaches for Ersari's butt and she swats his hand away.

"I guess psychopathy runs in the family," Brickman says.

Ersari pushes the pilot away. "I'm sure the name-calling, like jerking off, makes you feel better on some level, but what's it going to be, pay or die?"

Brickman sucks in a deep breath. "We're prepared to meet your terms as long as you hold up your end and stand down."

"Excellent decision," Ersari says. "My assistant will text that dear little Margaret of yours a link to upload your proof of the troop withdrawals. Have you dipped your pen in her ink yet?"

Brickman turns beat red. Margaret puts a hand on the back of his neck.

"Are we clear?" Ersari asks.

Brickman clenches his fists. "That takes time. We have to draw up a plan and organize it so nobody gets hurt. We'll start the planning today and the first troops will move out in the next couple of weeks."

"You have forty-eight hours to pull all your troops out. Miss the deadline and say goodbye to Cleveland and seventeen other cities."

"We sent the money, but we need more time to move thousands of soldiers and billions in hardware."

"Forty-eight for the troops or else..." The line goes dead.

MISSED PUTTS

At 2:30, Margaret assembles fourteen heads out of the twenty-
two departments that comprise the Department of Homeland
Security. Most people know that Customs and Border Protection, TSA, and FEMA belong to DHS. But many, including
those in Congress, don't realize that when DHS was formed
after 9/11, it absorbed the Coast Guard, Secret Service, the
Nuclear Incident Response Team, Center for Domestic
Preparedness, the Science and Technology Directorate, the
Office of Cybersecurity, and the Office of Infrastructure
Protection. The scenarios for what could go wrong if critical
personnel were to lose consciousness for a half-second would
impact and demand responses from all of them.

Margaret left off departments like the Plum Island Animal
Disease Center, the Animal Plant and Inspection Service, and
a few other four and five-letter departments. She's sure she'll
get blowback later from those excluded because egos always
want to be *in the room*. However, fourteen department heads
plus the Director of Cyber Command, the Secretary of
Defense, the Secretary of State, and the FBI director are

attending. With Michelle and Monica included, the meeting is unwieldy enough as it is.

Roughly half of those invited are physically in Conference Room Two, and the other half are small boxed-in faces on a wall-size video-conference screen. Margaret's assistant wheels in a cart with carafes of coffee and fresh-baked Danish. The warm sweet smell of them goes unnoticed.

Roger Brickman enters through a back door. Without a smile, he raises two hands to calm the chatter and sits. "OK, ladies and gentlemen. Glad you could make it one way or another. We're on a tight timeline. Could be days, but is more likely to be hours. We'll know that soon. The question before you is this..."

Margaret loads a slide up on the wall screen.

National Security Question—Priority One
If all critical personnel (pilots, surgeons, etc.) were to lose consciousness for a half-second, what could go wrong?

Margaret rolls out the last line on the slide:

How do we prevent accidents, deaths, and potential destruction from a half-second global loss of consciousness?

An uproar, like a tsunami, washes over the room. Brickman raises his hands again and shouts, "Shut up!"

Others hiss, "Shhh." The din settles.

"This is how we're going to do this. We're going to brainstorm part one of the question—what could go wrong. Then we'll prioritize the list in terms of most to least cost in human lives, disruption, and destruction. Finally, we'll assign an action and an owner, one of you, to each priority item. Is that clear?"

There are nods as Brickman tries to read their faces. He picks up a grimace from Sandra Weatherford of the National Infrastructure Protection Center. "What is it, Sandra?"

Weatherford squirms in her seat and says, "And how many months do we have to figure this out?"

Brickman jumps on the question. "We're going to do it all right here, right now. We'll take whatever time we need, but that will be limited by changing facts on the ground. Let's not waste time complaining. Fire off whatever *what-ifs* you can think of now, and Margaret will type them out on the big screen. Go!"

Monica, who is sitting behind the table full of bureaucrats, raises her hand.

Brickman smirks. "This is Monica Sunborn. She's, er... a consultant for the department."

"I have a few," Monica says. Then she rapid fires faster than Margaret can type:

"Pilots, not flying-by-wire, crash on landing or taking off.

Helicopters crash

Surgeon scalpels slip, nick arteries

Bus drivers blow through red lights and crash

Trains miss stop signals

Tailgating drivers of cars and trucks on highways pile up."

Margaret raises a hand to slow Monica so she can catch up.

"I have more," Monica says. "Should I continue?"

"No, let's give the others a chance, and if they miss anything on your list, you can add it at the end."

Monica's cheeks turn pink. She nods.

For thirty minutes, the assembled fire out scenarios until the ideas peter out.

"C'mon, in brainstorming, some of the best ideas come at the end. Anymore?" Brickman asks.

Monica raises her hand again. Margaret smiles.

Brickman sighs. "Yes, Monica. What else have you got?"

Monica kicks into high gear again.

"Astronauts docking at International Space Station lapse and crash.

Soldiers firing at the enemy miss and hit innocent civilians.

And, of course, if you're about to putt on the 18th green, you'd miss."

The golf catastrophe draws a collective chuckle.

"This is serious," Brickman says. "I don't think golfers will make the top priority list. Anyone else?"

The department heads offer a few more, followed by an uneasy silence.

Daniel Kennedy's face is ashen. "Wait, whatever you come up with here applies not just to us, but the rest of the world. I'd need to alert all global leaders, even our enemies. Half of them won't believe it, and we'd need time to get to them all and give them time to prepare."

"Yep, makes sense," Brickman says. "It's a bitch, I know. When we're done here, you can take whatever you come up with to your people."

"How much time do we *really* have?"

Brickman checks his watch. "Forty-hours tops. That's the deadline we have when the threat becomes real." He rises. "OK, there's more, but this gives us enough to start with. I want you to discuss each one for a maximum of five minutes each. Margaret, you time them and stop the discussion at five. When you're done, I want you all to assign a severity number to each item on the list from one to ten. Ten being the most critical and severe. Then you'll give your tallies to Margaret. Last, as a group, we'll take the top fifty most critical, decide on an action, and I'll assign it to one of you.

"For example, you can bet aviation will be high on the list. So, the action might be to ground all the planes or just keeping them all in the air on autopilot during the half-second outage. In that case, we'd have Ruby Dykstra from TSA get with the FAA ASAP to coordinate. See, I can do government-speak with the best of them."

A nervous laugh and Ruby says, "Will you give us an exact time for this interruption?"

"I was waiting for one of you geniuses to ask that question. The answer is *yes*. We'll be in control of the timing. We'll contact you all as soon as we have a time certain," Brickman answers.

Ruby persists. "But why have an outage in the first place?"

"That one is above your clearance levels. Just trust me, we wouldn't take this enormous risk unless we were stopping an even greater threat."

"Like what happened in Char;otte or at the State of the Union?" another asks.

"Eighteen times worse," Brickman says. "So, get to work. I have to duck out for a few minutes to check on something. Michelle Hadar will be your moderator in the meantime. Go."

Brickman turns and exits out the rear door. All the department heads turn and stare at Michelle.

Ersari studies the monitors that cover the walls of her new headquarters aboard the *Spirit of the Earth*. She has Cleveland on Screen One and other cities in an array on the other screens. In her mind, she replays what only took place a few hours ago.

It was like a dream. Her smartphone pinged with a cha-ching sound. She flipped it open and smiled. "Well, I'll be damned."

The pilot swiveled in his chair and looked up at her. "What is it?"

She turned the screen toward him. "Take a look at this."

His eyes widened. The message from their Swiss Bank said *New Deposit confirmed: $10,000,000,000.00.*

"God bless America," he said. "Don't mess around. Disperse the funds to all our other accounts."

She tapped the screen to initiate an automated action scattering pieces of the paid extortion money to fifty-two other accounts held by shell corporations across the globe from the Caymans to Romania. A few minutes later, the stream of confirmations came in. "It's ours now," she said. "I really didn't think they'd pay it. Now for the troop withdrawals."

"I don't know," the pilot said. "That was way too easy. They're up to something. I'm just not sure what."

"We got the money. Maybe we should hit Cleveland anyway. Just to shake them up," she said.

The pilot snarled. "Then they'd have no reason to trust us. They'd blow us out of the water."

"You're right. We're getting what we want. I just want it to hurt more, don't you?"

"We'll get that chance. Be patient, my sweet one." He reached for her waist and she stepped back.

"We agreed. That nonsense is over. Try that again and you'll pay."

The pilot licked his lips. "Understood. I'll look forward to it."

Ersari's phone rings with the Skizzy Mars' *Pay for You* ringtone. It snaps her out of her daydream. She answers.

"Just confirming, you got your money, right?" Brickman asks.

"We did, but you knew that. Now what about the troops?"

"What, not even a thank you? I'm sending you a link to a video feed now. You can see them packing up."

She clicks the link and sees a carousel of pictures labeled Stuttgart, Germany; Mons, Belgium; Durres, Albania; Orzysz, Poland; Campia Turzii, Romania; and more. In each frame, trucks are moving out, planes are lifting off, and tents are collapsing and being packed. "I'll need to verify this," she says.

"Of course," Brickman says. "Just hold up your end of the bargain or you better know how to swim."

"I don't like threats," she says.

"Look who's talking," he says.

She checks her watch. "You have forty-six hours left to get out all, not some of your troops. If you try to hide them or fall short, say goodbye to several million U.S. citizens. They won't remember what country they're in, or even their names when I'm done. Not sure how you handle that one."

Brickman bites his lip. "I have a meeting to get back to. I'll be in touch. Let's just stay on track here."

"It's all up to you." She clicks off.

Kennedy assassination. Everything stopped dead in its tracks. Schools, transportation, meetings, even surgeries. Everyone was glued to their TVs."

"OK, so what? What's that got to do with this?"

"You're right that there's no way your team can shut everything down piecemeal. You might save a few lives but lose a heck of a lot more. We need something dramatic, global even, that freezes everything all at once."

"Agreed. What's your idea?"

"We can't and we wouldn't recreate a 9/11, but we could fake an assassination of the president."

"Sam, you've really lost it now."

"Hear me out. I was only a kid when Kennedy was assassinated. Like everyone else that day, I remember exactly where I was. I was six years old and waiting at a bus stop with my mother in Irvington, New Jersey. Suddenly people poured into the streets, stopping traffic, and yelling, 'Somebody shot the president! Somebody shot the president.' There was a collective wail from all the strangers on that street and across the nation. My mother grabbed me by the hand and led me to the window of a nearby appliance store where we watched the breaking news on the TVs in the window along with a gathered crowd. We were riveted, waiting for the inevitable bad news that came from Parkland Memorial Hospital. Everything stopped—not just here, but all over the world."

"Yeah, that was terrible, but what's that got to—? Wait, you want us to fake an assassination of President Longford?"

"Yes, and I know you employ an entire team that has studied and created deep fake propaganda videos. I've seen a few you made of foreign leaders saying incendiary things they would never say."

Brickman groans. "That's classified."

I ignore his knee-jerk reaction. "I am suggesting you create fake videos of an assassination of President Longford. That you circulate it to the news media. That you do it in the next hour and then issue follow-up reports of her death over the next two hours. You can always take it back afterward or blame it on a Russian disinformation campaign. The point is to distract the nation so completely during the shutdown that it freezes ninety percent of all activities. But you've got to do it in the next hour, which will give the news time to spread and paralyze the nation and the rest of the world."

"In my twenty-two years in the service of my country, that is the craziest fucking idea I have ever heard."

"Thank you. Got a better one?"

"We can take more time, right? I mean, Frank can push the button whenever we ask him to up to Ersari's forty-eight-hour deadline." He looks up at the five wall clocks that show Washington, London, Moscow, Beijing, and Tokyo times. "We have forty-three hours left."

"Do you want to take all that time and risk Ersari's either figuring out what we're up to or setting things in motion just out of spite?" I ask.

Brickman scratches his head and looks at Patricia Sutherland, Director of Cyber Command, and Rick Koselke, his deputy director of the Office of Cybersecurity and Communications. "I know enough to know creating these types of videos takes time, a lot of time. Can we do this that fast?"

Sutherland blushes. "We actually have this scenario queued up."

"What? Why would you have this in the can?"

"Some of our computer science interns created presidential assassination videos as a training exercise. We never envisioned them being used for real," she says.

"I want to see these videos now. Then if my sanity departs, I'd need to convince Longford to let us engage in this charade.

I'm sure she would jump at the chance to be knocked off after the year she's had. Thanks, Sam. You've just taken me out of the frying pan and dropped me into the septic tank."

"Mixed metaphor, but you're welcome."

"Fuck you, Sam."

76

NOT A ROSE GARDEN

President Longford, alone in the Oval, stands at the window overlooking the rose garden. There are no flowers there, it being the dead of winter, but the green grass still peeks through the light snow covering. The sky is a crisp, oblivious blue with a smattering of cotton ball clouds. Maybe there is an answer far out there that will give us all peace someday, she thinks. For now, it seems my job is dodging bullets.

The president's chief of staff, Donna Swenson, gently knocks and enters, breaking the president away from her daydream.

"Secretary Brickman is here to see you, Madam President."

Her eyes still fixed on the sky, the president says, "Send him in."

Breathing heavily, Brickman enters. "Madame President?"

With her back turned, she says, "Roger, I don't believe any one man or woman, no matter how strong and capable they may be, can do this job."

Still standing, Roger says, "That's why you have us, the cabinet and advisers, behind you."

"Yes, and you are very capable, but there is only one final decision maker who can make or break us all. That's me at the moment, but it shouldn't be that way. It's a structural flaw. The founding fathers didn't contemplate a federal government with two million employees, over a hundred agencies dealing with everything from nuclear, chemical, and domestic threats to feeding the poor. Otherwise, they wouldn't have put one person in charge. I mean what if the electorate makes a mistake, like electing a smooth-talking charlatan or a thief or a counterspy for that matter. We'd all be screwed."

"There're checks and balances."

"Really, Roger? Don't be so naive." She turns and faces him. "Forget what I said. It's just the tired musings of an old lady. Sit down. Now, why did you want to see me? Any update on Ersari's latest threat?"

Brickman clears his throat. "You know we paid her the money, right?"

"Yes, to buy time, you said, some very expensive time. So what's next?"

"In less than two hours, Einstein and Sunborn will have a way to shut her down. There's only one problem, and it's a big one. In order to pull it off, they need to shut everyone's consciousness down for a half-second."

"They can do that, for everyone in the whole world?"

"Yeah, it's complicated. They can do it, but it must be one hundred percent of everyone to stop Ersari. It's our only option right now. Einstein will initiate on our signal. Our concern is the massive damage that a half-second unplugged can cause, like pilots crashing, surgeons cutting arteries—"

"Or releasing the dead man's switch."

"Huh?"

"Some maniac with a bomb holding down a button that when released blows up a bunch of people."

"I know what a deadman's switch is. We just hadn't thought of that one."

"I guess it's our job to imagine the worst that can happen and stop it, right?"

"Yes, which is why I'm here. I just met with my agency heads, plus FBI and State. We came up with a long list of what-could-go-wrongs. We can't stop them all in time here, not to mention around the globe."

"Are you sure the medicine isn't worse than the disease here?"

"We're sure. Plus, the medicine, as you call it, is a once-and-done. Yet, Ersari's threat, left unchecked, could lead to an ever-growing string of catastrophes."

"You're paying her off. What makes you believe she'll hold up her end of the bargain and quit attacking us?"

"By paying her off, do you mean you're actually willing to cave and pull all our troops out of foreign countries?"

The president blows out a breath. "Oh yeah, that. I was just thinking about the money. No, we can't undermine global security. I know we're just buying time or faking it there too."

"OK. So back to the worst that can happen. Sam Sunborn has come up with a crazy idea that may shut almost everything down and save more lives during the half-second outage."

"I'm listening."

Brickman interlaces his fingers. "You may want to sit down for this. I have a video to show you."

He pulls out his tablet. Longford takes a seat on the sofa next to him. "What's the video?"

"It's your assassination."

77

HOW'S EVAN?

My eyes dart from screen to screen. There are four virtual monitors in front of me now. One camera is hacked aboard the *Spirit of the Earth,* watching Jennie Lee Ersari's every move. Another is in the Oval. Brickman has bigger balls than I gave him credit for. He's showing the president the deep fake video of her bogus assassination. I play the phony video up on another monitor. The image I see is her walking across the South Lawn of the White House to board Marine One, her helicopter. A fake news anchor is in the foreground reporting that the president is flying to Camp David for the holidays. There is a dusting of snow on the ground. Her hair is blowing from the blast coming off the chopper's rotors. I can almost smell the exhaust from the engine. She waves to no one in particular off-screen. This ritual walk to Marine One is a scene we have witnessed a thousand times before, starring the president du jour.

As Longford ascends the six steps to Marine One's door, she hesitates. Her grip tightens on the handrail. Blotches of red blossom on the back of her camel hair overcoat, like rose petals opening in slow motion. She falters, tumbling backwards down the steps. The image wobbles and shakes. A half-dozen secret service agents in dark suits rush to the president, their bodies blocking the camera's view. The image flickers and goes to white snow. It's a harrowing scene that looks so real, I can't be sure it's a fake.

My anxiety meter goes into the red zone. *Breathe*, Frank's voice echoes in my head. I try to calm down and remember I suggested this plan. But how did they create that video this fast? Just curious—I'll find out later. On the fourth screen, the DHS department heads and cabinet secretaries are arguing over their what-could-go-wrong and what-do-we-do-about-it lists. At the head of the table, Michelle fights to keep the discussion focused. Sitting in the back, I see Monica taking notes.

I ring her cell. She looks down and takes out her phone. She nods to Michelle and quietly creeps from the room. She closes the door behind her and steps into the faintly lit hallway.

"What is it?" she asks. "I can't talk long."

"Hello to you, too. How's it going there?"

"The usual bullshit and ego battles I remember from my corporate years. Nothing changes. Hopefully, we can agree on some meaningful actions. Brickman left after you called. Michelle's trying, but I don't think they will decide anything until he returns."

"I know. I've been watching your room, as well as Brickman, pitching my idea to Longford. It's a wild-ass Hail Mary, but there's not enough time for a methodical, logistical response."

"I'm not sure I should be here. What am I contributing?" Monica asks.

"I heard you. You had more ideas than all of those other donkeys, I mean experienced professionals, offered."

"Thanks, but as you said, there may not be enough time for what we're discussing to do any good. Besides, I miss Evan. I'm a mother first. I've been away too long. Whatever happens, I'm going home tomorrow. I won't get sucked into this never-ending crisis vortex and swirl down the drain. I watched it happen to you. Firefighters only see fires until they get burned."

What can I say? Maybe she's right in one way, and maybe not in another. "Life is all about decisions. Sometimes we make mistakes." I want to say good intentions have to count for something, but I think better of it. I change the subject. "How's Evan? Have you spoken to him today?"

"I tried calling him and Charlotte twice. Neither of them answered. Then I got stuck in this meeting. It could be the shitstorm going on around me, but I have a bad feeling. Will you keep trying them while I go back inside? When you reach him, just text me to let me know he's OK."

"Remember, you wanted him to think I'm dead so he and you could move on."

"I changed my mind. Just keep calling."

Her worry hits me deep in the gut. "Sure, I'll do it right now and keep trying until I reach him."

"Thanks, gotta go."

I close my eyes. "I love you."

"I know," she says.

78

BREAKING NEWS

Breaking News flashes across the crawl on CNN, Fox, and MSNBC. The video of the president being shot plays on a loop as the stunned reporters fight back tears. Social media blazes with tweets and posts of concern, outrage, and conspiracy theories.

To sell the story, Marine One makes the ten-minute flight to Walter Reed where the president's body double is rushed on a covered gurney inside. Only her imposter's face with ghostly white makeup is exposed. A mass of reporters is being held back by police and Secret service agents just beyond the entrance.

Besides having made the video in advance, the astute interns, with support from their supervisors, had rehearsed a Code Brown with the head surgeon, Dr. Jim Jorritsma, and two of the nurses. They hurried the body double into isolation in the Presidential Suite. The hospital has a dedicated space with its own ICU, kitchen, dining room, sitting rooms, and secure conference room, all on reserve 24/7/365 exclusively for the president and her staff. It is heavily guarded by Secret Service and under full White House control. What seemed like a whimsical exercise by the interns, that no one involved thought would ever happen, is now in high gear.

Brickman, now back in the meeting at DHS, finishes briefing the department heads and secretaries. "I assume you have made your calls alerting the FAA and initiated other measures you could identify." Heads nod and Brickman continues. "I asked Michelle to have you make your calls from here and remain for a reason. We must keep the fake video and the president's condition top secret until this is over. Accordingly, Michelle will now collect your cell phones and you will remain here for the next two hours until this is concluded."

Monica hesitates and then drops her phone in the basket Michelle passes around. All she can think about now is Evan, her sweet little boy, with neither his father nor his mother there to protect him.

A roar of protests erupts with shouts. Ten people are talking at once.

"Quiet," Brickman shouts over the din. When the group settles down, he continues. "Don't feel bad, you're not alone." He turns to face the screen and addresses the seven remote-attending department heads. "If you haven't seen them already, a U.S. Marshall will arrive at your location. You will hand him or her your phone and remain in place with the marshal until I give the all-clear. Understood?"

The bewildered faces on the screen are silent.

"Good," Brickman says. "Now I believe our little ruse is having the desired effect. Let's check the news." He nods to Michelle, who taps a remote.

On the large wall monitor, the image of Dr. Jorritsma appears at a podium outside Walter Reed. Despite the winter chill, he stands bare headed in his white doctor's jacket, his thinning silver hair blowing in the breeze. Following the script the White House provided, he says, "Ladies and gentlemen, I'll read a brief statement. No questions at this time." After stating that the president is in critical condition, the situation is fluid, and it is touch-and-go, the reporters barrage him with questions. The doctor offers a faint smile, waves, and walks back through the hospital's front door.

The news anchor makes a few comments and then shows a scene of New York's Times Square filled with speechless onlookers, their heads up gazing at the billboard displays showing the hospital and replays of the shooting. Similar scenes of life on hold in Tokyo, London, Paris, Sydney, and Cairo carousel across the screen. A new crawl scrolls across the bottom of the screen: "The F.A.A. has grounded all planes in the U.S... Washington, D.C. is on lockdown."

Brickman looks at Secretary of State Kennedy. "I know we've got our hands full here, but how did you make out with the international calls?"

"Yeah, thanks for that lead time. We contacted all our embassies and asked the ambassadors to do whatever they could to shut things down. With so little time and the climate of distrust for America, I don't know how effective their last-minute entreaties were. Our allies seemed receptive but were unsure if they had enough time to do much. China and Russia seemed to smell blood in the water. So Chuck has put our troops in the air and on the ground on high alert."

"Good, I think we're as ready as we can be under the circumstances. I'm giving the green light to Sam Sunborn." Brickman looks at his watch, 5:15. I suggest you all stay seated. Blink will happen in approximately nine minutes."

79

OPERATION BLINK

The seas are choppy in the North Atlantic as a storm front moves through. The ten-foot waves splash over the *Spirit of the Earth* and the usually stable cargo ship sways side-to-side. The crew battens down the hatches. To steady herself, Ersari grips a stanchion inside her control room, her eyes glued to the wall screens. The news of the assassination attempt on the American president and the reaction around the world flicker by. "Can you believe this bullshit?" The ship rocks hard to port, and she stutter-steps to keep her balance. "What does this mean for our deal and our plans?"

"It's a temporary distraction," the pilot says.

"I don't believe this is happening," she says.

"Maybe it isn't," he says.

"What do you mean?" She points at the screen. "Can't you see it?"

"What if they're faking it to throw us off?"

"Huh? The reporters, the doctors, the hospital, everything? They couldn't pull all that off so seamlessly in a few hours. If you could do it at all, it would take months of planning."

"I told you they're up to something. We just haven't figured out what it is yet."

Captain Vorderstrasse makes his way to Ersari, grasping handholds along the way. "Aye, Ms. Ersari. Who were ye talkin' to right then?"

Ersari snaps out of her daydream. She stands alone. The pilot is a fantasy, an alter ego of sorts, that seems so real to her, especially now when she needs him. "I was thinking out loud, Captain. Sometimes it helps me work to speak my thoughts."

The captain smiles. "Aye, if I did that, I'd been slapped by every lass in Dublin." Sensing this was no time for humor, the captain asks, "Where to now, Miss? We're taking on some water. We can't sit here in 'dis storm."

They both turn toward a sidewall monitor showing weather radar. The sweep of the Doppler radar refresh shows the storm moving rapidly to the east.

"Head west, back toward Baltimore. Once you clear the storm, hold your position until I give further instructions," Ersari says.

"Aye, aye Miss," the captain says, making his way from handhold to handhold until he reaches a phone. He barks several orders to the bridge, hangs up, and nods to her. *The money's good, but what in the blazes have I gotten into?* he thinks.

"It's almost time, Frank," I say.

Frank's gaze flicks from one virtual display to another. "I'm ready."

"I'm waiting for a signal from Brickman. Question, you're going to shut down the consciousness of everyone on the world for a half-second and—"

Frank grins. "I've shaved that down to .3146 seconds."

I laugh. "Your lucky number, I suppose. Anyway, what happens to us, you and me, during that split-second blink?"

"You and I are digital. So we're not conscious in the physical sense. Besides, I've got to perform the critical task during that .3146 on Jennie Lee Ersari. That's the point of this whole thing and all the attendant risk that goes with it."

"But what if you're wrong? You flip the switch, and it shuts us down too?"

"I thought of that. I don't believe that will happen, but I'm setting an automatic script to run the task just in case I can't do it for some reason. To be more precise, with a window of only a fraction of a second, this requires micro-finite timing. No human could do it manually and hit the mark. I have to rely on my program to thread that micro-second needle."

"Understood... OK, I got the text from Roger. It's a *go*."

"Right, I'm starting the timer now."

Frank and I stare at the digital stopwatch on our screens. Brickman, the secretaries, the DHS department heads, Monica, and Michelle fixate on the digital timer on their wall monitor. In defense and security headquarters from London to Paris, Nairobi to Beijing, Buenos Aires to Moscow, those responsible for protecting their countries and its citizens all focus at the same countdown.

10... 9... 8... 7... 6... 5... 4... 3... 2...

80

OOPS!

Beads of sweat sprout on Brickman's brow. The tension in the room is molasses thick and smells like rotten eggs. Monica gazes up at the ceiling as if looking for some kind of divine signal. Michelle says a silent prayer from the Quran.

5... 4... 3... 2. The timer freezes at two, the number blinking in the dead silence of the DHS conference room and rooms just like it around the world.

"What the fuck?" Brickman shouts.

His outburst startles and shakes everyone in the room as if breaking a spell.

Being the only one left in the room with a cell phone, Brickman speed dials me. "What's going on?"

"Hold a second," I say and look at Frank.

Frank holds up one finger.

"Breathe, Roger," I continue. "I'm guessing Frank found an issue, and he's fixing it now."

"Guessing? Issue? Sunborn, we're all fucked, and this was your idea, remember."

I'm not sure what to say. Funny how when things go wrong,

"Aye, aye." Keator rings off and swirls a finger in the air. The two security guards, Deter Horst and Jennifer Blank, manning the door, move in on Ersari. She thrashes and kicks Horst in the groin. He doubles over. Jennie Lee grabs Horst's Glock and waves it in the air. Blank backs away. The other men and women, the techs, duck under their desks.

"Calm down, ma'am. We don't want anyone to get hurt," Blank says.

Ersari fires a shot that barely misses Blank and clanks off the hull. She spins in the other direction, blindly firing two more shots. Horst looks up and then charges, tackling Ersari like a middle linebacker. She tumbles facedown on the steel floor, the gun bouncing from her hand. She struggles to rise, kicks Horst in the face, and breaks free. Blank rushes toward her. Ersari growls at her, baring her teeth, and charges. She knocks her down and seizes her throat. Horst, wielding a steel pipe, raises it up, then drops it hard across the back of Ersari's head. The crunch of metal meeting bone echoes throughout the chamber. Ersari crumbles to the floor, motionless. Drops of scarlet ooze from her nose and mouth.

81

WAKE UP CALL

Our sense of time is quite different from actual time if time exists at all. Frank and I are alert and scan the scenes from around the globe. That .3146 seconds seemed to me like a month in slow motion.

A rogue wave of anxiety ripples from my stomach to my head. "Frank, is it over? Did it happen? Did it stop? Did you do what you had to?"

Frank points to the scene of the burning wreckage of Aeroflot 777 that was on route to Vladivostok, ambulances, fire trucks, people on stretchers, faces covered. His eyes well up. "It's over, but at what cost?"

I put a hand on his shoulder. "I can see the downside. It's all over our screens. It makes me want to throw up, but did we stop her?"

Frank taps a few keys and the image of Ersari pinned to the floor aboard the *Spirit of the Earth* appears. A man and a woman are holding her down. "Yes, that part seemed to work. During that .3146 seconds, my program shut down the memories, and effectively the consciousness, of everyone on the planet including Ersari. That allowed me to unlock her encrypted memory password, log in, and change it. Her mind and her memories are permanently disabled. She is out of commission, but that doesn't mean she didn't have some failsafe backup that would kick in, like a dead man's switch that we don't yet know about."

"Maybe, but you did it. I'm going to check in with Brickman and Monica."

Brickman shakes his head from side to side. Is this what a stroke feels like? he wonders. He looks around the room. "Are you all OK?"

There's a low rumble of voices.

Brickman seems startled by Monica's tortured expression. "Monica, are you OK?"

"A wicked headache," she replies, her hands shaking. "I want my phone now. I need to make a call."

Michelle queues up the news feeds from around the world, then hands around the bin containing everyone's phones.

"Check in with your departments. I need damage reports," Brickman says. "Michelle, get me an update on Ersari."

Kennedy from State looks up from his phone. "I've got a hundred plus texts from our ambassadors. Our allies and enemies alike are pissed. This is a shitshow. I hope it was worth it. I've got to get back to my office. I hope this doesn't lead to something much bigger."

"Like what?" Monica asks.

"Like the Russians or the Chinese consider what we did an unprovoked attack and decide to strike back. Think chemical, nuclear, cyber." Kennedy stands. "I've got major cleanup to do. Buckle up, friends."

Brickman nods. Kennedy exits, slamming the door behind him. The others hurriedly check their phones and look up at Brickman. He gets the silent message. "OK, OK. Go do what you must."

The department heads and staff rush out the door. Only Monica, Michelle, Hagar from Defense, and Roger Brickman remain. Brickman holds up his phone. "A text from Sunborn. He says Ersari is down. His concern now is any backup plan she may have had."

Hagar slams his fist on the table. "Well then, do I order the Nebraska to take out Ersari's ship?"

"Do your own assessment, general, and let's coordinate our response. If Ersari is down, that should give us a window to figure out what to do."

Hagar looks at the scenes of plane crashes and car accidents flashing on the screen. "If our enemies think we did this as an attack on them, we're in for it. You better get the president right away. Kennedy won't be enough—she has to calm things down now."

"You're right," Brickman says. "She's probably bouncing off the walls as it is. Let's both head over to the White House. I'm sure she'd be calling us to the Sit Room anyway."

"She's back at the White House?" Hagar smirks. "That was a quick recovery."

"She never left. Remember, the assassination was all a big ruse. She'll need to deal with the fallout from that too," Brickman says.

"She'll have a lot of 'splainin' to do," Michelle says.

"I'll see you there in ten," Hagar says, turns, and leaves.

Brickman stands and heads for the door with Michelle

when he notices Monica still sitting, catatonic in her seat, staring blankly at her phone. "Monica, Monica." He shakes her. "What is it?"

Monica grunts. "It's Evan, my son. There's been an accident."

82

KABOOM

For Delbert Bascue, life has gone from the mundane to the surreal to total insanity in less than seventy-two hours. He watches as the two guards and a medic help Jennie Lee Ersari from the room. The sound of the hatch closing reverberates in the still air. Bascue pops a Tic Tac in his mouth. The minty taste and smell seem to clear his head. He flips open his notebook and scribbles a few lines. *The reporter is back*, he thinks. "Captain V. Now what happens?" Delbert asks.

"I'll await orders from her second," V says.

"And who would that be?"

"Gobshite, I was never a knowin' what you're supposed to be. Well, what are ye doin' here?"

"Ms. Ersari, um, hired me to record this whole thing. I'm a reporter."

"Are ye now?"

"Yes, so who is her second-in-command?"

"Well, no harm, I suppose. You ain't a goin' nowhere. It's that guy she calls Pickles. What kinda' name is that? I paged him. Should be here in a minute. Then you'se can ask him all y'ur questions. I got a ship to sail."

Suddenly, there are three blasts from what sounds like an old car horn. A young hairless man wearing a headset turns to Captain V. "We've got two incoming."

V grabs the comm and bellows to the bridge, "Evasive maneuvers now. Decoys overboard."

Seconds later, an ear-splitting explosion and the *Spirit of the Earth* rocks from the first impact. It throws those standing to the deck. V staggers to his feet. "Status?"

"We're hit midship, taking on water," the radioman says. "Ten seconds till—"

The second torpedo from the Nebraska blows a basketball-size hole in the bow, then detonates. Fire and smoke erupt into the outside air. The ship lists to starboard and then rocks forward. Water fills the engine room, killing all power and filling the lungs of the six engineers below. The stern of the ship rises up as the bow sinks below the surface. The red and blue cargo containers tumble like Legos, crushing the ship's mast and tumbling into the salty water.

Screams and shouts fill Ersari's computer quarters as the icy waters rise to shoulder level. Delbert climbs on a tilting desk to keep his head above water. He gasps for air. Images of Richelle and Sherry flicker past in his mind. He's pushing a young Richelle in a swing at the park. He turns to Sherry who tilts her head and flashes him a warm smile. She gives him a lingering kiss on the lips. And then he closes his eyes for the last time. *I wish I had a cigarette*, he thinks.

The cameras are hastily arranged in the Oval Office. President Langford sits at the Resolute desk. The irony that the desk was made from the oak timbers of the sunken HMS Resolute is not lost on her. Donna Thompson, Longford's communications director, lowers her hand and points at Longford.

She begins. "Ladies and gentlemen. I come to you from the Oval Office to address not only the citizens of the United States but all the citizens and their leaders around the world. We have just faced down the greatest threat to global humanity, greater than the world wars, greater than all the pandemics. Time was not on our side. We had to act in the best interest of the greatest number of people. I wish we'd had more time to prepare, more time to coordinate efforts both internally and externally with both our friends and our adversaries to minimize the costs of the actions we had to take."

Longford raises a glass of water, takes a sip, and continues. "I know the cost in lives and property was steep. My heart goes out to those innocent victims and their families affected. I implore leaders around the globe for patience, and you, the people, for understanding as I explain what has transpired in the last forty-eight hours, the attempted assassination, the actions we took, and..."

A tiny stream of bubbles rise as the Triton submersible, the *Kiss Off*, puts several hundred yards distance between itself and the sinking *Spirit of the Earth*, carefully obscuring its sonar and visual signature by keeping the cargo ship directly in line between itself and the USS Nebraska. As soon as the cargo ship drops below the surface on its way to a watery grave, the Triton kills even its quiet electric thrusters and waits.

After the better part of an hour, the Nebraska turns one-hundred and eighty degrees south-by-southwest heading back to base.

The man in black pants and black turtleneck swirls his finger in the air and the Triton's pilot restarts the motor. "Where to, sir?"

Pickles answers, "Time for Plan B. Set a course ninety-two degrees southwest."

"Destination?"

"We're going to do a little sightseeing... on the Potomac."

83

POSTMORTEM

I know it before I pick up Monica's call. "I'm so sorry, sweetheart. I wish I could've been there."

"I understand now. I fell into the same foolish trap you did, and now I've paid the ultimate price, Evan's death," Monica says.

I lower my voice to a whisper. "We paid."

"I'm not getting into it again with you. I have two funerals to plan, yours and his."

"Please tell me what happened."

"I'm back home and here with Charlotte right now. She's a total wreck. Evan was kicking a soccer ball around in the front yard. He chased it into the street. An asshole driving a BMW was doing sixty in a thirty-mile-an-hour zone, slammed into our little boy, tossing him fifty yards into a tree. It killed him on impact. This is all too much, Sam."

I hear Monica choking back tears. I have a powerful urge to hug her, to comfort her, to feel the moisture of her tears on my cheeks, but I can't do it. If there's a hell, I'm in the tenth circle.

"Monica, it's no consolation, but you did help save countless lives, maybe millions..." I regret saying that the second the words leave my lips.

"Yeah, we agree on one thing. It's no consolation."

"We still have each other, right?"

"Not anymore. Tell Frank to break that link between us."

"OK, but you'll need to go back to the lab so Bart can remove the chip in your neck." I can't believe I just said that. I mean, I wanted to tell her, but timing is everything.

"What? What are you talking about, a chip? How did he do that?"

"It's part of what Frank did to give you the connection to my memories. He didn't tell me either until after he inserted it."

"How long have you known about this chip, and why didn't you tell me?"

I take a deep breath and sigh. I don't know what to say.

But before I can answer, Monica says, "It doesn't matter. I don't want to see you or hear from you again. I loved you then, but it's over now. Goodbye, Sam."

"But Monica—" The line goes dead.

"I'm glad that's over," Michelle says as she sips her double espresso outside the Hard Times Cafe in Old Town Alexandria. The air is unseasonably warm, the sky turquoise, and the aroma of fresh-baked bread lingers.

"I just wish we hadn't lost so many lives and flushed ten billion dollars down the toilet," Rich says.

"It could've been much worse," Michelle says.

"Ugh, I hate that phrase. It usually goes along with *thoughts and prayers*. But you're right. It could've been catastrophic. Now the politicians and generals will come up with another line I hate, *a proportionate response.*"

"Don't be such a downer. We'll always have enemies. We're the good guys trying to do our best, remember? But there's still something I don't get."

"You, the M.I.T., Ph.D. genius don't get something?"

"Maybe it's because I'm a girl, not smart like you..." She takes a bite from her cranberry muffin and throws the other half at Rich, hitting him in the nose.

Rich gapes at her, mouth wide open. "Hey, what's that for?"

"Old time's sake," she says.

They both laugh.

"OK, seriously, what don't you get?"

Michelle finishes chewing and wipes her lips with a napkin. "If Ashaki had the secret to hack people's memories and Ersari stole it from her, how do we know she's the only one with the secret besides Frank? Wouldn't her bosses, the Russians, have the neural weapon now too, which means they might use it against us?"

"That same anxiety kept me up last night. So I called Anthony George at NSA at 2:00 am. He wasn't too thrilled."

"And?"

"They had been all over this. While Ersari was aboard the *Spirit*, they intercepted her communications with the Center. The Russians wanted Ersari to turn over the neural weapon she had stolen from LaSalam, but she wouldn't do it."

"Did he say why?"

"Think about it. If she turns over the deadliest weapon humankind has ever discovered, what would they need her for? She kept it as insurance in case the Center had any ideas about making her disappear."

"A fair assumption, knowing the way they operate. But why would they stand for her holding out on them?"

"I'm sure they didn't like it and would try anything and everything to get their hands on that weapon, but for the moment they had no choice but to play nice with her. After all, she could've turned the weapon on *them*. For now, our assumption is that Ersari's secret weapon died with her and only Frank Einstein has access to it. Likewise, our government would like to put its mitts on that technology. They've tried, but Frank is adamant about at least trying to put that genie back in the bottle."

"Hard to believe she didn't share the secret with someone or hide it away somewhere."

Agreed, but that's a problem for another day," Rich says.

Michelle strokes Rich's cheek. "How about we go away for a weekend? We both need a break. They just made West Virginia's New River Gorge into a national park. It's only a few hours from here. The whitewater rafting on the Gauley is supposed to be spectacular."

"That's exactly what I need, more excitement." Rich snickers. "Besides, it's still cold outside."

Michelle slips her hand under the table and inches it up Rich's thigh. "I'll give you something warm *and* exciting."

"Now, you're talkin'." He grins.

A few moments later, Rich's phone vibrates. He looks down. "We've got to go."

"What is it?" Michelle asks.

"Something's happening on the Potomac."

"I'm so sorry about Evan," Frank says. "Is there anything I can do?"

I'm frozen, paralyzed. "You can bring him back."

"That was the plan, I mean the backup just in case," Frank says.

"I know. I need a minute. How will I explain this to Monica? She'll hate me even more."

Frank snickers. "Remember how I told you that even though it's accepted theory, I don't believe evolution is real. That we're way too complex beings to have evolved from fish and amoeba?"

"Yeah, I remember, but what has that got to do with Evan and Monica?"

"We're even way more complex than we think we are. Our ability to adapt transcends even the miraculous machine that is or was our bodies. Look at us. Evan will adapt to being digital— it's a good thing we uploaded him last year, and Monica will adapt to his being alive, at least the same way you are, in the Cloud."

"But she never adapted to me being digital."

"She will. If she still wants to be connected to Evan, she'll adapt."

"And what about me? Will she adapt to me?"

Frank nods. "That may take longer. I agree with you—at first, she will be very angry with you, but then she will be thankful for what you did with Evan. And I promise I will keep working on some safe way to get you, and now Evan, back physically to Monica and all the smells, tastes, and touches you sorely miss."

"I'm going to hold you to that," I say. "Because I have lived physically and now digitally, I now fathom deep in my gut that as humans, in whatever form, we are more than the sum of our parts. You and I are not just ones and zeros. What that extra essence is, that soul? Well, I'll need to get back to you on that."

The End

<<<<>>>>

AUTHOR'S NOTE

Most of the science and technology in this book are currently available and being deployed. Other aspects, such as the Zero Point Field and universal consciousness, are theoretical. Meanwhile, Google, Facebook, Amazon, and Elon Musk's Neuralink are investing billions of dollars to develop the capability to digitize and upload our brains to the Cloud. If you are as curious as I was about some of this amazing stuff, here are some links to further information and insights on the topics mentioned in *Still Not Dead.*

Frontotemporal Dementia — What Happened to Lee? https://www.wired.com/story/lee-holloway-devastating-decline-brilliant-young-coder/

A New Way of Looking at Consciousness: https://www.ncbi.nlm.nih.gov/pmc/articles/PMC6085561/

Indistinguishable Obfuscation: https://www.

quantamagazine.org/computer-scientists-achieve-crown-jewel-of-cryptography-20201110/

Complete Guide to Facial Recognition Technology: https://www.pandasecurity.com/mediacenter/panda-security/facial-recognition-technology

What is Amnesia? https://www.medicalnewstoday.com/articles/9673

Rescue Radar™: https://www.sensoft.ca/products/rescue-radar

Smell-o-Vision: https://www.smithsonianmag.com/innovation/smell-o-vision-astrocolor-other-film-industry-inventions-that-proved-to-be-flops-180968295/

Neuralink Digital-to-Brain Connection: https://neuralink.com/

Brain Implants That Could Change Humanity: https://www.nytimes.com/2020/08/28/opinion/sunday/brain-machine-artificial-intelligence.html

Persistent Surveillance Systems: https://www.wsj.com/articles/when-battlefield-surveillance-comes-to-your-town-11564805394

Is the Internet Conscious? If It Were, How Would We Know? https://www.wired.com/story/is-the-internet-conscious-if-it-were-how-would-we-know/

Triton Deepview Submarine: https://tritonsubs.com/
subs/deepview/

**The Future of Bioprinting: A New Frontier in
Regenerative Healthcare** https://www.medicaldevice-
network.com/features/future-of-3d-bioprinting/

Persuading the Body to Regenerate Its Limbs:
https://www.newyorker.com/magazine/2021/05/10/
persuading-the-body-to-regenerate-its-limbs

LIKED STILL NOT DEAD?

Check out more adventures of Sam, Michelle, Rich and Al in the *NOT SO DEAD Series* or the *NOT SO DEAD Trilogy* by Charles Levin.

If you enjoyed *STILL NOT DEAD*, please consider leaving an unbiased review on Amazon, Audible, Goodreads or Bookbub to help spread the word.

You can learn more about this book and the author at www.charleslevin.com

Contact or follow the author at

Contact: charleslevin.com/contact

Facebook: facebook.com/Charles.Levin.Author

Instagram: @charleslevinauthor

Bookbub: bookbub.com/authors/charles-levin

Goodreads: goodreads.com/author/show/18896291.Charles_Levin

ACKNOWLEDGMENTS

I realized after writing the first Sam Sunborn novel, *NOT SO DEAD,* that writing a book is like digitizing your brain. A published author is uploading his or her mind, emotions and memories to the Cloud and interacting virtually with the readers. Thoughts to keystrokes to the printed or digital word to your eyes to your brain. It is a miracle, a techno-thriller in itself. But I did have help from other very talented and generous people. So maybe part of their minds are in this book too. For their help, I am extremely grateful. It takes a lot of talented people to make a great book.

Ben Hanafin for sharing his extensive knowledge as a helicopter pilot and inventor of the sHeli-Port.

The Captain and crew of the USS Nebraska and Pat Powers for hosting me for a few days at sea--a hundred miles out and six-hundred feet down. Sleeping in a bunk wedged between two live nuclear missile silos is not something I will soon forget.

Geoff Parker for his *half-second* ideas and suggestions.

Brian Buckley for sharing his decades of experience and detailed knowledge as a firefighter.

Judy Roth for her relentless editing and Gabriella Swartwood for her keen eye in catching everything we missed.

Ann Keeran for being a very insightful beta reader and cheerleader.

And the many readers who volunteered their names for characters to be "murdered in my next book."

And finally, Amy Levin, who endlessly supports my crazy endeavors.

ABOUT THE AUTHOR

Charlie is an author who has written three thriller novels, NOT SO DEAD, NOT SO GONE, and NOT SO DONE. Charlie's 26-year background in tech, degree in philosophy, and love of fast-paced thrillers are the brew that created them.

He lives in New Jersey with his wife, Amy, and has two sons, too far away in California.

 facebook.com/Charles.Levin.Author
 twitter.com/charlielevin
 instagram.com/charleslevinauthor

"In my twenty-five years of practice, I have never..." Lark says.

Dr. Saul Geier looks at his former student, long since an accomplished psychiatrist. He studies her unkempt, auburn hair and the powdered whiteness of her complexion interrupted by swollen hazel eyes. Then, he turns his gaze out the floor-to-ceiling windows of his tenth-story office on Fifth Avenue. "We've known each other for a long time, Susan. We used to discuss cases often until you surpassed your mentor. I don't take it personally. It's a point of pride for me that you've done so well. But why, after ten years, come to me now?"

Susan Lark clenches her fists and sucks in a deep breath. "It's not only that I'm stumped, which I am, but I might be losing my mind too. I didn't know whom else to turn to."

Geier's face seems to smile with wrinkles, his blue eyes piercing. "You probably didn't know since we lost touch, but I'm retiring today. I think at age ninety-two, it's finally time to hang it up. I don't know how many patients I've seen over the last sixty years, but most are gone now. I think what I'll miss most is this view of the city, the four seasons over Central Park, the blossoms in the Spring, the Winter snow blanketing the ponds and meadows, the bikers and joggers and baby carriages, the hawks and geese taking a rest stop during their southbound Fall journey. I have relished the seasons of life right here."

"I'm sorry to hear that. You did a lot of good over the years, and not just for your patients. I don't know where I'd be now without your guidance and your wisdom."

Geier takes out a pouch of Captain Black and taps some tobacco into his Stanwell. He hangs the pipe unlit from the corner of his mouth. He promised his wife he would quit smoking. So, for him, the smell of fresh tobacco is the next best thing.

"It's nice to hear you say that, but I'm tired. I look forward to sitting out on my deck in Montauk and, staring out over the waves, inhaling the salt air. That's enough for me now. But my door will always be open to you. It just won't be here. OK, so tell me about this case."

Susan hands Geier the patient's intake form. He reads the form aloud to himself, "Anxiety, depression, sleep changes, racing thoughts, gets exercise running. She's a writer--nothing terribly unusual here. Let me see your notes."

Susan's face flushes. "I can't do that."

"Why not? You know I'll keep them confidential."

"I destroyed them."

"What?! You can't do that. It's a cardinal sin--you could lose your license for that."

"I know that, but I couldn't risk someone ever reading them."

Geier rubs his fingers through his thin gray hair. "OK, then just tell me what's going on."

Susan stands and walks to the window. "You're right, it's a glorious view. You can see Central Park and all of Upper Manhattan from here." She turns back and points at the intake form. "About a month ago, that patient walked into my office. I had an immediate visceral reaction to her appearance. Yes, she was attractive, mid-forties, slender, and with a confident posture. My reaction was not sexual. Maybe, it was her haunting black eyes that seemed to go right through me. As if she's known me all my life, but we'd never met before. It was eerie."

"OK, you'd already lost your objectivity, I see. It happens."

"Yes, but aren't we supposed to observe everything about our patients, especially appearance and body language?"

"It's a fine line, isn't it? Go on."

Susan looks up as if reading something on the ceiling. "Angela Auger was a writer. She wrote fiction, thrillers."

"You're using the past tense. Is she dead or just no longer a patient?"

"I'll get to that. Anyway, she tells me a story about her writing that gets more and more disturbing, bizarre really."

Geier looks back at the form. "I know this name. I believe I read a few of her books."

"You probably have. She was very talented; a few of her novels made the bestseller lists. I think her greatest knack was making her readers want to turn the page. Once you started one of her novels, you couldn't put it down. Like me with potato chips and romance novels."

"That was my experience." He looks down at the end of his pipe and gives it a tap as if stoking the unlit flame... "For me, the equivalent is apple cider donuts. Sorry, continue. So she was a good writer. I'm not seeing the problem yet."

Susan sweeps the tangled hair from her eyes, then recounts the plot from one of Auger's novels. "Here's the plot from one of her recent novels. The villain, a foreign terrorist, genetically engineers a virus that turns into a pandemic. She then aligns herself with a white nationalist group that successfully pulls off a domestic terror attack on the U.S. Capitol. Sound familiar?"

Geier dumps the tobacco from his pipe in the trash and refills it. "Sure, those things happened and she wrote about them. So what?"

"You don't get it. She wrote about those things before they happened. Like she foresaw them. The real pandemic started just as her book was hitting the store shelves and the attack on the Capitol happened a few months later. As her fictional scenarios unfolded in the real world, that's when her anxiety attacks started. She couldn't reconcile whether she had an unusual power to predict disasters or if it was purely an accident."

"Go on," Geier says.

"When the weight of these events hit her, she stopped writing for a few months. But to Angela, writing was like breathing; she had to do it or she would die. So, tentatively, she started again. She wrote a short story about an assassination attempt on the First Lady that included a scene where a bomb exploded at Union Station. Even before her editor reviewed it, both things happened. She became paralyzed by her own thoughts, fearful of writing them down."

"You are familiar with schizoaffective disorder, which might explain her delusional belief that she could see the future?"

"I am, and it was the first thing that occurred to me. Still, her delusions went a treacherous step further. She came to believe that not only did she have the power to predict the future, but she in fact was writing the future---that what she wrote caused those horrible things to happen."

... For more, look for *The Last Appointment* at Amazon.com or Barnesandnoble.com